BLEND

Praise for Georgia Beers

Right Here, Right Now

"The angst was written well, but not overpoweringly so, just enough for you to have the heart sinking moment of 'will they make it,' and then you realize they have to because they are made for each other."—*Les Reveur*

What Matters Most

"There's so much more going on, from the way they flirt to how they each learn who the other really is, the way their feelings come about to how the conflict is resolved and where the relationship is at by the end of the book. All the right romantic elements are there, packaged in a way that kept me interested, surprised, and often smiling."—*The Lesbian Review*

A Little Bit of Spice

"As always with Ms Beers's novels, this is well written and edited, well paced and flowing. Definitely one for the reread pile…in fact, one of my favourites from this author." —*The Lesbian Reading Room*

Lambda Literary Award Winner *Fresh Tracks*

"Georgia Beers pens romances with sparks."—*Just About Write*

"[T]he focus switches each chapter to a different character, allowing for a measured pace and deep, sincere exploration of each protagonist's thoughts. Beers gives a welcome expansion to the romance genre with her clear, sympathetic writing." —*Curve magazine*

Finding Home

"Georgia Beers has proven in her popular novels such as *Too Close to Touch* and *Fresh Tracks* that she has a special way of building romance with suspense that puts the reader on the edge of their seat. *Finding Home*, though more character driven than suspense, will equally keep the reader engaged at each page turn with its sweet romance."—*Lambda Literary Review*

Mine

"From the eye-catching cover, appropriately named title, to the last word, Georgia Beers's *Mine* is captivating, thought-provoking, and satisfying. Like a deep red, smooth-tasting, and expensive merlot, *Mine* goes down easy even though Beers explores tough topics."—*Story Circle Book Reviews*

"Beers does a fine job of capturing the essence of grief in an authentic way. *Mine* is touching, life-affirming, and sweet." —*Lesbian News Book Review*

Too Close to Touch

"This is such a well-written book. The pacing is perfect, the romance is great, the character work strong, and damn but is the sex writing ever fantastic."—*The Lesbian Review*

"In her third novel, Georgia Beers delivers an immensely satisfying story. Beers knows how to generate sexual tension so taut it could be cut with a knife....Beers weaves a tale of yearning, love, lust, and conflict resolution. She has constructed a believable plot, with strong characters in a charming setting."—*Just About Write*

By the Author

Turning the Page

Thy Neighbor's Wife

Too Close to Touch

Fresh Tracks

Mine

Finding Home

Starting from Scratch

96 Hours

Slices of Life

Snow Globe

Olive Oil & White Bread

Zero Visibility

A Little Bit of Spice

Rescued Heart

Run to You

Dare to Stay

What Matters Most

Right Here, Right Now

Blend

Visit us at www.boldstrokesbooks.com

BLEND

by

Georgia Beers

2018

CREDITS
Editor: Lynda Sandoval
Production Design: Stacia Seaman
Cover Design by Ann McMan

Acknowledgments

Huge thanks to Via Girasole Wine Bar in Pittsford, New York. Nicole, Sue, and Mike not only taught me so much about wine, wine bars, and cheese plates, but when I told Nicole I needed to research a wine bar, she invited me into her business with open arms and introduced me to my Happy Place. I'm pretty sure it won't be long before I have my name engraved on a chair there.

Thank you to my editor extraordinaire, Lynda Sandoval. With each book, she makes me a better writer.

Thank you to Len Barot, Sandy Lowe, and everybody at Bold Strokes Books for making me look good.

Thank you to my friends and family for the support and encouragement in this wonderful, frustrating, amazing, solitary career I've chosen, specifically Melissa, Rachel, Carsen, Nikki, and Kris. They keep me going on those days when I'd rather give up and watch Netflix.

And last, but never least, the biggest of thank yous to my readers. Your support means more than you know.

CHAPTER ONE

W hat do you think?" Lindsay Kent leaned an elbow against the marble bar top and watched closely as Paul Richardson gazed into his wine glass. He swirled it, stuck his nose in, and inhaled deeply before taking another sip of the rich, dry Amarone.

"Good Lord, that's delightful," he said, seemingly to himself.

"Right?"

"I was hoping, at that cost, it would be outstanding. It does not disappoint."

"You've just got to trust me, Mr. R."

"You haven't steered me wrong yet." He smiled at Lindsay. "And you should know I'm not happy that I love this wine. It's going to hurt my wallet."

Lindsay chuckled. "I know. We don't have it often for that very reason."

"Why's it so pricey?"

Lindsay pulled out one of the barstools and took a seat on the edge. "Because it's not only hard to make, it's risky. The grapes are harvested ripe, then dried, so they're on their way to being raisins."

Paul nodded. "I can taste that."

"It's all about the skin quality of the grapes. If they're handled too much they'll be ruined, and the winemaker can lose his entire batch. So it's delicate work. It's dicey and takes a long time, thus the price."

"Well, it's worth it."

"I'm glad you think so." Lindsay stood back up. Paul Richardson was one of her regulars at Vineyard, the wine bar she'd been working at for three years now, managing for nearly two. He was a tall, sophisticated-looking man in his sixties with thinning silver hair, always dressed in a suit and tie, always pleasant and kind. He came in every Monday, Wednesday, and Friday after he finished work. He always let Lindsay recommend a wine for him, and he sat at the bar and proceeded to have two glasses of wine and a cheese board. Never more, never less. He rarely had the same wine twice.

Lindsay patted his shoulder and moved to a table in the corner to check on the four women who'd been laughing since they arrived.

"Hey, Linds?" Kevin Short, one of her employees, caught her attention as she passed. "Mrs. B. wants to see you when you get a minute."

"Sure."

Lindsay checked on the foursome, then stood near the window for a moment, gazing out at Black Cherry Lake and the late March sunshine that glinted off the water. It had been a particularly brutal winter, but the past couple of days of sunshine had begun to melt the remaining small piles of snow, bringing the promise of impending spring. The temperatures had stayed above freezing for the past week, and Lindsay could feel herself breathe again as she imagined the crocuses and daffodils and tulips that would start to pop their colorful heads up through the soil over the next few weeks.

A gentle smile on her face, she headed to the back office to see what her boss, the owner of Vineyard, needed from her.

Ellen Bradshaw was a very attractive woman of sixty-five. Her chestnut hair was cut in a simple bob, and at 5′2″, her nose poked Lindsay in the shoulder when they stood next to each other. She was ensconced behind her public school metal desk where she spent the majority of her workday. A small Bluetooth speaker nearby was playing the movie soundtracks Pandora station that Ellen was partial to. Lindsay tapped on the door frame just as the low brass tones of the Darth Vader theme sounded from the speaker.

"Well, that's ominous," Lindsay said as Ellen looked up and waved her in with a smile.

"Come in, Lindsay. Close the door. Sit down." She indicated the navy blue plastic chair in front of her desk. Lindsay sat, feeling, not for the first time, like she'd been called into the principal's office. "Did Paul like the Amarone?"

"Loved it. Didn't love the price."

"None of us love the price."

"I'm really hesitant about us keeping that as a regular selection. Not many people will pay that much for a glass of wine." Lindsay made sure to keep her expression soft.

"I know." Ellen finished up tapping on her keyboard, then slid it away and folded her hands on top of her desk and looked at Lindsay. A beat went by. Two.

"Okay, this is also ominous," Lindsay commented, waving a finger around Ellen's general posture. "Are you firing me?" She said it only half joking because Ellen was kind and fun and easygoing, but right then, she was looking incredibly serious.

"Of course not," Ellen reassured her. "Don't be silly."

Lindsay blew out a breath. "Oh, good."

"I need to discuss something with you."

"Okay."

And then they sat in silence while Ellen studied her folded hands and Lindsay tried not to squirm in her chair as worry blossomed in her gut.

"Mrs. B.," Lindsay finally said, leaning forward. "Are you okay? You're scaring me."

Ellen looked up then and smiled. Lindsay knew the difference between Ellen's genuine smile and her fake one—she'd seen the fake one used on many a difficult customer in the past—and this one was the real thing. "First of all, I don't know why I bother telling you to call me Ellen since you never do." Her expression was one of affection, and Lindsay returned it. "Second, I'm taking a trip."

Lindsay's eyebrows flew up into her hairline. "A vacation? Finally? Well, it's about damn time, that's all I have to say about that." She scooched forward so she was perched on the edge of her chair. "Where are you going? For how long?" Ellen's hesitation made Lindsay squint at her. "I'll ask again. Are you okay? You're not sick, are you?" Ellen was like a second mother to Lindsay, had been since she'd taken a chance and hired the girl with no experience and very little knowledge of wine.

The genuine smile was back, much to Lindsay's relief. "Oh, no. Not at all. In fact, I'm incredibly healthy, and that's made me realize that maybe I need to do a little exploring."

Lindsay sat back in her chair and blew out a small breath of relief. "Go on."

Ellen mimicked her position by sitting back in her own chair and visibly relaxing a bit. "Well, Tom's been gone for more than two years now."

At the mention of Ellen's deceased husband, Lindsay nodded. She'd only worked for him a short time before he'd passed away.

"And I sit in this tiny cube of an office like veal, six days a week." Ellen's half-grin gave Lindsay permission to chuckle. "I don't want to do that anymore."

"I can't tell you how glad I am to hear that. I mean, you don't even have a window."

"I know, right? Well, I'm taking some time off, Linds, and I'm leaving you in charge of Vineyard."

Lindsay blinked at her while her brain took time to absorb the words. "What? For how long?"

Ellen was nodding, her face brighter and happier than Lindsay had seen in a long time. "That's right. I may be gone for a while. I want you to run Vineyard. You and Piper." At the mention of Ellen's daughter, Lindsay had to catch herself and make a conscious effort *not* to grimace. "Though I'm sure she'll have no interest. But she'll be available if you run into any issues or need help. She's very business-minded."

Lindsay nodded, letting Ellen's praise of her daughter settle before asking some questions. "So…how long is a while?"

"I honestly don't know, and that's kind of the beauty of it. Might be three months. Might be a year."

"A *year*?"

"I'll keep in touch. Don't you worry." Ellen studied her then; Lindsay could feel the weight of her gaze. "Lindsay, when I say you're in charge, I mean it. I know you've got ideas you want to try, changes you think we should make, updates. And I know I haven't exactly been open to those changes, so this is your chance. Go for it. Experiment a little. Try the new things you've been sending me endless links about." She winked. "All I ask is you don't run my wine bar into the ground while I'm gone."

Her musical peal of laughter did little to ease the pressure Lindsay suddenly felt. But larger than the pressure was the simple excitement that coursed through her system like electricity, and she could barely sit still in her seat. "I don't even know what to say." It was the truth. Vineyard meant so much to her. Mrs. Bradshaw's faith in her meant so much more. "I won't let you down."

"I know you won't."

And just like that, Lindsay's head was filled with the unnerving combination of worry and ideas. New ideas. Worry that she'd mess up. Ideas she'd tucked away. Concerns about establishing authority. Ways to make Vineyard more profitable. Ways to bring in a younger, hipper crowd. Her brain was suddenly overcrowded, and she needed a pen and paper, ASAP. "When do you go?" she asked.

"Late next week. First stop, Orlando. Do you know, I've never been to Disney?"

Lindsay tilted her head. "Well, that's tragic."

"I know!" They smiled at each other, their eyes locked. "I trust you, Lindsay," Ellen said softly then. "I'm not worried."

Her words gently made their way into Lindsay's head, into her heart, and abruptly, the worry vanished. "I'll take good care of the place."

Ellen clapped her hands together once, effectively ending the conversation. She stood, and Lindsay followed suit. "Okay. I need to talk to the others. And I'll have a chat with Piper tonight, get things all squared away so I can pack." Her face was bright with joy, with anticipation. Lindsay couldn't remember seeing her like that since Mr. B. had died.

Her hand on the doorknob, Lindsay turned back to her boss. "You look happy, Mrs. B. Really happy. It's nice."

"Thank you, Lindsay." Ellen's expression was tender, her smile soft.

❖

"This is going to be so much fun!" Although Bridget D'Amico kept her voice at a stage whisper, actual low volume was nearly impossible for her, and Lindsay was pretty sure the whole of Vineyard could hear her. She was small and bouncy, her skin olive and her hair and eyes dark and sleek, like her Italian father's. From her Irish mother, she'd gotten her first name.

Lindsay couldn't help but soak in some of Bridget's enthusiasm. She was the perfect employee; the customers loved her. She had a great sense of self-deprecating humor, but she knew her wine, and she had a head for business. Mrs. B. had talked to her a little while ago, just before she headed home for the night, and Bridget was as happy for her boss and as excited about the prospect of more responsibility as Lindsay was.

Finished pouring the three glasses of red in the flight, Lindsay hooked the metal carrier on them and handed them over to Bridget. "There you go." She pointed at each glass as she spoke. "The Pinot Noir, the Rioja, and the blend."

"Got it." And Bridget was off.

Lindsay stood behind the small bar and surveyed the space. It was rectangular; not huge, but not tiny. The bar had eight stools. Another bar ran along one side of the building that lined the windows overlooking Black Cherry Lake and the unused patio there. Frankly, Lindsay didn't think they took enough advantage of what was actually a pretty spectacular view, and she pulled out the small notepad she'd stuffed into her back pocket earlier and jotted a note about that. There were twenty small tables that could be dragged together to create seating for larger parties, and Lindsay had no intention of messing with the furniture. Mr. and Mrs. Bradshaw had spared no expense there, the tables solid, dark wood, the matching chairs upholstered with cream cushions decorated with grapevines. The rest of the interior of Vineyard was nice, if a little dated, and she scribbled more notes about possible paint, wall decorations, table décor.

She needed to step carefully, though. No—she *wanted* to step carefully. For Mrs. B.'s sake. Vineyard had a super prime location, and Lindsay firmly believed that was the main reason it had survived this long. It certainly wasn't because it had changed and evolved with the times or because it catered to the ever-changing landscape of wine drinkers. But Mrs. B. had a tough time with change. Big change, anyway. And her trust in Lindsay, her leaving Lindsay in charge and telling her to run with some of her ideas, was huge. The last thing Lindsay wanted to do was take advantage of that trust.

"All right, Lindsay," said Kate Childs, a blond in her forties, sitting at the bar alone. "One more, then I need to get home to my dog. What do you suggest?" Kate was another regular, a suspense novelist who often came in during the afternoon for a glass of wine while she wrote. "Some writers prefer coffee shops," she'd said to Lindsay one day when she'd pulled out her laptop. "I prefer wine bars while I work." Lindsay had chuckled and they'd started up a conversation about modern-day thrillers.

Lindsay knew Kate was partial to whites, but not too sweet. "I've got a new Sauvignon Blanc from New Zealand. Want to give it a whirl?"

"You know I love the Kiwi wines." Kate closed her laptop and slid it into a bag. "Hit me."

They were approaching closing time, which was 8:00 p.m. Tuesday through Thursday and 9:00 on Friday and Saturday. Vineyard was about a quarter full; Lindsay could count the number of patrons easily. Kate had had a particularly great session of writing, she'd told

Lindsay a bit ago, and was there later than she'd expected to be, so her presence at this hour was unusual, but welcome.

Bridget returned with the flight carrier and hung it up behind the bar. As if privy to Lindsay's thoughts, she said, "I still think we should stay open later." She seemed to be musing out loud, as she didn't wait for a response from Lindsay, just took a cloth to a nearby table and began wiping it down.

Lindsay slid the glass of white to Kate, watched as she sipped, then nodded her approval and scrolled on her phone.

Sucking a large, slow breath into her lungs, Lindsay looked around. It had been almost four hours since Mrs. B. had given her the news, and Lindsay couldn't help the feeling that this was the start of something new for her.

Something big.

Something important.

CHAPTER TWO

Mom. Come on. You're kidding, right?" Piper Bradshaw sat at her desk and gazed out over the downtown cityscape, phone to her ear. Clouds of dull nickel gray were moving in rapidly, likely confirming the morning meteorologist's rain predictions. She watched them as they slid across the sky, blotting out the blue and the sun and any slight bit of cheer the remainder of her day may have held. "Why? Why do you feel the need to gallivant all over the place?"

Ellen sighed at her daughter's words. "First of all, I have worked nonstop since your father passed away. I think I deserve a break, don't you?" Without waiting for a response, she went on. "Secondly, I don't consider a well-earned vacation 'gallivanting.'"

Piper could envision her mother making air quotes around the word. She sighed as she grabbed the underwire of her bra and tugged at it, her snug-fitting dress starting to feel constrictive after nine hours of wear. "I know. I'm sorry. I just…I'll miss you." That was the truth. "What about Vineyard?"

"That's the other thing I wanted to talk to you about."

Something in her mother's voice made Piper brace herself just a bit.

"I'm leaving Lindsay Kent in charge of the day-to-day running of things."

"Lindsay? The hippie?" Piper couldn't catch the scoff that burst from her lips. "Why would you do that?"

Ellen's tone hardened. She hadn't kept a business running all on her own by being a marshmallow. "Lindsay is not a hippie, and I made that decision because I own the place."

Feeling chastised, Piper went on. "I know. I know. But…" She let her sentence dangle, doing her best to back off and find the right path to tread with her mom.

"What is your problem with her, anyway? She's smart. She's good to the customers. She's a fast learner."

Piper opened her mouth, closed it, then opened it again. "I just don't think she's right for the atmosphere of the place. She's super casual. I don't think she gets wine drinkers or how a business runs or…" Again with the dangling. *Why can't I finish a damn thought?* Her mother was the only person on earth who could make Piper feel unsure of herself.

"Well, you're wrong." There was no room for argument now and Piper knew it. "And you'd better change that attitude, young lady, because the two of you will have to work together. I'm leaving both of you to handle the business while I'm away. You will have access to the business account and the money. Any changes that cost money will have to be agreed on by both of you."

Piper was nodding even though nobody could see her.

"Unless you'd rather I leave that responsibility to Gina."

At the mention of her big sister's name, Piper chuckled. "Mom. Please. My sister the college professor wouldn't know the first thing about running Vineyard."

"Then I guess you're going to have to take care of it."

"I will."

"Good. Come by tomorrow after work so I can reintroduce you and go over some of the details, okay?"

Piper agreed to the meeting and hung up the phone. Before she had time to dwell on the topic at hand, her intercom buzzed.

"Ms. Bradshaw? You wanted to go over that report before I left."

"Okay," she said to Charlotte, her admin. "Come on in." Thank God Piper had dinner with Matthew tonight. *At least he'll be level-headed about this.*

❖

"Sorry I'm late," Piper said, as she kissed Matthew O'Keefe on his bearded cheek. "I had a morning meeting run long, and it threw off my entire day."

Matthew was a big man, bulky and kind. The parents of his kindergarten students called him a big teddy bear, which his husband found endlessly amusing. He stood from the high-top table and wrapped

Piper in a hug. "No worries. I'm still on my first drink, so you're safe. The tradition is still alive." He signaled to the waitress. "A vodka tonic for the lovely lady, please."

Piper held him at arm's length, took in his khakis and navy blue oxford. "You look good. Lost the tie already, I see." She winked at him as she slid out of her trench coat and hung it on the back of her chair along with her purse.

He reached to the pocket of his coat and pulled the end of a light blue tie out far enough for her to see. "By two o'clock, that thing is choking the life out of me."

"Sounds like my bra." Once she was all settled in her seat, she propped her elbows on the sleek black surface of the table, set her chin on her fists, and smiled at the man who'd been her best friend since junior high. "God, it's good to see your face."

"Back atcha. And also, you look incredible." Matthew's eyebrows went up high as he took in the red dress that hugged her hips and framed her figure like it was made for her.

"Thanks. I had a couple client meetings today. Gotta dress to impress." She didn't add that she couldn't wait to get home and into her slouchy lounge pants and ratty sweatshirt. "How are you?"

"I'm good." Matthew smiled and sipped his beer.

"What dark concoction are you drinking today?" Piper asked, taking the glass from him so she could sip.

"It's Red Barn's new vanilla porter. I love it."

Piper tasted it, then wrinkled her nose as she handed it back, and he chuckled.

"You don't like beer, P. Why do you insist on taking a sip of every one I drink?"

Piper shrugged. "Like you said, tradition." The waitress arrived with Piper's cocktail and a couple menus. "How's Shane? It's been, what? Six months? Seven? Still lost in a haze of wedded bliss?"

"Married life is awesome. You should give it a try some time."

Piper snorted as a response. Another sip of her drink and she said, "Wait until you hear what my mother told me today."

"Aw, how is Mrs. B.? I haven't seen her since the wedding."

"She's taking a vacation." Piper said it as though it was an unbelievable piece of news.

"Good for her! It's about time. Where is she off to and for how long?"

"That's just it. She's off to Disney first, but then she said she's going to travel some more after that and she hasn't decided where yet. She said she might be gone for months. Maybe a year!" Piper felt her eyes widen in disbelief, just as they had when her mother had first told her. She still couldn't believe it.

"I'll say it again. Good for her."

Piper made a face at Matthew. "Of course you say that. She loves you and you love her. You two have an unhealthy love fest for each other."

Matthew gave a mock-gasp and pressed a hand to his chest. "I take offense to the word 'unhealthy.'"

"Figures."

They grinned at each other for a moment, two old friends enjoying their biweekly time together. Finally, Matthew asked, "So, why does this have your panties in a twist?"

Piper grimaced. "Ew. Don't say panties."

"Why not? That's what they are."

"No. We hate that word."

"We?"

"All of womankind."

"I think you exaggerate. But whatever." Matthew finished his beer. "Knickers? Undies? Briefs? Wait, you're not a boxer girl, are you? Thong?"

Piper clamped her hands over her ears but couldn't stop the laughter. "For the love of God, stop!"

"Fine." Matthew grinned widely, then asked, "Why are you so bothered?"

"Mom is leaving me and Lindsay Kent in charge." She stressed the two names of Vineyard's manager.

Matthew shook his head slowly, obviously unaware who she meant.

"Lindsay. The blond hippie chick my dad hired just before he died?"

Recognition dawned on Matthew's face. "Oh, her. Okay. Been a while since I was in there, but I remember now. She's cute. And so not a hippie."

"Is too."

"I think you need to look up the definition of that word."

Piper waved him away with a *pfft*. Before she could say more, the waitress was back and they placed their dinner orders and a second round of drinks.

"Isn't she the general manager now or something?"

Piper shrugged with feigned indifference. "I guess."

Matthew narrowed his eyes at her. "You haven't liked her since Day One. How come?"

Their drinks arrived. Matthew picked his up and sipped, his gaze never leaving Piper. She felt that stare, felt it physically. Matthew always could get her to talk to him. She took in a deep breath and gazed out the window by their table while she honestly pondered his question. Once she'd let it out slowly, she turned back to him. "I'm not trying to be unreasonable. There's just…there's something about her that rubs me the wrong way."

Matthew blinked at her for a long beat of silence.

"What?" Piper finally prodded.

He shook his head. "I'm just marveling at how much you sound like the women who refused to vote for Hillary Clinton." He changed his voice to a whine. "'I don't know what it is. I *just don't like* her.'"

Piper groaned. "Fine. The first time I met her, she was…" She searched for the right description. "Overly giddy. Like, way too friendly, kind of flighty. A little flaky. Smiled too much. Like a hippie."

"Oh, my God, she was super friendly *and* smiled a lot? What is her *problem*?"

Piper glared at him. "Maybe you should not mock me."

"Maybe you should get to know her."

"I don't want to."

"Fine." Matthew tossed her word back at her with a roll of his eyes, then made a sound that said he gave up. "Also, why do you even care? You never go to Vineyard anyway."

Piper found herself inexplicably uncomfortable with this subject all of a sudden. Mostly because Matthew was right. Since her father had passed, she rarely set foot in Vineyard. It was too hard. She didn't know how her mother managed to. "I don't know," she said finally, waving a dismissive hand. "I'm just being ridiculous."

"Well, that's not news."

She swatted playfully at him across the table. "Hey!"

He laughed as he dodged away from her. Their dinners arrived and the conversation halted until they were each chewing.

"I think you just need to chill," Matthew told her. "You know?"

"That's funny. Have you met me?"

"Good point."

"I have to meet with my mom and Lindsay there tomorrow. Go

over details. I can hardly wait." Piper shoveled a bite of salad into her mouth.

"Open mind, P. Open mind."

"I know." But her voice softened.

After a moment or two of just chewing, Matthew asked quietly, "You okay?"

Piper held his gaze, amazed as always by the deep levels of kindness visible in his brown eyes. She smiled and nodded, suddenly determined. "Yeah. I am."

"You know...I'm happy to go with you. If you want. I'd love to see your mom..." He let his words trail off, leaving the idea there for her to grab.

She chewed, swallowed, took a sip of water. Only after all of that did she tell him, "I'm going right after work. I'm not going to ask you to come, but if you want to, I won't stop you."

Matthew arched one eyebrow and tilted his head. "You're ridiculous."

Piper laughed because he knew her so well. "I so am."

It was nearly 9:00 by the time she left Matthew and headed home. Edgar made it very clear to her how dissatisfied he was with these hours, meowing noisily at her the second she entered the house, circling her black heels impatiently as she stood at the counter.

"All right, all right," she said down to him. "I'm sorry." She bent and scooped him up before he could dodge her, protesting loudly as she showered him with kisses. She'd found him as a kitten, huddled near the dumpster at the back of her office building two years ago. She'd just lost her father, and her partner, and was living on her own for the first time in a long time. And suddenly, there he was. A little black and white ball of fur, his meow so small and high pitched, it sounded like he'd inhaled helium beforehand. He had a white face with a little slash of black just under his nose, and it looked so much like a mustache that she'd named him after Edgar Allan Poe. He turned out to be exactly what she needed at the time: companionship without too much maintenance.

Piper kissed him once more, then set him down and finished getting his dinner together. When she set it on the floor, he pounced on it like he hadn't eaten in weeks, and she rolled her eyes. "You're such a drama queen."

In her bedroom, Piper kicked off her heels and eyed the brand-new life vest leaning against the wall. It had arrived yesterday and was still wrapped in plastic, as she'd had no time to examine it. The outer fabric was navy blue and the vest was ultra-thin, made of some newfangled, revolutionary material, and supposedly much more breathable than most. It had cost her an arm and a leg, but she had a feeling it would be totally worth it the next time she was gliding across Black Cherry Lake in her kayak well before 6:00 a.m. Pulling it from the plastic, she unfastened it and put in on right over her dress, then stepped to the free-standing, full-length antique mirror in the corner.

It was sleek and definitely thinner than her current vest. Once fastened, it was comfortable along her neck, didn't feel like she was wearing the shoulder pads of a linebacker. The weight of it was surprisingly light and Piper was suddenly seized with such an urge to kayak that she had to consciously remind herself it was dark out right now. And thirty-nine degrees.

"Soon," she said quietly, as she took off the vest. The end of March was when she paid close attention to the weather. The lake wasn't frozen; it never froze all the way across—it was much too big—but at this time of year, it was completely thawed, coastlines and all, and she started to get that itch.

This weekend, maybe.

Piper took off her dress and hung it carefully in the closet. While she didn't consider herself a neat freak by any stretch, she did take very good care of her wardrobe. Mostly because it cost her a fortune. Some people collected art. Some people spent their earnings on vacations. Piper loved clothes, and she was willing to spend the money on a dress or a suit or a pair of slacks if they fit her well. Being in a large corporate office, she needed to look as professional as she could and garner all the respect possible. Managing other managers was never easy, especially when most were male and older than her.

Slipping into her slouchy gray sweats and worn-to-the-point-of-falling-apart black sweatshirt felt like heaven (just because she enjoyed dressing nicely didn't mean she was comfortable after wearing those nice clothes for twelve or thirteen hours). Piper headed back downstairs long enough to make herself a cup of chamomile tea and grab her laptop. Then she headed back up to her bedroom where she stacked pillows against the wrought iron headboard, spread work out around her, and clicked on the wall-mounted television.

The calm, soothing voice of *The Barefoot Contessa* made for a nice soundtrack to Piper's report reading. Edgar curled up against her hip and began to purr.

"Those pork chops look really good," she said to him, when she glanced up at the TV. "Maybe I should try making them." She watched for another twenty seconds before snorting. "Yeah, right." When she turned to Edgar, his expression said the same thing.

She refocused on her work, tried hard to concentrate, but her mind kept pulling her back to her mother's impending trip, the upcoming meeting, and Lindsay Kent.

Tomorrow was going to be interesting.

CHAPTER THREE

It was a typical crowd for a Thursday evening. The after-work crowd that had come in for a glass of wine with their coworkers had pretty much headed home, and now the occupied tables were mostly people out for a nice night of wine and cheese. Maybe eight or ten customers, total.

It should be more.

That thought ran through Lindsay's head often, at least once a shift.

Her brain short-circuited right then, though, as she glanced at the door and saw Piper Bradshaw on her way in.

Piper Bradshaw was uptight. Everybody thought so.

Piper Bradshaw was kind of snobby. Everybody thought so.

And Piper Bradshaw was fucking hot. Everybody thought so. Including Lindsay, which didn't make her happy, given the uptight and snobby parts.

Today she was wearing black slacks, a rust-colored top unbuttoned at her throat, and a long, black coat. Her brown hair fell in gently spiraled waves past her shoulders, her dark brows accenting eyes that seemed to take in everything around her in an instant. She wasn't tall—Lindsay put her around five-five—but she had a presence that commanded attention when she walked in. She was a literal head-turner, and Lindsay watched as four people shifted their positions to watch as she entered. Piper's heels clicked as she crossed the wooden floor to the corner table where Ellen sat with a notebook in front of her.

As Piper took off her coat, Ellen threw a nod in Lindsay's direction. That was her cue to bring three glasses of wine to the table and join them.

"I see Princess Elsa has arrived," Bridget whispered as she stood next to Lindsay and poured an order for her customer.

"I'm hoping this is all just a formality." Lindsay spoke just as quietly as she filled three glasses with the new red blend that had just been delivered that morning, her suggestion to Ellen. "I mean, she rarely shows her face in here at all. I don't see her suddenly becoming a regular, you know?"

"I'm keeping my fingers crossed for you." Bridget scooped up her wine and was off to serve.

Lindsay grabbed her three glasses and carefully crossed the room to the back corner table. When she finished setting them down, she found herself looking into a gorgeous pair of—not brown as she'd originally thought—hazel eyes. She'd never seen that color before… sort of the color of weak iced tea, but with a bit of copper thrown in to brighten the overall effect. Framed by very dark, very thick lashes and accented with various shades of subtle brown eye shadow, they were easily the most stunning eyes she'd ever seen. Lindsay's breath hitched.

"Lindsay, you remember my youngest daughter, Piper." Ellen's voice yanked Lindsay harshly back to the present. Piper's expression showed satisfied amusement and Lindsay felt her face warm with embarrassment at having been caught staring.

"I do." Lindsay held out her hand. "Good to see you again." Piper's grip was firm, a little too firm if Lindsay was being honest, but her skin was soft. Lindsay took a seat.

"I've talked to each of you individually," Ellen began, her hands flat on the notebook. "So you both know the basics. I really don't have a lot to talk about, but I wanted the two of you to be in the same space so you understand that you will work together."

Lindsay glanced at Piper, who was looking down at her glass as she spun it in slow circles with both hands. She had nice hands. A silver ring that looked like several rings looped together sparkled from her right forefinger. There were no rings on her left hand. Delicate-looking skin. Neatly shaped nails polished with a dark color—black? Yeah, she had *really* nice hands.

"I don't understand what you're doing, Mom." Piper's voice was quiet but firm, the kind of voice that would get the attention of an entire room without the volume ever increasing.

Ellen sighed and Lindsay got the impression they'd been through this already. "I'm sixty-five, I'm tired of working, and I'd like to do some traveling before I croak. What's there to understand?"

Lindsay rolled her lips in and bit down on them to smother a smile. "And you're just going to leave Daddy's business?"

"It's *my* business now, Piper."

Piper made eye contact with her mother and their gazes held. Lindsay felt like she was intruding on a private family moment, so she sat silently and sipped her wine.

Several beats went by and Lindsay was finally clear on where Piper got her determination and confidence, because she turned away first and Lindsay gave Ellen a mental point.

"Fine," Piper said, and the slight tone of sad defeat made Lindsay feel a little sorry for her. "What do you need from me?"

With one nod, Ellen opened the notebook. "You won't have to do much. Lindsay's going to take care of the day-to-day running. Right?" Ellen smiled at her protégé.

"Absolutely," Lindsay said. "I got this."

"You, Piper, already have access to the bank accounts, so we're just going to keep it that way. Lindsay can handle all the regular expenses. She knows how everything works. But if she needs something unexpected that costs money, she'll need to run it by you."

That was the one part of the whole arrangement that didn't thrill Lindsay. She was perfectly capable of running Vineyard. Easily. And it wasn't like she was going to tear the place down and rebuild while Ellen was gone, so the idea of running some of her new ideas by Piper—and then needing her approval to put any of them into action—was less than ideal. They'd only met a handful of times, but Piper didn't like Lindsay. She'd made that abundantly clear. The staff didn't call her Princess Elsa for nothing. It was as if everything she touched turned icy. And really, Lindsay couldn't have cared less if Piper didn't like her. It hadn't mattered one bit in the grand scheme of Lindsay's life. Until now.

Piper was nodding. "That makes sense." She turned to Lindsay. "You got that?"

"I do."

"You come to me for approval. I'll keep track of your daily spending. If something looks suspicious or unusual, I'll be coming to see you. Understood?"

Lindsay wasn't sure if it was meant to sound like a threat, but it sure did, and she had to take a moment, count to five in her head before responding simply, "Yes." Her jaw began to ache from clenching her teeth.

Ellen sipped her wine, then looked from one of them to the other and back again. Something that might have been amusement zipped across her face, but it was too fast for Lindsay to analyze. "I'm expecting you two to work together."

Lindsay nodded. "No problem." *If your daughter keeps her uppity self out of Vineyard altogether, things will be just fine.*

Ellen sipped again, then looked at Lindsay and lifted her glass slightly to indicate the wine. "This is good."

Lindsay felt her face light up. "Right? Told you."

"This is the new blend?"

As Lindsay nodded, Piper's brow furrowed. "You're selling blends now? Dad hated those. He said they were made by vintners who were too cheap to get the real varietals right."

Lindsay wet her lips as she turned to Princess Elsa and her scowl of disapproval, and she smiled. "Blends have come a long way over the past few years. There are some very prominent—"

She was interrupted by Piper's upheld hand. "I don't need a lesson, thank you. I'm aware of how wine is made."

Lindsay bit back a snarky retort that would have included something to the effect of *how could you possibly be aware of anything with your nose that far up in the air?* Instead, she said simply, "Taste it."

Piper let out a little sigh, and Lindsay took it as her dissatisfaction at being told what to do. But to her credit, Piper picked up her glass, sipped, let it roll around before swallowing. "It's good." She said it almost grudgingly, and Lindsay smiled, though she was pretty sure it didn't reach her eyes.

"Blends tend to be a bit less expensive as well. I'd like to bring in some more, pull back on the super-expensive wines we carry."

"Vineyard is sophisticated," Piper said, those gorgeous eyes flashing at Lindsay. "That means the clientele is sophisticated. Sophisticated people don't want to drink cheap wine."

Lindsay opened her mouth to reply, but Ellen held up a hand. "Enough," she said, using Piper's earlier method of speaking very firmly, but quietly, so that only Piper and Lindsay heard and understood. But her eyes flashed not unlike Piper's had, and it was obvious she was irritated by their behavior. "You two are grown women, and you're going to have to figure out how to work together. I'm not going to worry about it. I'm telling you both that right now. I will *not* be basking on a beach in Florida wondering if you two have killed each other yet. You're adults. Work it out." She gently closed her notebook, and

Lindsay was surprised by the relaxed smile on her face. "I leave next Friday. Wish me safe travels." She held up her glass.

Lindsay and Piper both touched their glasses to hers. "You're going to have a great time," Lindsay said. "I'm so happy for you."

Piper nodded, but apparently had nothing to say.

Thankfully, the awkward silence was broken by a big, burly man with a beard who appeared at their table. "They'll let anybody in here, I see."

"Matthew!" Ellen jumped up from her seat and threw herself into his arms. "Oh, my God, it's good to see you. It's been so long. And Shane." Another man sidled up next to the first. He was taller and thinner, with dark hair and striking blue eyes.

"It's good to see you, Mrs. B." He, too, wrapped Ellen in a hug.

"How are you?" Ellen asked.

Lindsay watched the exchange with amusement. Piper's expression had softened and relaxed, so it was obvious she knew these two as well. That was confirmed when she stood from her chair and hugged the man named Shane. She gave Matthew a playful shove. It was so interesting to watch Piper change. She went from that chilly Princess Elsa persona to an actual warm-blooded human being who was happy to see her friends, in a matter of moments.

I guess it's just me she doesn't like.

Lindsay gave a mental shrug, trying her best to pretend that didn't bother her, and stood to leave the Bradshaws to their friends, but Ellen grabbed her arm.

"Lindsay. Meet these two handsome young men." Lindsay met the kind eyes of the bearded one Ellen introduced as Matthew. "Matthew was like the son I never had when the kids were in high school. He and Piper were inseparable. Still are. He spent as much time in my kitchen as he did his own. Right, Matty?"

"True story." Matthew reached a hand out and Lindsay shook it. "Matthew O'Keefe."

"Lindsay Kent," Lindsay said. "Nice to meet you."

Matthew turned to the other man, but before he could say anything, Ellen chimed in with, "And this is his gorgeous husband, Shane."

Shane also shook Lindsay's hand, gave her a friendly smile and nod.

"Well, I'll leave you to your visit," she said, but Ellen was already chatting animatedly with the men. As she turned, Lindsay caught Piper looking at her, then she looked away quickly and pretended to be engrossed in the conversation. With a nod, Lindsay headed back behind the bar.

"Get a little intense over there?" Bridget asked in low tones, as she sidled up next to her.

"How do you do that?" Lindsay asked her, brow furrowed.

"Do what?"

"Appear out of nowhere and know exactly what's going on." Bridget grinned up at her. "Mad skills."

Lindsay shook her head good naturedly. "I wouldn't say intense." She kept her voice low and her eyes on the foursome that still stood near the table chatting. "I'd say that Princess Elsa doesn't like people knowing more than she does."

"Unsurprising."

"Yeah…" She continued to watch the action, again amazed by the very obvious change in Piper's demeanor, still annoyed by the fact that it rankled. She laughed at something Shane said, the sound very feminine, and laid a hand gently on his arm. Matthew and Mrs. B. were standing a bit away from them, their heads together in quiet conversation. "Anyway," she said to Bridget, "Mrs. B. leaves next Friday morning. I think we should have a staff meeting on Saturday just to touch base with everybody. Can you send out a text?"

Bridget nodded, her eyes also on the Bradshaws and their friends. "Not a problem, boss."

Lindsay gave a look. "I prefer Queen."

"Oh, these next few months will be fun." Bridget rolled her eyes, then bumped Lindsay with a shoulder and went to wait on a table for two.

❖

Her mother and Shane were going on and on about some new yarn shop they'd both discovered and which knitting projects they were each working on. Piper smiled and sipped her wine. Which was better than good, though she'd never say it out loud and let Lindsay Kent know she was right.

"I still don't get your issue with her," Matthew said, as if looking straight into her brain. His voice was low, meant only for Piper. "First of all, she seems very nice. The customers seem to really like her. Second, have you looked at her? She's *really* sexy." He gestured with his bearded chin toward a table about ten feet away where Lindsay was talking and the two customers seemed fully engaged, large smiles on their faces.

Piper followed his gaze. She didn't want to let her eyes roam over the way the dark jeans hugged Lindsay's ass. She didn't want her gaze to linger on what looked to be very soft, super-smooth skin of Lindsay's forearms, bared by the rolled-up sleeves of her light denim shirt, which stood open. And as she turned and Piper got a glimpse of the front of her, she certainly didn't want to look at the surprisingly ample breasts covered by a white V-neck T-shirt.

But she did all of those things.

She didn't even stop looking when Lindsay moved to a different table, tucked a hank of her blond hair behind her ear, and bent forward slightly to listen to what the woman sitting there was saying.

"Yeah," Matthew said, and when Piper turned back to him, a knowing smile had taken up residence on his face. "I see you *have* looked at her."

"Shut up," Piper hissed. "You know nothing." She finished off her wine, really wanted another glass, but didn't want to call Lindsay over.

So damn Matthew did it for her. Piper watched in horror as he lifted his arm and signaled to Lindsay, who glanced at Piper before smiling at Matthew and walking toward their table.

"Hi there," she said, and Piper saw a small mole on her right cheek she'd never noticed before.

"Well, hello again," Matthew said, a wide smile on his face. "I think the lovely Miss Piper here needs a refill. And I'd like a glass as well."

"The blend or something different?" Lindsay asked, hands clasped in front of her.

"The blend," Matthew said at the exact same time Piper said, "Something else."

"Of course," Lindsay said as she looked at Piper, and those two words said a lot more than that.

"I'd like a glass of the Castle Rock Pinot Noir, please," Piper said, looking Lindsay in the eyes, surprised by their greenness.

"Of course," she said again as she took Piper's empty glass. "Be right back."

"I don't understand you." Matthew shook his head.

"Who, me?" Shane asked, surprising both of them.

Piper shot a pleading look at Matthew, which he seemed to get, thank God.

"Yes. The yarn and the needles and the stitches and the patterns. I don't understand it."

And they were off on a discussion about the joys of making your own hats and mittens and giving them to others. Piper listened absently but was very aware of Lindsay's approach. Which didn't make her happy.

"The blend for the gentleman. And the Pinot for you." Those green eyes snagged Piper's and held them for a beat. Two. Three. Piper wanted to look away, but somehow...couldn't. "Enjoy," Lindsay finally said, and was gone.

Piper swallowed and poked the inside of her cheek with her tongue. When she finally turned her attention back to Matthew, he was studying her over the rim of his glass.

"Interesting," was all he said.

"Shut up." Piper sipped her wine. It was delicious, but part of her wished she still had the blend, which she had zero intention of telling Matthew.

Matthew still looked at her, his gaze a mix of amused and gleeful, and she had to fight to keep from squirming in her chair. He finally broke the eye contact and nodded, sipped his wine. With a knowing grin, he said, "Uh-huh. I can't wait to see what happens next."

CHAPTER FOUR

S o far, so good, Rocket, my man." Lindsay flopped onto her couch and toed off her shoes as her big lug of a yellow Lab put his paws in her lap and demanded attention, his firehose tail sweeping everything off the coffee table in one swoop. "Dude, seriously. Have a little respect for my stuff."

"Well, I would, Mom, if you were home more often," Lindsay then responded in the low-pitched, rumbly voice she used when she did what she considered her impression of Rocket. *"Have some respect for me."*

"I know, I know. I'm sorry. Come up here." She patted the couch, and Rocket pulled the rest of his eighty-five-pound body up next to her and dropped his head into her lap. Crossing her feet at the ankles and propping them on the now-empty coffee table, she lay back against the couch and dug her fingers into her dog's fur, just enjoying the peace and the unconditional love.

"So," she said, after a few moments, "that's the end of the first week without Mrs. B., and I think it went really well. I met with all the staff. We've got Bridget, Kevin, Christi, Zack, and Sharon. Plus, I'm meeting with the cheese guy and a wine distributor Monday." She glanced down into her lap at the sweet brown eyes of her dog, who seemed to be paying very close attention to everything she said. So she scratched his belly and went on. "Nobody seemed weirded out to have me in charge. I mean, I was sort of in charge anyway, as general manager, but they could always go to Mrs. B. if they had a problem. Now they only have me. And they seemed all right with that. Which was a huge relief."

It was a decent staff. Bridget, Kevin, and Sharon knew their stuff. Zack and Christi were younger, but vibrant. Fun. And they brought in some of their friends on occasion, who then brought in more of a younger crowd, something Vineyard could really use.

"I feel like Mrs. B. was finally starting to get that, you know, Rocket? That wine is being consumed by the younger set now?"

"I do get that, Mom. You're super wise about wine and stuff."

"Right?" She moved her fingers to his ears and massaged them gently. "Too bad her daughter doesn't get that. Oh, well. She's made no appearances, so I'm hoping it stays that way."

And right on cue, her brain tossed her the image of the last time she'd seen Piper. The black slacks and rust-colored top and heels that clicked all the way across the floor. Those hazel eyes and dark, dark lashes. Those dimples that didn't show nearly enough because she didn't smile nearly enough, and that perfect, perfect hair.

"I'd like to mess up that hair," Lindsay whispered aloud, which made Rocket snap to attention, sitting up on the couch and looking at her expectantly. She chuckled. "Dude, just because I whisper doesn't mean I'm talking to you." But that face and those eyes...she couldn't resist and took his square head in both hands, kissed the bridge of his nose. "But you're right. I totally was. I'd like to mess up *your* hair. Yes, I would." And then Rocket's tail was whacking loudly against a throw pillow and his ears were up and his head was cocked and he was the most adorable, loving thing in the world to Lindsay. She hugged him tightly and told him so.

Lindsay wasn't a night owl by nature, but working the hours at Vineyard had sort of turned her into one. They closed at nine—something she was going to change in the next week or two—and once she cleaned things up, took care of the money, and got the place ready for the next day, it was often 10:30 before she got home, wired and hungry and not at all ready for bed. Part of the drawback to that was she tended to lose touch with some of her friends who had normal-business-hour jobs. A glance at her phone showed two missed calls and three unanswered texts from friends and family, but it was too late now to text back. She'd try to do that in the morning.

Tonight was no different than most in the wired and hungry department. In the kitchen, she sautéed some cherry tomatoes in a little olive oil, then scrambled in some eggs. Once topped with a little oregano and some parmesan cheese, she slid it all onto a plate, poured herself a glass of cabernet, and returned to the living room to watch a little TV with Rocket. This was when she did her best thinking.

Eggs devoured and a *Modern Family* rerun on the television, she pulled out her little notepad, along with a larger one (she preferred pen and paper to a computer screen when brainstorming...and she couldn't doodle on a laptop while she thought), and began to list the things she wanted to address around Vineyard.

"I have to be careful, Rock. I don't want to make too many changes too fast, you know? Gotta ease into some of these things." She was going to give the staff a week or two to get used to the new hierarchy, then talk to them about staying open an hour later. Then two if the first hour was worth it. That could mean more hours for her, she knew. She couldn't expect the staff to suddenly be available more than they'd originally thought they'd be needed. But she had a feeling Bridget and maybe Kevin would be more than willing.

The Cab was very good. Peppery but smooth, with a long, lingering finish. She'd order more tomorrow, jotted that on the list. Her phone dinged to indicate a text and she picked it up. It was from her stepbrother, Josh, apparently having no qualms about texting when it was nearing midnight.

Got a few pals together. Looking to come by tomorrow after work.

Lindsay couldn't remember the last time she'd seen Josh face-to-face. Months ago, easily. She remembered him asking her lots of questions about wine, and she hadn't been sure if he was actually interested or was just making conversation. With a shrug, she texted back.

What time? I'm there from 12 to 9.

A few seconds went by while Lindsay watched the bouncing dots that indicated Josh was typing.

4 of us. 7?

Lindsay jotted in her schedule to reserve a table.

Perfect. I'll save space for you.

She knew the twentysomethings of today were drinking a ton of wine. There were countless articles on it, and Lindsay was pretty sure she'd read them all. So it wasn't really about educating them on wine; they already knew they wanted to drink it. It was more about getting them into the wine bar, drawing them in with something. Setting, atmosphere, music. *Then* she could educate them, which would help to keep them coming back. All of it played a role. Lindsay just had to be the director and make it all work seamlessly. Josh and his friends would give her a golden opportunity to practice.

It was a challenge she was up for.

Finally ready to give her brain a rest, she set aside all her notes and her empty plate, picked up the half-full wine glass, and paid attention to the television. Tomorrow was Saturday and not a day that she should be worrying about business, but she was. A restaurant at the other end of the lake, Lakeshore, had started serving wine flights last month, and it concerned her that her customers might be going there. It was a bigger place, more modern, but Lindsay had also found, during a covert visit, that it was kind of generic. A bit…sterile and lacking in personality. Still, healthy competition had pros and cons. Lindsay wanted to focus on the pros.

Might be time for another visit.

❖

Saturday morning dawned clear, the sun very slowly making its way to the horizon, like an elementary school student trudging around sleepily, dreading the impending schoolday. Sluggish and lazy, taking its sweet time.

Black Cherry Lake was cold. There was no doubt. Piper had her water shoes on but decided to launch from the dock rather than the shore. No way was she walking waist-deep into early April waters. In fact, she almost didn't come, cursing at her alarm when it went off at 5:45. She certainly didn't have to be out here so early. It was the weekend and she had all day. But there was something about the peace of the early morning, especially when there was no wind, like today. The lake was like glass, everything was quiet and so very peaceful— with the exception of the birds and ducks gradually reappearing after a winter away. And you couldn't beat the sunrise. Piper had lost count of how many mornings she'd glided across the lake in her bright green kayak, lifted her paddle out of the water, and just drifted in utter silence as she watched the sun appear and get the day started.

Nothing gave her more peace.

After her father died, she was out here almost every morning. The days had suddenly felt so loud, and frankly, she was angry that the earth kept spinning, that everybody just went on with their lives when she'd lost the most important man in her world.

Now, two years and change later, she didn't miss him any less, but she'd become very good at shifting her thoughts to other, less painful things. She also no longer hated the entire planet and everybody on it. And these early-morning glides through the lake were her salvation in a life of demanding bosses and needy clients and numbers and quotas and too many people relying on her. On top of all that, she got to add in worrying about her mother as well.

Getting herself situated in her seat, Piper adjusted her new life vest—which was even thinner and more comfortable than she'd hoped—and pushed off the dock. A few fishermen dotted the lake within her view, their small rowboats as quiet as her kayak, and for that, she was grateful. Nothing spoiled her tranquil mornings faster than the obnoxious buzzing of a motor. The waterproof bag between her feet contained her cell phone (which was on silent), a bottle of water, and an energy bar for later. Her paddle made very little sound as she sliced it into the water and pulled, gaining enough momentum until she was moving steadily along the water, a satisfying burn in her shoulders and arms telling her she was working the right muscles. To her left, a fish jumped, the small splash seeming loud in the quiet of the morning, the ripples making larger and larger circles until they faded.

Once she fell into a rhythm, her thoughts drifted back to her mother. *What the hell is she doing? What the hell is she* thinking, *traipsing all over the country? She has responsibilities here. She has two daughters. She's got grandkids. She has a* business, *for Christ's sake. How does she think it's okay to just up and go?*

And then Piper felt immediately guilty. She was an intelligent woman, and it wasn't hard for her to understand exactly what her mother was doing. She was breaking free. She was giving herself permission to live again. She'd been devastated when Piper's father had died and she'd stayed holed up for months before finally venturing out somewhere other than home or Vineyard. It was time. She was due some happiness. She deserved it. Piper knew all of that.

Still...

She was approaching near center of Black Cherry Lake, and the sun was starting to show itself over the tops of the black cherry trees for which the lake was named. A grove of them framed the east end of the water, their blossoms preparing to burst into an explosion of beautiful white flowers. Piper pulled her paddle out of the water and laid it across her kayak, just let herself drift as she breathed in the crisp morning air. Spring was her absolute favorite. It spoke of rejuvenation and new beginnings, and if there was one thing Piper loved, it was wiping the slate clean and being able to start again. After such a long, cold winter, she was even more excited to be in the early throes of it.

Inhaling a long, slow lungful of fresh lake air helped her to find her center, and she exhaled just as slowly. Her mother had trusted her to take care of some things while she was away, and it was time for Piper to step up. She hadn't been back to Vineyard since the initial meeting with her mother and Lindsay Kent; she hadn't had the desire or the need. But now she realized that her stubbornness was misplaced. She was in charge, and she at least needed to make an appearance once in a while. She made a pact with herself that she'd go tonight. Maybe drag Matthew and Shane with her.

Yes. It was time to make sure Lindsay Kent knew Piper was around.

❖

Despite the light weight of the kayak, getting it on and off her SUV by herself was still an awkward maneuver for Piper. She'd managed to get it pretty much down to a science, but she was always glad there was nobody around to hear her grunt and groan and swear or see her struggle with the balance as it tended to tip one way or the other before she got it under control.

Her arms were already burning from the exertion of the paddling—this was her first outing this year, and her muscles had gotten soft and lazy over the winter.

"Gonna be sore tomorrow," she said to herself, as she unlocked the door from the garage to the house she lived in alone.

Edgar sauntered into the room and began weaving around her ankles—his feline way of saying hello and that he loved her (and possibly a request for something tasty. Treats, food, whatever—just something good).

Kat had moved out three years ago this month. Piper hadn't been ready for that then, and she still didn't like to think about it now. They'd picked the house out together, though Kat's credit was lousy, so Piper's was the only name on the deed. That actually made things easier when Kat had left. Easier legally. Easier financially. Not easier emotionally. It had taken Piper months before she could even breathe. Her feelings for Kat had run deep, deeper than she'd realized, and Kat's reasons for leaving had made perfect sense. And were also devastating for Piper to actually hear. Just when she was starting to feel somewhat human again, her father had died and sent her spiraling right back down into the depths of darkness and pain and hopelessness.

It was getting better, though. Several months ago, Piper had finally hired a painter to come in and change the color in almost every room. She rearranged some furniture, got rid of some altogether, and bought an entirely new bedroom set. She had the carpet pulled from the living room and had hardwood installed, which gave the room a whole new look, exactly what she'd been going for. The house was no longer hers and Kat's. It was just hers, and she'd wanted it to feel that way. No, she'd *needed* it to feel that way. And now it did. It still felt a bit empty, but she was doing better with that.

In the bedroom, Piper had just stepped out of her clothes, ready to shower, when her phone rang. Grabbing it from the nightstand, she saw that it was her big sister. She swiped to answer. "Hey, G."

"Hi there, Pipe-sicle. You kayak this morning?" Gina knew Piper better than anyone, could often verbalize Piper's thoughts before Piper had a chance to. It was creepy and unnerving and comforting all at once.

"I did. It was chilly, but worth it. The sunrise was gorgeous." Piper stood in front of the full-length mirror and eyed her naked body's profile critically.

"Mom called to say she was having a good time and was heading to New Orleans tomorrow."

Piper's brow furrowed. "New Orleans? What happened to Florida?"

"She's apparently done there and ready for the next stop."

"I...what is she..." Piper fought to find words. "How many stops are there?"

"No idea."

"I thought she was just bouncing down to Florida for a while. I mean, I scolded her for gallivanting, but I didn't think she actually *was* gallivanting."

"I think that's exactly what she's doing." Gina paused. "Why do you sound so freaked about it? This is good for her."

Piper sighed, unable to come up with an answer. "I don't know. It's just...weird. Don't you think it's weird?"

"I think it's different. And sometimes, different is exactly what you need."

"I don't know..."

"She's happy, Piper. She's having a good time. Let her."

Gina was right. Piper knew that. Gina was way better at emotions and feelings; she always had been. She just...got stuff. Things that

Piper completely missed, Gina caught, analyzed, and reported back so Piper understood. Gina was her emotional translator. And thank God, because Piper needed one more often than she cared to admit.

"Fine. I'll try. But I'll still worry."

"That's acceptable." Gina's chuckle was warm and didn't make Piper feel ridiculous. "What's your plan for this lovely April Saturday?"

Piper grabbed her robe off the hook on the bathroom door. She rarely wore it but was getting chilly parading around in her birthday suit while on the phone. "I've got some cleaning to do. I need to hit the grocery store. And I thought I'd scoot by Vineyard tonight, check on things, make my presence known."

"Ominous."

"No, just being responsible. Mom left me in charge, so…"

"I thought Mom left you and *Lindsay* in charge."

"Po-*tay*-to, po-*tah*-to."

Gina laughed heartily this time. "Go easy on her. She loves that place as much as Mom does."

"Yeah, yeah." An image of Lindsay Kent, with her tousled blond hair and ridiculous green eyes, invaded Piper's mind's eye. "I just want her to know I'm watching her."

"What are you, Big Brother? Relax, Piper. You'll give yourself a panic attack."

"Yeah, yeah," Piper said again.

"Why don't you meet me and Brittany for dinner? We're going to be down at the lakefront. Eat with us and then you can zip over to Vineyard. Hell, maybe I'll go with you. God knows my daughter will have had more than enough of me by the time our meal is over. She's meeting some friends at the coffee place."

Piper didn't have to think about it. She accepted the invitation in an instant. "I'm in. I feel like I haven't laid eyes on my niece in ages. Apparently, fifteen-year-olds are way too cool to be seen with their old aunts any more. I'm sad for me."

Gina scoffed. "Please. Aunt Piper is infinitely cooler than Mom. At least you've got me beat."

"Well, then, I'm sad for you instead."

They made plans to meet and Piper finally got to hang up and get her now goose-bumped body into a warm shower.

It was shaping up to be a pretty great day.

CHAPTER FIVE

G ood evening, my queen." Bridget's voice was teasing as she bumped Lindsay with a hip behind the bar.

"I could *so* get used to that," Lindsay replied with a grin. "How are you?"

Bridget's shift was just beginning and she tied a black waist apron behind her back. "I'm not bad. You?"

"I had a really good day." It was the truth. Lindsay's Saturday had been relaxed and enjoyable. "I took Rocket for a hike in the park near the cherry grove. Haven't done that in a long time. It's just been too muddy. Then I read a little bit, did some research, came in a little bit early and opened at two. We've been steady all day, which is awesome."

"The nicer weather is bringing people out of their houses finally."

"I think that's it." Lindsay nodded. "Now, let's find a way to keep them coming back."

"How's Zack doing?" Bridget asked, pointing with her chin at the tall redhead taking care of the corner table.

"Not bad. This is his first Saturday, which is why I started him early, but he seems to be handling it okay so far." Zack was young, but at twenty-seven, not that young. Lindsay pegged him as one of those guys who'd decided college wasn't really for him, hoped to learn a trade, hadn't found one he liked, and was just kind of drifting. She could relate to that. He didn't know a lot about wine, but he was a quick study and willing to listen and learn. And he had a terrific smile that made the customers comfortable. "He's got about another hour and he's off for tonight. He's good, though. He'll pick things up."

Bridget nodded and they both watched for a beat before she asked,

"Hey, have you been to Lakeshore lately? I heard they're doing wine flights now."

"Yeah, I saw that. I'm going to take a trip over there this week, check out what they're offering."

"Maybe you should send the new girl," Bridget suggested. "What's her name?"

"Christi?"

"Yes. Her."

"Why?"

Bridget shrugged. Her dark hair was in a ponytail and her dark eyes were big when she turned to Lindsay and gave her a look. Lowering her voice to a whisper, she said, "Because the Lakeshore dudes might know who you are. You don't want them to think you're spying on them."

"We're not on *Bar Rescue*, you know." Lindsay chuckled and gave Bridget a one-armed hug. "But thank you for the suggestion. The queen shall take it under advisement."

Bridget groaned as she moved out from behind the bar to help Zack with the crowd. "You're insufferable."

"I think you meant 'Long live the queen.' But I translated you."

Bridget tossed an eye roll at her over a shoulder and chuckled.

Zack came behind the bar. "I know which wines to pour, but can you help me with the flight carrier?" he asked. He was kind of the perfect person to bring in a younger crowd. Tall and redheaded, a bit on the scruffy side, but handsomely so, not like he needed a shower.

"Sure. Let me know when you're ready." The door opened and a group of women looked around. "Be right back," she said to Zack and crossed to the newcomers. "Hi there. Welcome to Vineyard. Table for five?"

By the time Josh and his friends showed up for their 7:00 reservation, Vineyard was half-full. This was a better-than-usual crowd, but Lindsay didn't want better-than-usual. She wanted the place filled to capacity. *Okay, that might be lofty*. She wanted it pleasantly busy. After that, she'd aim for filled to capacity.

"Follow me," she said to her stepbrother after she hugged him. He looked great in his khakis and red sweater, so grown up. She couldn't get over the fact that he was an adult, had been one for years now, that he had a grown-up job and friends who were also adults. To Lindsay, he would always be a boy…the boy she wasn't. "These are the specials for tonight," she told the group that consisted of three guys and one woman, all around Josh's age. "We have flights and wines by the bottle or glass. We've also got cheese boards, so take a look and somebody will be by with water."

"This place is cool," Josh commented as he tossed his head to get his sandy, always-a-bit-too-long hair out of his eyes and looked around.

"I told you." Lindsay grinned at him, then left them to peruse their options.

By 8:00, Lindsay had already made the decision not to call last call at her usual 8:45. Vineyard was still two-thirds full and she was perfectly willing to hang out and wait on the remaining customers if they wanted to stay past nine. It would be a good experiment. She'd let Bridget go home at her usual time and work the last hour herself.

She was standing behind the bar, contemplating this schedule shift when a glance at the door had her heart picking up speed.

Piper Bradshaw stood there with another woman, one who looked like a softer, friendlier version of her. Piper wore her usual workday attire that made her look like she'd walked right off the cover of *Businesswoman Weekly*. Tonight it consisted of black dress slacks, a white top, and a black and tan scarf knotted loosely around her neck. Without her heels, Lindsay guessed Piper and the other woman—who wore jeans, a sweater, and flats—were almost exactly the same height. Piper looked around with those unique hazel eyes and her gaze locked on Lindsay's. And held.

Lindsay cleared her throat and approached them. "Piper. Hi. How are you?"

Piper gave a cool nod. "I'm well. You remember my sister, Gina?" she asked, indicating the woman standing next to her. Gina's hair was a shade lighter, strands of gray shot through. She wore little makeup and had missed out on the dimples Piper had, but she had kind brown eyes and an inviting smile. Way more approachable than Piper. "Gina, this is Lindsay Kent."

Gina stuck out her hand and Lindsay grasped it. "It's been so long, but it's nice to see you again, Lindsay. My mom speaks very highly of you."

"Well, that makes me happy. Nice to see you as well. You guys want to sit and have some wine?" Lindsay indicated a couple of empty tables. "Wherever you'd like." They chose a table near the windows. Lindsay left them with selections and went to get them water. As she poured it, she marveled at how neither Piper nor Gina popped into Vineyard. Pretty much never. She'd been working there for nearly three years and she'd only met Gina at Mr. Bradshaw's funeral. Which didn't mean she never came in—Lindsay didn't work every single hour they were open. But she was surprised by the apparent disinterest the daughters had in their parents' business.

Though Lindsay couldn't explain why in that moment, she had the sudden feeling all that was about to change.

❖

"God, this place reminds me of Dad." Gina looked around Vineyard, took in the wood beams, the solid furniture, the sconces.

"Yeah." Piper didn't mention it was exactly the reason she didn't come very often; she didn't want to talk about their father. She didn't want to get into a discussion about emotions and feelings with her sister. Not here. She settled on a wine, saw Lindsay approaching with two water glasses. She wore dark jeans, black ankle boots, and a black long-sleeved V-neck T-shirt with the sleeves pushed up to just below her elbows. A thin silver bracelet hung from her wrist. She wore no necklace, and the expanse of skin left bare and visible by the V-neck drew Piper's eye without her permission. She forced her focus toward her sister. "You decided?"

Gina blinked rapidly as if pulled out of a dream. "Oh. Yeah."

Lindsay set down the waters. "What can I get you?"

Gina smiled at her. "We'll be quick. We know it's almost closing time."

Lindsay waved a hand dismissively, and Piper watched as the bracelet caught the light and glimmered. "No worries. I'm not shoving people out." She turned to Piper. "In fact, I'm thinking of lengthening our hours, especially on weekends."

"Really." It wasn't a question, more a statement. Piper cocked her head.

"I'm thinking ten during the week, maybe eleven on Fridays and Saturdays. I'm not sure yet. I might experiment a little bit." Lindsay gave a shrug, and Piper saw her throat move as she swallowed. Was she nervous?

"That would mean longer hours for the staff, which means more pay," she pointed out.

Lindsay agreed. "Yes. But it also, hopefully, would mean more business. Which means more money coming in, so…"

"That would cover the extra staff time," Gina concluded.

"Exactly." Lindsay pointed at her as if she'd won something.

"I'd like a glass of the Malbec, please," Piper said, inexplicably needing to hurry this along.

"Oh." Gina glanced down at the wine selections on the sheet in front of her, obviously surprised by the abrupt shift. "The Meritage, please."

"Good choice," Lindsay said, and Piper almost rolled her eyes at the blatant support of yet another cheap blend. "Can I bring you ladies some cheese?"

"Oh, no." Gina waved her off. "We just had dinner and I am stupid full. Plus, we had some wine with our food, and I might be a tiny bit tipsy."

"Good for you." Lindsay chuckled, then turned those hypnotic green eyes on her and raised her eyebrows in expectation. Piper was annoyed to feel a catch in her throat. She shook her head, not trusting words to actually form.

"Okay. Be right back." And Lindsay left them alone.

"She's great," Gina said, her eyes following Lindsay's retreating form.

"She's okay." Piper picked up her water and glanced around the wine bar, noting the number of empty tables. A table of four was laughing loudly, an empty board in the center where Piper assumed some cheese used to be. Three women huddled over their table and talked in hushed tones.

Lindsay returned with their wine. "Let me know if you need anything else."

"She's really pretty," Gina said once Lindsay was out of earshot. "Any chance she plays on your team?"

Piper just looked at her.

"What? I'm just asking an innocent question."

"Your questions are rarely innocent, big sister of mine."

Gina sipped her wine. "Oh, that's good. I was simply wondering if you and she have that in common. That's all."

Piper sighed, recalling her mother telling her when she'd hired Lindsay how nonchalant she was about her sexuality. "Yes, I believe we do."

Gina's eyes widened, her expression one of massive disbelief. "And you haven't asked her out yet?"

Piper grabbed her arm. "Would you keep your voice down?" she growled through clenched teeth.

"Sorry."

Gina's stage whisper was so loud, Piper couldn't help but smile. "You have the alcohol tolerance of a housefly. You know that, right?"

"I do!" Gina pouted and hung her head for a beat. Then she snapped it back up and said, "But don't you think she's really pretty?"

Piper followed her sister's gaze back toward the bar where Lindsay was chatting with a gentleman sitting there alone. She laughed at something he said, the toss of her head exposing a long, elegant throat. Then she lifted a hand and tucked some blond hair behind her ear, and Piper swallowed hard.

"I love her hair," Gina said, as if reading Piper's thoughts. "Not too long, not too short, tons of different blonds, and the style just seems…"

"Effortless," Piper said quietly.

"Yes!" Gina pointed at her much like Lindsay had done earlier. "Effortless. That's exactly it." They both leaned slightly toward each other across the table and stared for a bit longer, until Gina whispered, "We're, like, two creepers staring at this poor girl who has no idea we're analyzing her look."

It was funny for about a second and a half, and then Piper caught herself and sat upright. "How's your wine?" She picked up her own glass, realizing she had yet to touch it, and took a gulp that was much too large.

Gina blinked in obvious confusion over the whiplash-inducing change of subject. "It's good. I said that already."

They sat in silence for long moments, Gina still surreptitiously watching Lindsay and Piper making a massive effort to look at anything *but* Lindsay. After ten minutes, she was surprised to hear herself say, "Is it weird to be here? For you?"

"You mean because of Dad?" And just like that, Gina seemed completely sober as she rested her brown gaze on Piper's lighter one. With a reach across the table, Gina closed a hand over Piper's forearm. "I know it's hard for you. It's hard for me, too. But he loved this place, so I love it."

"But you don't come here any more often than I do."

Gina's smile was sad. "I said it's hard for me, too."

Piper nodded and glanced around one more time, an odd ball of emotion settling itself in the pit of her stomach. "Can we go?"

They'd barely touched their wine, but Gina seemed to get it. "Sure."

Piper made eye contact with Lindsay, who hurried over. "We're ready for our check."

Lindsay's brow furrowed. "What check?"

Piper gestured at the table with a hand. "For our wine?"

"As if I'm going to charge you. Your mom would have my head." She smiled, and for the very first time, Piper didn't feel like it was forced. Instead, it was soft and tender and went all the way up to those green eyes, causing the corners to crinkle slightly.

"You're sure?" Gina asked, looking from Piper to Lindsay, then settling her gaze on Piper. Which Piper felt.

"Absolutely. I'm glad you guys stopped in. You should come back." Lindsay took their glasses, told them to get home safely, and left them.

The sisters stood and put their coats on. Once outside the door, Gina leaned close. "You two would make beautiful babies," she teased.

Piper groaned. "Oh, my God, shut up."

Gina just laughed and laughed.

Later that night, Piper poured herself a glass of the merlot she'd opened a day or two before and took it upstairs with her. She kicked off her heels, removed her slacks and hung them in the closet, and took off her top. In the en suite bathroom, she ran a hot bath and just dipped herself in long enough to warm up. Despite the fact that she'd been out on the lake that morning, the damp, cool evening had left a chill in her bones she couldn't seem to shake. Once in her striped flannel pajamas, she got into bed, propped up some pillows, and grabbed the latest Julie James book off her nightstand.

She sipped her wine, mentally chuckling at how shocked some of her work colleagues would be to know she read romance novels. They probably thought she read business books (and she did; two sat on her nightstand at that very moment). Books about how to fire somebody or how to ask difficult questions during a job interview. Most of them didn't know she kayaked either. She was pretty sure they all thought of her as cold. A bossy bitch. Of course, if she were male, she'd be a hero and they'd love her, ask her to join them for Happy Hour. Didn't matter, though. She was very, very good at her job and wasn't going anywhere anytime soon. They had their assumptions about her, and that was fine. She let them believe what they wanted. Didn't matter. Even the whispers about an impending merger didn't rattle her. She was tougher than most of her male coworkers and she knew it. So did some of them.

Edgar chose that moment to come visit, curling himself into a warm, purring ball against her hip. She gave him gentle scratches for a moment, then turned back to what she'd been doing. Wine glass back on the nightstand, she settled in and began to read. She'd made it about five pages in when one word caught her eye and wouldn't let go.

Effortless.

Her thoughts instantly deserted that novel and took her back to Vineyard, to Gina talking about Lindsay, to Piper using the word to describe Lindsay's look.

Effortless.

Piper hated to admit it, but Lindsay Kent was one of those women who—it seemed to Piper, anyway—had to hardly try at all. While it was true that she thought Lindsay should dress more professionally, more upscale in order to project the sophistication of the wine bar, she was also envious of that ability to throw something on and look great. Piper's routine was *not* effortless. She spent both time and money on getting herself to look the way she thought she should for her job. Her clothes weren't cheap. Neither was her hair stylist. She was not a natural when it came to putting an outfit together, so she tended to buy right off the mannequin in the store or the model on the website. It took a lot of painstaking *effort*, and for that, she disliked Lindsay Kent just a bit more.

Lindsay's hair was ridiculous, frankly. The color was gorgeous, the many different shades of gold all blending harmoniously. The cut was…well, it was simple, to be honest. Nothing at all fancy. It was layered, the ends skimming her shoulders. Like the rest of her, her hair was casual and fun, carefree. And when she tucked it behind her ear…

Piper swallowed hard and grabbed her wine, almost toppling the glass in her irritation.

"Enough," she said aloud. Edgar opened his big yellow eyes to look at her. The empty room echoed her voice back to her and then the silence settled back in. "Enough," she said again, but this time, it was a whisper.

Piper was hard on herself. Harder than anybody else. It was probably her biggest flaw, but she couldn't seem to help it. She was her own harshest critic, her own worst enemy. She excelled at beating herself up over mistakes, misjudgments, whatever. Her father used to worry she'd give herself a heart attack from all the stress she took on. Sometimes, she agreed with him. She could hear him in her head sometimes. Like now.

Baby girl of mine, you have got to ease up on yourself. We all make mistakes, even you. So what? Let 'em go. Move on. Just breathe. Just be.

Whenever she started to worry too much, to freak out, she'd do her best to close her eyes and channel him, try to hear his voice. *Just breathe. Just be.*

With a sigh, Piper dropped her head back against the headboard. "God, I miss you, Dad," she whispered. "I miss you so much." The book in her lap, she sat like that for a long moment before saying, "And this is when it's good to have a cat." She smiled softly at the black and white ball of fur next to her. He looked up at her, yawned widely, but held her gaze with those big eyes of his. He got her. Edgar totally got her, she was sure of it, and for that, she loved him more than she could ever put into words. His company, the warmth of his presence, it kept her grounded, especially at moments like this when her emotions threatened to wash her away like a shell on the beach. She reached out, ran the back of her finger along his soft cheek.

She finished her wine, brushed her teeth, and settled back into bed. Giving up on the book, she clicked on the TV and turned out the lamp. Deciding on a Hallmark movie she'd already seen but had enjoyed, she snuggled down into the covers to watch and hopefully, drift off to sleep. But the lead was a blond woman, tall, casually dressed in jeans and a T-shirt.

That was all it took.

Lindsay invaded her thoughts once again.

Piper groaned. "Goddamn it."

❖

Back at Vineyard, Lindsay locked the door behind the last customers. It was after eleven, but she didn't care. She considered her experiment a success. There hadn't been a lot of customers. Two tables, and one was her brother's, so she wasn't even sure she could count that. But the other table had stayed and Lindsay believed they were happy not to be ushered out at nine o'clock on a Saturday night. Bridget had stayed until almost ten...nearly an hour past her scheduled end time. There hadn't been enough customers to keep her busy, but she stayed anyway.

Once she'd finished turning the chairs up onto the tabletops and sweeping the floor, Lindsay stood in the middle of the wine bar and looked around. All four walls were wood, and that made it feel dark. Not necessarily a bad thing, but brightening it a little bit might make it more inviting. She studied the far wall—the only one with no windows, as it butted up against the next store. Maybe something cream? She wouldn't need more than a couple gallons of paint...

Lindsay wasn't sure how long she stood there staring at the wall, but a car door slammed outside and jerked her back to the present. Tomorrow was Sunday and the wine bar was closed (something she also wanted to change). It wouldn't take much time, energy, or money to paint this wall. And if she did it all herself, she wouldn't have to run anything financial past Piper Bradshaw.

Taking the broom and dustpan to the back to stow them in the closet, Lindsay thought again about how fascinating the difference was between Piper and her sister. Physically, they actually looked very much alike. It was obvious to anybody who looked that they were sisters. The fascination came in the soft versus hard, the casual versus sophisticated, the approachable versus the standoffish. How two women with similar genes could be so different was intriguing.

Lindsay only had stepsiblings, so nobody to compare her face to, nobody who shared the same genes as her. Maybe that was why she couldn't get the Bradshaw sisters out of her head. Lindsay could see Mrs. B. in both of her daughters, but Gina definitely resembled her more, and Lindsay decided it wasn't so much a physical similarity but rather the friendly approachableness she exuded. Just like her mom.

Piper, on the other hand...

Lindsay shook her head, not wanting to waste time there. Piper had come by, so maybe she'd gotten her fix, done her duty, and Lindsay wouldn't see her again for a while. Fingers crossed, because Lindsay had the feeling that it didn't matter what ideas she had, Piper was going to oppose them all. Why, she had no clue. But she was a good judge of such things, and she'd read Piper like a book. Piper didn't like her and resented the power her mother had given her. Part of Lindsay was curious, that part of her that had thought at one time she wanted to be a psychologist. She wanted to analyze Piper, dig in, dig down, figure her out. But a larger—and more reasonable—part of her scoffed. She needed to let that go. Piper Bradshaw was insignificant in the grand scheme of Lindsay's life.

Besides, she had plans for this place. By the time Mrs. Bradshaw came back, Lindsay wanted Vineyard to be the hottest place on the lake. And that was going to take some work.

CHAPTER SIX

I still can't get over how amazing that looks." Bridget sat at one of the tables in Vineyard, Lindsay on her left and Mike, the distributor for Lollypop Wines, setting up his supplies opposite her. She gazed at the wall across from them, the wall that used to be weathered wood and was now weathered wood painted a warm cream color. "It brightens up the room without taking the warmth."

"Yeah?" Lindsay asked. "Good. That's exactly what I was going for."

"And it feels bigger in here."

Lindsay nodded, unable to keep her grin from widening. "Well, my shoulders are killing me and Rocket still has paint on his pads, but we got it done. I'll put the pictures and stuff back up when we're done here. Should be dry by now."

Mike opened a bottle with his wine key and Bridget gave a tiny half squeal of delight.

"I can't believe I get to do the tastings with you," she stage-whispered as she grasped Lindsay's arm.

"Mrs. B. always said a second opinion was a good thing. Did you eat a big breakfast? We've got two of these this morning."

"French toast, baby."

"Excellent."

Mike poured them each a small amount of wine and began to pitch his product, a new red blend.

Wine tastings were part of the job, a part that Lindsay wasn't privy to until she'd worked at Vineyard for over a year. They were more than just picking wines that tasted good. Taste was subjective. What one person liked, another might hate. The tastings were more about what they could teach the customers as well as what would sell. That's why

Mrs. B. had always had at least one other person taste with her. Once that second person was Lindsay, it had stayed that way. And with Mrs. B. gone, the person Lindsay trusted most was Bridget.

They tasted several wines over the next three hours, both from Mike and from a second distributor who came in after him.

"This is unusual," Lindsay'd told Bridget. "Mike had to reschedule, so we ended up with back-to-back tastings, which is not ideal." By the time the second distributor had packed up her stuff and departed, Lindsay was feeling the wine even though she'd ended up spitting some out. She was pretty sure Bridget was as well.

"That was awesome," Bridget said, shelving the clean glasses she'd removed from the commercial dishwasher in the back. "I learned so much."

Her smile was contagious. "That's how I felt the first time I tasted with Mrs. B. When she first taught me that trick for telling how acidic a wine is."

"You mean that thing where you hold it in your mouth, swallow it, breathe through your nose, and see how much you salivate?"

Lindsay chuckled as she wiped down the bar with a disinfectant spray. "That."

"That was so cool."

She tossed the cloth over her shoulder, folded her arms, and leaned the small of her back against the bar. "Tell me something," she said to Bridget.

Bridget looked at her and must have decided her stance was serious because she stopped what she was doing and faced Lindsay. "Okay."

"We tasted a lot of Old World versus New World wines today. What did you think?" Lindsay had her own opinion but wanted another. Yes, Bridget was fairly new to the game, but she was quick and she was smart. She'd picked up very quickly that Old World wines were mostly European—Italian, French, Spanish, German—and New World wines were from the US, Australia, New Zealand, South Africa, Canada.

Obviously taking time to really think about the question, Bridget inhaled slowly and then let it out. "I liked both," she said finally. "I really did. And I was surprised by a lot of things."

"Like?"

"Like the fact that the Old World stuff was subtler. I expected them to be the bigger, bolder wines. I was surprised that the New World stuff fit that bill better. I was also surprised to learn that 'fruit-forward,'" she made air quotes, "doesn't necessarily mean sweet."

Lindsay nodded. "That's a big misnomer."

"You know what I was doing in my head during comparisons?"

"Tell me."

Bridget broke eye contact and went back to shelving glasses as she spoke, almost as if she was embarrassed. "I was assigning celebrity names that fit each wine."

Lindsay furrowed her brow in confusion.

Bridget laughed at her expression. "Like, that one from Italy? The Primativo? That was Robert De Niro compared to the Zinfandel from California. That one was more...Tony Soprano." When Lindsay still didn't comment, Bridget went on, her hands flailing animatedly as she spoke. "Like, the Primativo was subtle and had staying power. It was a more constant presence. Like De Niro. And the Zinfandel, that hit hard. It was a punch to the mouth. Big and loud. Like Tony Soprano."

Lindsay brought a hand to her mouth.

Bridget threw a rag at her. "Don't mock me."

Lindsay held her hand out, traffic cop style. "No. No, I'm not mocking you, Bridge. At all. No, this actually gives me a great idea for marketing some of the newer wines. Can I use that? Your celebrity naming thing? I think they're great descriptors."

Bridget's face went from slightly pouty to totally lit up. "Yes. Absolutely."

"What did you think of the blends?"

"As opposed to the single varietals?" At Lindsay's nod, she narrowed her eyes in thought. "I liked them a lot. Some, I liked even better than the standards. From what the distributors were saying, a lot goes into making the blends."

"Exactly," Lindsay said with a nod, remembering her attempt to tell Piper Bradshaw that exact thing. "I mean, they're not going to replace traditional wines. Duh. But I think they've come a long way and I'd like to get more of them in here. I think the younger demographic is more open to blends than the older, traditional crowd."

Bridget nodded her agreement and went back to the glasses while Lindsay's head spun with new ideas.

"Hey, I'm going to go grab us some food," she said to Bridget, who tossed her a look of relief.

"Oh, thank God. I was going to have to break into one of the baguettes in the back."

"Any preference?"

"You know, Zack is always talking about the burgers at Lakeshore. He says they're to die for." Bridget grimaced. "Is that too far?"

Lakeshore was on the other end of the lake, but to be honest, Lindsay relished getting out and breathing in some fresh air. "Not at all. Be back in a bit. Hold the fort."

Lindsay loved Black Cherry Lake and she loved the lake path that Vineyard was on so much that she often forgot there was an entire "rest of the lake." She hopped in her car and took her time driving along the water, catching glimpses of spring boaters, braving the still-cold water to catch some fresh fish. The lake path, where Vineyard stood, was a simple concrete sidewalk that ran along the shore of one end of the lake in a horseshoe shape. Parallel to it was a long stream of businesses, from stores to restaurants to bars to ice cream places and coffee shops. The entire lake path ran about three miles, and during the summer, it was hugely populated. Near one end was Black Cherry Park, which boasted a large gazebo where live music filled the warm evenings and food trucks and vendor tables and a beer garden would keep customers full and happy as they listened or danced.

The other end of the lake was like a slightly off mirror image of the lake path. Rather than concrete, this one was asphalt. But it ran a very similar length, boasted several shops, restaurants, and bars, and had a park at one end where local picnics and weekend celebrations were held. *No gazebo, though*, Lindsay thought, giving her end of the lake an extra point.

The weather was cool and the sky the color of a submarine hull. Rain was imminent. Lindsay pulled into the parking lot of Lakeshore, tugged her jacket around her more snugly, and headed inside, wondering if the rain would hold off long enough for her to get back to her car without getting soaked. Lakeshore had opened at eleven, and she pulled on the heavy door, then stood to let her eyes adjust to the dim lighting.

Once she could see, she headed to the bar where a guy she'd never met polished the bar with a rag. He had brown hair and a Paul Bunyan beard, and Lindsay almost laughed out loud, as he looked like every stereotypical bartender she'd ever seen in a movie. But when he looked up and greeted her, his eyes were kind and smiling and she felt a little guilty.

"What can I do you for?" he asked, throwing the polishing rag over his shoulder.

"Lunch. Can I get some food to go?" She took the menu he handed her and looked it over quickly, even though she knew what she was getting. She ordered cheeseburgers and fries for both herself and Bridget, then took a seat at the bar.

"A drink while you wait?" the bartender asked.

"Just a Coke would be great."

He slid it her way, then went about his business as Lindsay spun on her stool and took the place in. It had been a while since she'd been there, but it was much like she remembered. Mostly wood, not unlike Vineyard but a bit more on the rustic side, and it looked as if it couldn't decide what it wanted to be: rural family restaurant, sports bar, or something classier. Booths lined the walls, tables scattered in the center like marbles tossed by a kid. It was about a quarter full, but it was still early. It was true she rarely came here, but since Mrs. B. had left her in charge, it was like something in her had clicked and Businesswoman Lindsay had been let out to play. She thought it important to know what other bars and restaurants were doing.

Turning back to the bar, she sipped her Coke and slid the cocktail menu out of its little holder. The wine flights were definitely new like Bridget said—it was obvious they'd been hand-added to the already printed menu—and she read over the options. Not bad, but one of them was an exact duplicate of Vineyard's...an Around the World flight of a Spanish Rioja, an Argentinian Malbec, and a California Zinfandel. Lindsay squinted at it. Even the brands were the same. A hell of a coincidence, to be sure.

Ten minutes later, food in hand, she was in her car and headed back to Vineyard just as the rain began to fall in large, wet splotches on her windshield. Once on her own end of the lake, she noted how the whole lake path was slowly waking up, in a sense. Several places closed down in the winter—the ice cream stand, the smoothie bar, for example—but were starting to open doors and dust off cobwebs, as if awakening from hibernation. Wouldn't be long before she could scoot down the path during the afternoon and grab a cone filled with the homemade black cherry ice cream they made at the Creamery.

"Cheeseburgers, ice cream, the cheese guy later," Lindsay mumbled as she walked. "My poor hips." With a self-deprecating grin, she went back to work.

❖

Rain pelted the window behind Piper's chair like somebody was throwing small pebbles at the glass. Her mind had been all over the place today, though she wasn't sure why. Well, no, that was a lie. She knew exactly why.

Her father.

He'd been on her mind so much lately, despite her attempts to keep those thoughts and memories at bay. Any therapist worth her salt would correctly remind her that her mother had just left on her first solo outing since the death of her husband, and that was affecting Piper in ways she hadn't expected.

That was the simple reason.

Piper groaned softly and slowly turned in her chair so she could watch the rainstorm from her sixth-floor office. It had started with thunder and lightning but had calmed down to a basic gray cloud, lots of water downpour.

The complicated reason—or reasons, plural, rather—were that work was stressing her out, she was worrying about her mom traveling alone, and she was a little bit lonely. That last one wasn't an easy thing to admit, and she tended to avoid thinking about it. But thoughts of her mother made her think of her parents together and what a great relationship they had and how she was going to be forty in a couple years and didn't have that yet and what if she ended up alone forever and—on and on and on. An endless loop of panicked self-pity.

These were things she talked to her father about all the time. Work. Politics. Life. Love. No subject was off-limits. Sometimes, Piper felt like it had been two years since she'd had a deep conversation with anybody at all.

Which would be very hurtful to Matthew. To Gina. To Piper's mom. She knew that. Didn't make it not true.

Her father had been the COO of a large real estate company for nearly thirty years before he'd retired. He'd gotten bored quickly, found a small bar for sale on the coveted lake path, and before anybody could say Cabernet Sauvignon, Vineyard had been born. He loved that place, put his heart and soul into it, spent a ton of time there. Piper used to go all the time, sit at the bar while he served his customers, talk to him about whatever crap she was dealing with at work. HR issues, sexist treatment, overly demanding clients. He had experienced all of them and he was her sounding board. Whenever she was unsure what to do, how to act, what to say, she'd go to her dad and he'd have just the right advice...or he'd help her come up with the solutions herself, which always made him that much prouder of her. Once her mother had retired from teaching, she'd joined him at Vineyard and it had been their hangout, the three of them. Even Gina would pop in every so often when she wasn't busy with the kids.

Tom Bradshaw had loved Vineyard. And now Piper was in charge.

She found herself subtly nodding as the rain began to let up and a hesitant ray of sunlight peeked from between gray clouds, then vanished again as if uncertain. Yeah, she needed to pay more attention to Vineyard.

For her father.

A knock on her office door pulled her back to the day at hand. One of her managers she'd asked to see reported for duty, a worried expression on his face.

"Come on in," she said, gesturing for him to enter, and she got back to her day.

❖

By six thirty, the rain had decided it still wasn't finished and hammered at the roof of Piper's SUV as she sat in the parking lot next to Vineyard. She couldn't see in the windows from her angle, so had no idea if it was busy. But the parking lot had exactly four cars in it, one of which she knew was Bridget's, so she figured the weather was keeping people away.

After ten minutes in the car, she gave up on waiting and reached into the back seat for an umbrella. It wasn't like she couldn't manage the forty-yard walk from her car to the door of the wine bar, but she was wearing heels and a very expensive suit she'd rather not get drenched. She pushed her car door open with her foot, popped the umbrella up, and hurried to the door, where there was enough of an awning to give her space. She folded the umbrella back up and stepped inside.

The inside of Vineyard was warm and inviting, as it always was. It also seemed…bigger tonight, which was weird. Piper squinted as she shed her wet coat. Two tables were occupied and a handsome man in a suit sat at the bar. Piper headed that way and took a stool. It took her several minutes before she noticed the painted wall.

"Hey there, Piper. How are you?" Bridget's voice was cheerful and friendly. Piper pegged her as one of those people you couldn't help but be at least a *tiny* bit happy around. "Is that rain ever going to stop?"

Piper turned to her, brow furrowed. "I'm starting to wonder."

"Can I get you something?"

"Yes, I'll have a glass of the Chateau le Prince Bordeaux, please."

Bridget grimaced. "We're not carrying that one anymore," she said, apology in her voice.

"Since when?"

"Last week?" When Piper didn't respond, Bridget said, "We have a California Cabernet that we're offering instead. I think you'll like it. It's got very similar notes to it." She bit down on her bottom lip and Piper realized she was nervous.

"Fine," she said with a slightly annoyed wave of her hand, which she then pointed at the wall. "When did this happen?"

Bridget followed her gesture. "The wall? Oh, Lindsay did that over the weekend. Doesn't it look great? Really brightens up the place." She took a bottle down and went to work with her wine key. "Fresh bottle for you," she said, with an uncertain smile.

"Is Lindsay here?"

"No, she ran home to feed her dog. She'll be back." A quick glance at the clock on the wall had her adding, "Any time now."

The cork released with a pop and the gentleman sitting two stools down commented, "I love that sound," with a smile.

Piper nodded and gave him a smile in return.

A tall, reed-thin woman approached the bar and stood next to Piper. "Hey, Bridget, can we get another bottle when you get a sec?"

Bridget looked over her shoulder at the customer. "Of the Stuffed Elephant?"

"Yeah, the one you recommended. It's amazing."

Bridget nodded. "You got it."

"I'm going to have to try that one next time," the man said.

"It's fairly new for us, but it's been going over really well. Lindsay's right; people love the blends." She slid Piper's wine in front of her. "Anything else? Want some cheese with that?"

Piper shook her head. "No. Thanks. I'm good."

The gentleman held up his nearly empty glass. "Cheers."

She smiled and lifted her own, then sipped.

"Bridget, I'm all set when you get a minute," he said.

"You got it, Mr. R." Bridget pulled out a tablet and touched the screen a few times, and that was the first time Piper had noticed the cash register was gone.

"What's that?" she asked, pointing.

"This? It's a tablet. It's how we do our transactions. Your mom loves it." Bridget smiled and handed the tablet to the gentleman, who signed with his finger.

"When did she make that change?"

Bridget shrugged. "I don't know…Two months ago? Three? It was Lindsay's idea. Makes things a lot easier on the waitstaff, and the app is super easy to use." She set the tablet down on the back counter. "Take it easy, Mr. R. See you Wednesday." Then she disappeared into the back.

Mr. R. donned his gray trench coat. "Time to brave the elements," he said. With a tip of his head, he bid Piper good night. He held the door open for Lindsay, who shook herself as she entered.

"Thanks, Mr. R. Catch you Wednesday?"

"Of course."

Lindsay turned her head and met Piper's gaze. Did her friendly smile falter just a bit? Piper wondered if she imagined it.

She crossed the floor, and Piper took her in as Lindsay shed her coat and carried it behind the bar with her. Dark jeans, a white button-down shirt, sleeves rolled up, several silver bangle bracelets jingling softly on her left wrist. Decidedly un-hippie-like, though Piper chose to ignore that. Lindsay's hair was tousled and a little wet, and she tucked a chunk behind her ear as she disappeared in the back, presumably to hang up her coat. She was back quickly.

"What are you having?" she asked Piper, indicating her glass.

"Not the Bordeaux I wanted."

Lindsay wrinkled her nose. "Yeah. That one is really pricey. Wasn't selling. Did Bridget give you the Cab instead?"

Piper nodded.

"And?"

"It's not bad."

One corner of Lindsay's mouth lifted slightly. "Not bad is good. I'll take not bad."

Without looking, Piper jerked a thumb over her shoulder. "You painted." She tried hard not to sound like a scolding parent, but wasn't sure she succeeded.

"I did. Like it?"

Piper opened her mouth to speak, but before she could, Lindsay continued.

"I think it makes it look both brighter in here and bigger. If the sun ever comes out again, it'll be even more obvious. Not that the majority of our customers are in here during the daytime, but you know what I mean. That wood sucked up a ton of paint, too. Took me three coats. I was beginning to wonder if I'd ever be finished." Her laugh was a bit shaky, like she was nervous. Piper wasn't sure if she was glad or sympathetic about that.

"Maybe you can run something like that by me next time." Piper had meant it to be a question, not an order, but again: failure.

"I didn't use money from the business account. I used my own." The nerves were suddenly gone from Lindsay's voice, Piper noticed. It had a very slight edge to it.

"Okay. Still. It's a change, and I'd like to be apprised."

"Fine."

Their gazes held for a beat. Two beats. Three.

"Hey, I left a couple messages for you in the office," Bridget said, obviously sensing the tension and wanting to alleviate it.

Lindsay nodded, her eyes still on Piper's. "Okay. Thanks." Then she looked away.

Piper picked up her wine and drained it, wanting to chalk that up as a win, but somehow, it felt hollow. As Lindsay went into the back, Piper mentally shook herself. That exchange had left her uncertain and weirdly confused. About what, she had no idea, and that confused her more. She pulled a twenty from her wallet and placed it on the bar under her glass, then left without a word.

❖

"There is no way I'm running every single thing I want to do here by her," Lindsay said quietly in the back office.

"Why are you trying to pace in here?" Bridget asked. "It's, like, six feet total."

Lindsay stopped. "Can you believe her? I've worked here for three years and I've laid eyes on her, like, three times. Now? Twice in a week."

"She's got some control issues, it would seem."

Lindsay scoffed. "You think?"

Bridget peeked out through the two doorways, a straight shot to the bar. "She's gone. You can relax now."

"Not the Bordeaux I wanted," Lindsay mimicked in a whiny voice.

Bridget listened, but made no comment.

"Mrs. B. and I are going to have a conversation next time she checks in."

Bridget shook her head with a sigh. "I don't understand you two." Then she left to take care of customers.

Lindsay blew out a breath of frustration. Was this how it was going to be now? Mrs. B. had given her free rein, but not really? "Hey, Linds, go ahead. Implement those changes you've been driving me mad with. Experiment. Knock yourself out. Oh, by the way, here's my daughter the pit bull. Good luck doing anything she doesn't want you to."

Seeing Piper on that stool when she'd walked in had been a shock. Mostly because the first thing Lindsay had seen was a pair of legs. Toned and shapely legs, gorgeous legs, crossed at the knee, the one on top bouncing gently, black high heel dangling from the toes of one foot. Her eyes had followed them up to the black skirt, then an emerald green top, then the obviously amused face of one Piper Bradshaw, all dark waves of hair and mysterious eyes. Realizing who it was sent Lindsay's joy at looking right out the window.

"Okay. Take a minute," she whispered to herself. "Just take a minute." She stood still in the middle of Mrs. B.'s office—which she was trying not to think of as hers, but sometimes did—and counted slowly to ten. Once she finished, she felt better. It was a little trick her college roommate, Angela, had taught her so many years ago when Lindsay would let things get to her. *Just breathe*, she'd say. *Just take a moment and breathe. Focus on the in and then the out. You'll calm right down.* She'd been right, and the exercise had served Lindsay well throughout her life.

Making a mental note to give Angela a call this week, Lindsay exited the office and went out into the wine bar. Only three patrons remained, and she sent Bridget home, then put her elbows on the bar and scrutinized the interior of Vineyard, her brain whirring with ideas.

CHAPTER SEVEN

"Hear that, Rocket?" Lindsay asked her dog in a voice just above a whisper. The yellow Lab sat at her feet, ears pricked, and cocked his head.

"I don't hear a thing, Mom."

"Exactly. The silence of nature." She took a deep breath of fresh, woodsy air. "Isn't it awesome?" With a reach down and a flick of her wrist, Rocket was off his leash and bounding through the trees. "Don't get too far ahead of me," Lindsay called, and as if he understood, the dog stopped and looked back. When Lindsay was about fifteen yards away, he bounded off again. She chuckled and shook her head.

This was her favorite. Her favorite time of day, her favorite hiking companion, her favorite place on the lake. She'd slacked lately, and she knew it. Rocket needed this. He was cooped up at home for long periods of time, but he was young and he needed the exercise.

The sun was just now coming up over the horizon, coloring the morning in a gorgeous haze of indigo and pink. Rocket broke through a copse of trees and headed down to the shore where he could slurp up water like he hadn't had any in weeks, the sound seeming extra loud in such a peaceful space. Lindsay caught up to him and grinned at him as he splashed in the water, but only about ankle deep.

"Cold, huh, buddy?" Her gaze slid from her dog up to the vast expanse of Black Cherry Lake. She saw a lone kayak gliding silently through the water. It was bright green, but that was about all she could make out from this distance, the unidentifiable pilot stroking strong and sure as the kayak moved cleanly along. The paddle barely registered a splash at all as it cut into the water and pulled the kayak forward. Lindsay thought she could make out a ponytail on the paddler, but wasn't sure; it was just far enough away. She stood there and watched for what felt like a long time, until the kayak had moved down the lake and she could hardly make it out any longer. "I'd like to try that some time, Rock. What do you think? Wanna?"

"You know I love the water, Mom." Her dog looked at her with that adoring face, the one that said Lindsay was everything in the world to him, and she laughed out loud.

"If we can just find me a girl who looks at me like that, I'll be all set. Get on that, will you, pal?" He ran ahead, began his forward-and-back, forward-and-back routine, and Lindsay followed him. "Don't forget to look behind all the trees!" she called after him.

Her thoughts turned back to the idea of a girl. The idea of actually dating a girl. It might be time. Of course, if she asked Angela, time was long past and her lady parts were probably covered in cobwebs and dust from lack of use. (Yes, she'd actually said that.) It had been…God, how long had it been? Two years? Three, since she'd had an actual relationship? She'd dated on and off, of course. She was human, and a girl's got needs. But nobody had…turned her crank (Angela again) in a very long time. And she'd been fine. When she met Mrs. B., she'd been a little lost, not sure where she was going or what she wanted. Kind of stuck. Mrs. B. was down an employee at Vineyard and was looking for someone part-time; Lindsay happened to walk in at just the right moment. To this day, she and Mrs. B. would laugh about it because Lindsay had very little knowledge of wine and Mrs. B. hired her on the spot. No references. No background. Nothing.

"There was just something about you," Mrs. B. had said dozens of times. "I trusted you in an instant. The Universe was talking to me that day."

Whether it was the Universe or God or just dumb luck, Lindsay had no idea, nor did she care. She'd found something to focus on and she'd thrown herself in, head first. Videos, books, classes. She'd read everything she could get her hands on about wine. Even before she was part of the tastings, she'd be sure to go in that day, even if she wasn't scheduled, just so she could watch and listen and learn. And there'd been no turning back. While she'd never refer to it as a "calling," Lindsay was certain she was right where she was supposed to be and doing exactly what she was supposed to be doing. There was a great comfort in that, not just because she knew not a lot of people experienced that in their jobs, ever, but because Lindsay herself finally felt like she *belonged*. She would be forever grateful.

Lindsay walked for another forty-five minutes through the woods and along the lakeshore. Luckily, she'd put Rocket back on his leash just moments before seeing a doe and her two fawns nibbling at the vegetation. The babies were so small, and Lindsay was able to stand still and watch for several moments before Rocket whined and scared them away.

"Oh, they were so pretty, huh?" she said to her dog, watching the display of grace as the deer leapt away in the trees.

"Pretty enough to eat, Mom."

"No eating the deer, pal."

The rest of the walk back was uneventful, Rocket refusing to keep any slack whatsoever in the leash, straining at the end of it the whole way. Once they broke through the edge of the trees to the parking lot, Lindsay was surprised to see the bright green kayak, still dripping, propped on top of a black Audi SUV. As she and Rocket passed by the back of the vehicle on the way to their own car, her eyes caught the bare feet of a woman sitting sideways in the driver's seat, apparently just having taken off her shoes. Lindsay's eyes followed up a pair of glorious legs until she saw the woman's face and actually let out a little gasp.

Piper Bradshaw.

Piper looked up from the sock she was bunching in her hand and seemed just as surprised as Lindsay. "Hey," she said.

"Hi." Lindsay was so surprised to see her there that words left her completely. Rocket whined and strained, wanting to say hi to this new person, and finally, Lindsay found her voice, resigning herself to small talk with this woman she didn't care to talk with. "So that was you I saw out there a little bit ago." Her eyes roamed to the kayak on the roof.

"It was. I try to get on the water as often as I can." Piper finished with her socks, tied on a pair of sneakers, and slid off the seat to walk toward Lindsay's dog. His tail picked up speed and his body shook with the excitement of a dog who'd never seen people before. Piper squatted down and let him lavish her, yet another surprise for Lindsay. "Well, aren't you a handsome guy?" she said quietly.

Lindsay had never seen Piper not in business attire. She wore skintight black pants—some kind of yoga or compression material—and a long-sleeve shirt made of the same material, just as snug and with hot pink accents on the arms. The outfit left little to Lindsay's imagination, for which she was inexplicably thankful as she studied the curves and dips of Piper's body: muscular thighs, small waist, rounded hips, generous breasts. And the hair. Lindsay couldn't get over the hair.

It was a simple ponytail, curling in almost a corkscrew from the elastic band to skim Piper's shoulder blades. Many strands had escaped during her ride, and they also had some body to them, framing Piper's face like ribbons on a package that had been curled with scissors. Business attire was gorgeous on Piper Bradshaw. Casual attire was just as attractive.

"What's his name?" Piper asked as she looked up and met Lindsay's gaze.

"My name is Rocket," Lindsay said in her Rocket voice, before she could catch herself. When Piper quirked an eyebrow at her, Lindsay cleared her throat and used her own voice. "He's three and he's full of it."

"You guys walk along the lake?"

"Yeah, the path is finally not quite as muddy. Though..." She glanced at her dog's dirty feet and where he'd pawed at Piper. "Sorry about that."

"No worries." Piper put her face right up to Rocket's and was rewarded with many kisses.

Lindsay watched in disbelief, unable to reconcile the untouchable, put-together, management-type Piper she knew with this casual, kayaking, dog-kissing, down-to-earth woman squatting in a parking lot and loving her yellow Lab. It was kind of freaky. "What about you?" she finally managed, pushing the words out past her incredulity. "I didn't know you kayaked."

"There are a lot of things you don't know about me."

Was that flirty? Because that sure sounded flirty. "That's very true."

Piper stood. "Well. I guess I'd better get home. Get ready for work." She looked down at Rocket, scratched his head. "It was nice to meet you, sir."

Lindsay gave a small smile before heading to her own car. Not before she saw an amused grin cross Piper's face, though. She was wiping down Rocket's filthy paws with a towel as Piper drove out of the parking lot and headed home. Lindsay recalled how she'd done the Rocket voice before she could catch herself, sighed, and shrugged. "Oh, well," she said to her dog. "If she didn't find me unappealing before, she certainly does now. Glad to have solidified that for her. Thanks for your help, man."

Rocket licked her face in response. *"Anytime, Mom. I'm here for you."*

Back home, Lindsay had her phone propped up against a sugar

bowl as she made herself some coffee and spoke to the screen. "Damn if she didn't look amazing in those pants, though. Wow."

Angela Jackson sipped her own coffee on Lindsay's small screen. She was traveling for work and was on the West Coast for the week, still in her pajamas, the dark circles under her eyes visible even against her dark skin. "You always were a sucker for a girl in a suit," she said, her voice gravelly.

"Did you get any sleep, Ang?" Lindsay had shared an apartment with Angela for nearly four years while Angela got her bachelor's in business and Lindsay floundered, trying to figure out what to be when she grew up. She knew Angela was a very light sleeper and had trouble sleeping away from her own bed.

"I hate these damn cross-country trips," she muttered and took another sip. "So, tell me about this kayaking woman of yours."

"Oh, you misunderstand, my friend," Lindsay said as she leaned her forearms on the counter so her face was centered on the screen. "She is no woman of mine. Do I like the way she looks? Of course. I'm not blind. But she hates me, and frankly, I'm not that fond of her either." She backed up and told Angela the entire story, starting with Mrs. B.'s announcement that she was leaving to travel and ending with Piper's most recent visit to Vineyard, along with her complaints.

"And then, there she was in a kayak," Angela supplied.

"And there she was in a kayak." Lindsay nodded. "My brain had trouble computing it."

"Because you thought she lived in suits and heels?"

"I think I did, yeah." Lindsay laughed and Angela chuckled along with her.

"Well, she's your boss's daughter, so that's enough reason to stay away."

"Agreed. Also, she's kind of bossy and uptight. So there's another."

"See? You got this. You don't need me." Angela's words were punctuated by a large yawn.

"You'd better drink that coffee faster or you're going to fall asleep on your clients."

"Shit."

"When are you coming home?" It had been far too long since they'd spent any quality time together. "I miss you."

"Next week," Angela said. "I miss you, too."

"Come by Vineyard when you're back."

"You got it."

They spoke about a few more mundane things, then hung up, and Lindsay felt the distance of her best friend strongly. She was pretty independent and didn't tend to depend on a lot of people, but Angela had seen her through a lot. Angela knew more about her than anyone, and *knew* her better than anyone. Too long away from her and Lindsay's world felt off-kilter. She put a note in her phone to make sure she got in touch next week. They needed some time together.

❖

"Therefore, we're going to stay open longer. It might be slow for a bit, but once summer hits, I think it'll work really well. We'll play it by ear until then."

Lindsay glanced at her staff. It was just before noon. Everybody was there but Bridget, but she was due in later and Lindsay would fill her in. Zack, Kevin, Christi, and Sharon all looked at her openly. "We're going to do noon to ten, Monday through Thursday. Friday and Saturday, noon to eleven. And I'm going to experiment with some Sunday hours a bit, but I'll cover those for now." She watched the nods. Nobody stood in protest. "I mean, it's not a huge change, but I think it'll be good. We need to be here for our customers. Nobody wants to go out for a glass of wine and get kicked out by nine, you know?"

"I think it's a great idea," Sharon said. She was a retired schoolteacher, an old friend of Mrs. B., and had worked at Vineyard part-time for over a year now. "I'm happy to pick up a few more hours."

"Hell, more customers mean more tips." Christi smiled, then fist-bumped Zack.

"Thank you, guys, for being so flexible," Lindsay said with a relieved grin. "There are more than enough of us to cover it all." She took a beat, then added, "I've got some other ideas I'm working on, nothing solid yet, but I'm thinking about music. Live music."

Eyebrows went up and mutters of surprise went through the group.

"Nothing definite. Just an idea. I think it might bring in more people, you know?"

A couple minutes later, she dismissed them from the meeting, happy with the reception and excited to implement the new schedule. Kevin helped her take down the rest of the chairs before he left, and when noon hit, she clicked on the Open sign and stood behind the bar, surveying the space.

God, she loved this place.

She scanned some more, squinting, envisioning. The metal sign hanging on the wall that read Vineyard in fancy lettering was chipped and marred. She made a mental note to do something about that. Then she went back to the overall space, trying to visualize, before settling on the front corner. It had potential for her next idea. In her head, she rearranged the layout of the tables, moving some completely, shifting some a few feet. It could work. She was sure of it. There was only one problem: it was going to cost money. Not a lot, and hopefully, once things got rocking, it would make that money back and garner a profit. But until then, she'd have an outlay of cash. And that meant one thing.

She needed Piper's approval.

"Crap." She blew out a breath. Not a phone call she wanted to make, even after the impromptu, decidedly pleasant visit this morning.

Maybe she'd think on it for a bit...

Kate Childs, the suspense writer, came in at two, found herself a table, and pulled out her laptop.

"What's happening in the world of murder and mayhem today?" Lindsay asked, as she approached her table. "And what wine goes with it?"

"My serial killer has killed again and my detective is mulling over the clues so far. Which amount to...not much."

"Uh-oh."

"Yeah, I think she needs a glass of Chardonnay to help with that."

Lindsay grinned. "I've got just the one to help get those mystery-solving juices flowing," she said, and went to pour a glass from a new vintner she'd tasted recently.

Bridget arrived at four and Mr. Richardson came in not long after that to join Kate and the three others who'd come in during the afternoon. Lindsay greeted him when she came out from the office after updating and revamping the very old Facebook page for Vineyard.

"Okay, Bridge, we're good to go. Can you help me keep it updated on a regular basis?" She called up the page on the tablet and handed it over.

"It looks great," Bridget said after a few minutes, then offered up some additional suggestions.

"This is why I keep you around," Lindsay said. "I want it to be updated in almost real time. When somebody is thinking of coming here tonight, I want them to be able to check and see exactly what the specials are. You know?" Bridget nodded, as did Mr. R., who was privy to most of their business conversations simply by proximity. When he asked for a refill on his Montepulciano, Lindsay cocked her head and looked at him. "Would you come listen to jazz here, Mr. R.?"

"Like, live, you mean?" At Lindsay's nod, he said, "I would."

"Good." Lindsay winked at Bridget. "I thought so."

"Told you." Bridget glanced at the door as a couple entered. "You've got a phone call to make," she said over her shoulder as she went to wait on them.

"Can't I ask a few more people first?"

Bridget's voice came from behind a wall. "Sure. You still have to make the call, though."

Lindsay groaned.

It was after 7:00 p.m., and Thursday had been a rough one for Piper. There was an HR situation with one of her managers. Her boss was on vacation and left way more slack for Piper to pick up than was fair. She was waiting on a report that had been due yesterday but had yet to show up, and she had to get uncomfortably firm with the person responsible for generating it. And she was told by upper management that she needed to let somebody go tomorrow. She was tired. She was stressed out. She was starving. Her new heels were torturing her feet. And Lindsay Kent wanted to talk to her. In person. That could mean nothing good, but Piper supposed it was just icing on the cake of a horrible, horrible day.

The first thing Piper noticed when she reached for the door handle of Vineyard was the new sign that announced new hours. Looked like they were opening a bit earlier and closing a bit later and…open on Sundays now? That meant payroll would go up. That was probably what Lindsay wanted to talk about…though it looked like she'd already made the change without consulting Piper first. She shook her head and blew out a frustrated breath before pulling the door and entering.

Peals of laughter were the first thing she heard as the door shut behind her, and Piper followed the sound to a table of women about twenty feet away. Five of them. They'd pushed two small tables together and the surfaces were littered with wine glasses, bits and pieces of cheese on two cheese boards, and a couple oval slices of baguette. Lindsay's back was to Piper, but the way she reached up and tucked her blond hair behind her ear was a surefire way of identifying her. Four of the women at the table were obviously two couples. Two of them held hands and one had her hand on another's thigh. The fifth one, who had brown hair and a pretty smile, looked at Lindsay with such an obvious gleam in her eye, and Piper wrinkled her nose at the sight. *Is she going to swoon now?* The woman said something and Lindsay laughed and Piper rolled her eyes. Turning away, she took an empty seat at the bar and waited for Lindsay to finish flirting.

Bridget came out from the back carrying a slate rectangle with three hunks of cheese arranged on it, a sliced baguette in the center. She stopped for a beat when she saw Piper at the bar. "Oh, hey, Piper. Be right with you." Piper watched her deliver the cheese to a table in the corner, and for a minute, she could see her father doing the same thing. But he'd stand there and chat for longer than necessary until her mother had to actually go get him. "They came for wine, Tom, not your stories," she'd say, and Piper could hear the affection in her voice, even now, in her own head. She shook the memory away, having no energy today to deal with that pain.

"Hey." Lindsay was suddenly next to her, her voice low and laced with...uncertainty? It seemed to always sound like that to Piper. She sidled around so she was facing Piper and the bar was between them.

"Hi."

"Wine?"

"Please."

"Can I choose for you?" Those green eyes held Piper's gaze. A challenge? A plea? Piper couldn't tell, but she was curious.

"Sure." Again, no energy to fight.

Lindsay gave one nod, then turned her back to Piper so what she was doing wasn't visible. After a moment, she turned and set a glass of red wine on the bar. She had a second one in her hand. "We're going to taste this together."

Piper cocked her head. "We are?"

"Yup."

With the stem between her fingers and the glass still on the bar, Piper swirled the wine.

Lindsay did the same, then held her glass up to the light. "Tears are slow."

"More alcohol."

With a nod, Lindsay added, "A nice ruby color."

Piper's turn to nod. Then they each put their nose in the glass and inhaled. "I get lots of fruit," she said, almost to herself. "Cherries, maybe a little blackberry."

"Me, too. I'm also getting vanilla. And something…I'm not sure." Lindsay's light eyebrows met in a V above her nose. Her eyes snapped to Piper's. "Citrus?"

Piper focused, sniffed again, then nodded slowly. "I'm getting that, too. Orange, maybe?"

"Orange! Yes. That's it." Lindsay smiled at Piper, who smiled back before she realized she was doing it. "Okay. Moment of truth."

Lindsay leaned on the bar so she was closer to Piper, and they both sipped. Then they both hummed in approval.

"High tannins," Lindsay observed.

"Not nearly as sweet as I expected, given all the fruit I smelled."

"Right? Same here."

Piper sipped again, held the wine in her mouth for a beat, then swallowed. "This is good."

"Agreed. I'm going to put in an order for more."

"Are you going to tell me what it is?" Piper asked.

Lindsay shook her head. "Nope."

Piper arched an eyebrow. "It's a blend, isn't it?"

Lindsay shrugged. "Maybe it is. Maybe it isn't."

Piper couldn't help it. She grinned. Widely. The wine was good. She couldn't deny it. It was complex and interesting; it had layers. She sipped again as she glanced up at Lindsay. Who was looking over Piper's shoulder. She muttered an "excuse me," and came out from behind the bar. Piper followed her with her gaze as she approached the table of women. Again, they were cheerful and laughing, and again, the Fifth Wheel had eyes only for Lindsay.

Piper grimaced and turned away, uncomfortable with her own discomfort. She shook her head and drank her wine with her back to Lindsay while eavesdropping on the conversation the couple next to her was having. He was bitching about work. She was bitching about home.

That must be a pleasant household.

Piper sipped again, trying her best to continue eavesdropping and not to be drawn to the table where Lindsay was.

She lost that battle in less than a minute and slowly spun on her stool.

❖

"So, Mindy here wants to know if that's your girlfriend." The redhead at the table of women had very intense eye contact, and she held Lindsay's gaze like a drowning person holding a life preserver.

Lindsay furrowed her brow. "If who's my girlfriend?"

Red jerked her head in the direction of the bar. "Corporate Barbie over there."

The others at the table looked at her expectantly and the cute brown-haired girl batted those doe eyes at her. Yeah, she'd be hard to resist in any other situation. Lindsay followed Red's gaze and realized belatedly that they were talking about Piper, who was watching them with those deep, unreadable eyes of hers. The uncomfortable chuckle burst out of Lindsay before she could catch it.

"Um, no. Definitely not." She shook her head as she picked up an empty cheese board.

"Too bad," Red said. "She's hot."

Nods went around the table with the exception of the brown-haired girl.

Lindsay smiled politely but made no comment. "Can I get you ladies anything else?" They'd arrived just before five, so seemed to be winding down after almost three hours. "I'll be right back with your check." It wasn't the first time she'd been hit on by a customer and it wouldn't be the last. She took it as a compliment and went on with her work, just like always. This time was no different.

Back at the bar, Piper was looking down at her glass, turning it slowly in her fingers. Her nails were newly polished, again with a very dark color...plum or black maybe. Lindsay was definitely a fan.

"Still liking it?" she asked, and gestured to the glass with her eyes when Piper looked up.

Piper nodded, but said nothing more.

"Okay, let me take care of this table and we'll get down to business." Lindsay took the tablet over to the table, tried not to hurry them along but also tried not to get too sucked into conversation with them. Piper seemed to be in a rare pleasant mood tonight, and Lindsay didn't want to squander her chance. The table tipped her generously enough to leave her just this side of uncomfortable, and she nodded her thanks, then skedaddled back to the bar, to Piper.

"Your fan club?" Piper asked, and Lindsay couldn't quite read the tone of her voice.

"Ha. No, just some customers. A couple are regulars."

"Mm-hmm." Piper polished off her wine.

"More?"

With a shake of her head, Piper said, "Okay. Why am I here? What change do you want to make now?"

This time, reading her tone was no problem. She was back to regular, uppity Piper, and Lindsay had to consciously control her expression to keep from letting her disappointment show. "I have an idea. It's going to take a little bit of an outlay of cash, but I think after a month or two, it'll pay for itself and then make a profit for us by bringing in more of a crowd." She paused for dramatic effect. "Live music."

Piper held her gaze. Blinked. Blinked again.

Lindsay raised her eyebrows.

"You want to bring in a band?"

"More than one. And just small. Like one-man or one-woman entertainers or even duos. Keyboards and guitar. You know?" It was difficult not to let the unimpressed look on Piper's face dampen her enthusiasm, but Lindsay worked hard. "Only on weekends. Fridays and Saturdays."

"There's no room." Piper made a show of looking around Vineyard, then faced Lindsay and held up her hands, palms up.

"That corner." Lindsay pointed, then laid out what she'd thought earlier in the week, how they could move tables, set the band up in the corner. "They'd be visible, but out of the way of my staff."

"We've never had live music here." Piper said it as though it made perfect sense, like it was a fact and that was that.

"I know. But what goes better with wine than a little light jazz?" Lindsay smiled, did her best to stay up and positive, sell the idea to this most difficult of marks. "Something modern. I think we could bring in a larger, hipper crowd with some music. Local bands. Lots of advertising."

"What kind of cost are we talking?" Piper wasn't happy with the idea—that much was obvious—and she asked the question as if it was an utter burden to even think about. But Lindsay had anticipated this possibility and was ready.

"Hang on." Lindsay held up a finger. "I've got it all written up for you." She zipped back to the office and stood there for a moment, hands braced on the desk's surface, head dropped down between her shoulders. Her heart was thudding and that annoyed her. Why did talking to Piper make her so nervous? Why did she feel like the poor student and Piper, the strict teacher? Lindsay was not weak. She was not a woman who ran scared or was easily intimidated. But Piper Bradshaw could make her feel both. "Goddamn it," she muttered, as she snatched her report off the printer.

Back out at the bar, Piper had her coat on. *So, apparently, we're not even going to discuss this.* Lindsay handed the report over. "I'll email it to you as well," she said as Piper took the paper with her manicured hands that Lindsay tried not to look at.

"I'll go over it and get back to you."

"Okay." What else could she say? She hated that she was at Piper's mercy as far as money went, but that was the way Mrs. B. had wanted it. Lindsay did her best to hold in her frustrated sigh until Piper was out the door.

"And how'd that go?" Bridget asked, as she passed by carrying a cheese board littered with scraps of bread and a dirty knife.

"I am honestly not sure." Lindsay pursed her lips.

"Unsurprising."

"I guess." Lindsay shrugged. While Mrs. B. would take a bit of convincing, Lindsay was sure she'd end up thinking it was something worth trying. She trusted Lindsay. Piper? Not so much. And Lindsay knew that, so she'd taken it into consideration when writing up her report (which she wouldn't have had to do for Mrs. B.). She'd included everything she could think of. Cost of paying the bands. Cost of advertising. Cost of possible extra staff if things took off. Estimated increase of clientele, which led to estimated increase of sales. She'd Googled anything she could think of to help her. How to pitch a new idea. How to impress an investor. How to increase your business. A lot of it was junk, but there were a few diamonds, and she'd polished them up and used them to the best of her ability, doing her damnedest to ignore how annoyed she was that she had to do it in the first place. She and Piper were supposed to be equal at running things, but Mrs. B. had thrown in that one clause, that one caveat about needing Piper's approval for things that cost money. That had instantly rendered them much less equal, even if Mrs. B. hadn't realized or intended it.

Oh, well. She couldn't dwell on it or it would drive her insane. Besides, she had a strategy planned out. Her ideas for Vineyard were extensive. She had lots of changes and alterations and tweaks to bring in more business and make more money. Her list was long. If she just kept bombarding Piper with a new idea every day or two, she'd get so overwhelmed that she'd probably approve some just to get them off her plate. Since Lindsay had never worked in business before, she had no idea if this would actually work. But it seemed like a good plan, so she was running with it.

Now all she could do was wait.

CHAPTER EIGHT

When Piper opened her email at home on her couch, she couldn't help but grin. Another one from Lindsay, this subject line read *Idea #5* with a smiley. The girl was persistent, Piper had to give her that. And—though Piper would never admit this, no matter how much somebody tortured her—oddly charming. This idea list had been going on for more than two weeks now, and the first of May indicated the official start of the summer season for all the businesses along the Lake Path. As Lindsay said a couple emails ago, it was time to kick it up a notch. And though Piper hated to acknowledge it, her ideas didn't suck. Well, most of them didn't. Piper was pretty sure a few were thrown in as either filler or an attempt at humor. Potted grapevines as décor was one. Wine Pong was another. They made Piper chuckle. Reluctantly.

Idea #5 was listed as better outdoor seating, and Lindsay went on to plead her case about how they weren't using their view of Black Cherry Lake to its full potential. Piper had to agree on that one. There were a few mismatched chairs scattered around on the makeshift patio, but her parents had never gotten around to really sprucing it up, mostly because they couldn't seem to agree on how best to lay it out. Once her father had passed, her mother seemed to lose any ambition to do anything with the space at all.

Might be time to remedy that.

She jotted a quick return email to Lindsay, doing her best to stay light and positive. Gina had brought to her attention recently that she had the tendency to treat all email like work email and that her responses could be abrupt, clipped, and cold. All things Piper felt she'd needed to be at work lately. It had apparently rubbed off on her nonwork persona. She chose her words carefully, asked Lindsay if they could meet and look at the patio together, decide what they'd need. Maybe early next week? Monday, perhaps? Being open on Mondays was another new idea of Lindsay's and Piper was curious to see how that was working so far. She sent the email just as her phone rang.

"You're alive," she said happily to her mother when she hit the answer button. "Where are you now? Timbuktu? The Bermuda Triangle?"

"Sweetie, do you think I'd be able to call you if I was in the Bermuda Triangle? Do you think the aliens would let me?" Her mother's voice was laid back and relaxed, yet she sounded happy and vibrant.

"Yeah, probably not."

"How's it going there? How's work? How's Vineyard? Tell me you haven't murdered Lindsay and hidden her body."

"Things are going fine. I have not murdered Lindsay." Piper flopped onto her back on the couch and stretched out her legs so her bare feet rested on one arm.

"You didn't say 'yet.' I'm kind of shocked. You're actually getting along?"

"We're managing."

"I had a feeling you'd like her if you got to know her a little bit." Her mother sounded…smug? Maybe a little self-satisfied? Piper couldn't quite put a finger on it.

"We're not best friends, Mom. We're adults who have to work together on occasion. That's what we're doing."

"Okay, okay."

Piper could picture her mother, hands up in surrender. It was the same body language she used every time she realized she might be pushing Piper's buttons a bit too much.

"As long as the place hasn't burned to the ground, I'll back off."

Piper softened her tone. "It hasn't. I promise." She took a breath and changed the subject. "So, tell me what you're doing? Where are you exactly?"

"I'm back in Florida, which is why I'm calling. I'm leaving on a ten-day cruise tomorrow."

Piper's eyebrows shot up. "What?"

"Yup. We leave here tomorrow afternoon and head to…let me think. Jamaica. A couple other places I don't remember. Key West. I met some friends here that talked me into joining them."

"Wait. You're going on a cruise with people you just met? Mom." Piper's worry ratcheted up.

"Piper, I'm fine. They're three widows, just like me. We have a lot in common and I think it's good for me to be around people who understand my situation."

Her "situation" being that her husband was dead. Piper got that part, she did. An internal battle began in her chest between being happy for her mom and being worried.

"I wanted to call," her mother went on, "because I won't have cell service on the ship."

Piper cleared her throat, did her best not to sound as uneasy as she felt. "You call me the second you're within range again. Understand? If I don't hear from you, I'm going to panic. I'll call the Coast Guard. I mean it."

Ellen's chuckle was warm as it rumbled over the phone. "Yes, Mom."

"Ha ha. Very funny. You know you'd feel the same way if our roles were reversed."

"I would." Her mother got serious. "You're absolutely right. I will call you as soon as I can. All right?"

"Fine. Does Gina know?"

"I just got off the phone with her."

"Okay. Good." There was a beat of silence. "Mom?"

"Hmm?"

"Have fun. Okay? Have a great time."

Piper could almost see her mother relax. "I will do my best."

They talked a bit longer, about mundane things, while Edgar walked across Piper's body and began to knead her stomach. He settled down in a ball of cat just as Piper ended the call.

"Grandma's going on a cruise with a bunch of single ladies, Ed." She stroked his cheeks as his motor kicked into high gear. "Does that feel weird to you? It feels weird to me. I mean…what if some guy hits on her? Tries to pick her up? Those cruises, they can be like singles bars." The reality was, she had no idea what a cruise was like, and she was probably being ridiculous. But the thought of her mom as the target of men was just…her body literally shuddered at the thought.

She wished it wasn't going on eight o'clock and dark out. This was exactly the kind of thing that sent her to her kayak. Gliding along the water was the only thing she'd found that truly reduced her stress to manageable levels. Between her job, which had become increasingly tense, and the worry about her mother, she was feeling a little bit… edgy. Grabbing her phone, she checked the weather for tomorrow, then gave a nod.

She'd be on the water in the morning.

❖

Lindsay had overdressed for their morning walk in the woods. She had taken her jacket off and tied it around her waist, leaving her in workout pants and a hoodie. They were almost back to the parking lot and it was a lovely morning, brisk temperatures in the high forties, but headed to near seventy. May was her favorite month. Well, mid- to late May. Early May was still too close to April, and April meant rain and wind and gray skies. Once it got to be mid-May, nature started to bloom, grass became greener, the sky seemed bluer, and the sun started to show up once in a while. Lindsay could feel her entire demeanor change with the weather. Spring was, by far, her favorite of all the seasons. It meant new life, a new start, freshness.

Rocket was doing his usual run-ahead, run-back thing, which Lindsay loved. Not only because it was adorable, but because he ran himself ragged and then slept for much of the day. She'd learned the hard way that the key to a happy and relaxed dog was plenty of exercise, that they got destructive or mischievous when they were bored. Lindsay had thrown away two pairs of sneakers, a pair of boots she'd been in love with, a bathroom rug, and two throw pillows to back up that theory. Once she started running Rocket through the woods or in a park or even playing lots of ball with him in the yard, he'd stopped eating her things. Thank freaking God.

A lot of people disliked spring, especially around the lake, because it was messy. Wet and muddy and brown. Lindsay knew this firsthand because, well, she had a dog. Not just any dog, a Labrador. And if there was one thing Labradors loved, it was water. Rocket was no different, and he preferred to walk as close to the lakeshore as he could, no matter how much he sank into the mud. He'd venture in daintily in the early spring (the water was cold) and then splash in like a surfer dude in the summer. He would swim for hours if Lindsay let him, and he was fun to watch. In the summer, he'd just get wet. In the spring, though, he'd get wet and caked with mud and leaves and any other dead vegetation lying on the ground near the water. The first few times it happened,

Lindsay had tried to keep him from going into the water at all, to save herself the hassle of cleaning up after him. But then she realized how much fun he had, how happy he was doing what he was bred to do, and she decided she was willing to deal, that his happiness and joy were worth the trouble. So she invested in a waterproof cover for the back seat of her Camry and she converted the small screened-in mudroom at her back door to a sort of shower area for Rocket, complete with a hose and a drain in the floor. Totally worth it.

Today was a "venture in carefully" day for Rocket, and Lindsay watched with a smile as he trotted in until the water reached his doggie knees. He stood still and looked out over the lake, his stance all handsome and regal. Lindsay wished she had a camera to capture the pose, but before she had any more time to regret leaving her phone in the car, Rocket broke into a series of barks and bolted full-force into the lake.

"Rocket," Lindsay called, scampering toward the shore. She skidded to a halt when she saw the lime green kayak gliding by, heading toward the shore near the parking lot, Rocket all the way in the water and swimming to it. "Thank God she's not in the *middle* of the lake," Lindsay muttered with a shake of her head. Piper was actually not that far offshore at all, probably because she was just about finished with her ride and was very close to where she'd exit the water, and Lindsay watched as she propped her paddle across the kayak and reached a hand out to pet Rocket. Strangely, Lindsay was almost happy to see her. She chose not to analyze that, and when Piper looked up and met her gaze, she was able to let it go. For the moment.

"Good morning," Piper called.

"Good morning to you. Sorry about that."

"Don't be. I wish my cat seemed this happy to see me."

Lindsay smiled. "He's probably going to swim with you to the end there."

"Well, I best keep moving then, huh?" And with that, Piper picked up her paddle and made her way the remaining thirty or forty yards to where Rocket could touch the bottom. She was careful with her paddle so as not to bonk him, and Lindsay warmed at the consideration as she trotted along until the path spit her into the parking lot and she could curve around to meet up with her dog and that pretty girl in the kayak.

It was still so odd to see Piper in clothes that weren't designer and didn't make her look like the poster girl for entrepreneurial women. Not that Lindsay didn't appreciate that look because she did, in a big way.

There was something untouchable about it, something unattainable. Maybe that's why this change, this other look, seemed so dramatic. The outfit was similar to last time, all skintight nylon, though today's bottoms were shorts and left Piper's legs bare from the knees down. As before, all her curves were on display, which Lindsay had no choice but to appreciate; the woman was beautiful. But overall? Out of everything? It was the ponytail. The ponytail was what made the change of styles seem so polar opposite. Something about all those waves harnessed into one elastic band, bouncy and loose as they hung from the back of Piper's head...something about that ponytail was what made her seem so much friendlier, so much more approachable. Lindsay tried to shake it all away, not wanting to stare, but finding it hard not to.

Yeah, Kayak Piper? Total turn-on.

"Isn't the water cold?" Lindsay asked as she approached the shore to grab Rocket's collar and clip his leash on.

"Very," Piper replied. She waded through water that was almost to her knees. "But I hate scraping the bottom of my kayak on the pebbles, you know? I mean, I could. It's made to withstand that. But the sound is just awful." She brought her shoulders up in a full-body cringe as she wrinkled her nose. "Makes it seem like I'm doing all kinds of damage." She tugged the kayak behind her as she exited the water, then pulled a small bag out of it. When she met Lindsay's curious gaze with those hazel eyes, she held it up. "Waterproof. My phone and a couple granola bars."

"Ah." Lindsay nodded.

And then Piper heaved up the kayak, held it over her head, and carried it to her SUV.

Lindsay swallowed. Hard. With a clear of her throat, she caught up and asked, "Can I help?"

Piper's face showed relief. "I'd love that."

Lindsay grabbed one end, and together, they hefted the kayak up and settled it into the two-kayak rack on the roof.

"I can do it myself," Piper explained. "Been doing it myself for a while now. But that doesn't mean it isn't awkward as hell. I need longer arms."

"That would probably help. Hard to find them, though."

"Right? Surprisingly, Amazon doesn't seem to carry them." Piper began strapping the kayak into the rack.

"And I thought they carried everything."

Piper smiled at her, Lindsay felt a flutter in the pit of her stomach that was not unpleasant, and for a moment, she wondered if this wasn't really Piper. She was so nice, so friendly. Was there a twin maybe? An alternate version of the Corporate Barbie persona? She immediately felt guilty for thinking such a thing, though, and was brought back to the present when Rocket shook, sending mud and lake water flying everywhere.

"Okay, pal, time to get you home and cleaned up." Lindsay glanced at Piper. "Unless you need more help."

"No, I've got it. Thanks."

"All right, then." A beat of silence passed. "I guess I'll see you Monday."

Piper nodded and gave her another smile and a little wave before she pulled on a strap to tighten it.

What is happening? was all Lindsay could think as she tugged Rocket to the car and her stomach continued with the fluttering thing. She belted herself in, a bit bewildered by it all, and they headed home.

❖

As Piper pulled off her kayaking attire, she found herself smiling at the muddy paw prints on her shorts. Having Rocket swim right to her was wonderful and reminded her how nice it might be to have a dog. Edgar was great. She loved her cat, wouldn't give him up for anything. But it wasn't quite the same. He was happy to see her when she got home because that meant it was time for food. And once he'd eaten, he was happy to cuddle her. But dogs were happy to see you, period. No caveats like "Feed me, and then I'll love you." Which Piper had to admit, she admired about Edgar.

And then her smile grew wider when her thoughts shifted to Rocket's owner.

Lindsay was growing on her. She had to admit that, even though she hated to.

As she pulled open her closet door and chose an outfit for the day, her brain handed her an image of Lindsay from earlier. It was the first time Piper had seen her in yoga pants, but she hoped it wouldn't be the last because they…were good to her. A simple white T-shirt had left her long arms bare. Lindsay's skin was pale, but more creamy than starkly white, and, Piper had noticed, very subtle freckles dotted her skin. The black jacket tied around her waist was casually cute, and she must have tucked her hair behind her ears a dozen times—something Piper now realized was a nervous habit.

Wow. She'd noticed a lot of detail about Lindsay today, and wasn't quite sure what to do with that.

Before she had a chance to mull over the why of it, her phone pinged, and she opened a text from Ian Parsons, another manager at her workplace.

Get here soon. Merger has a new wrench.

"Shit," Piper muttered. She typed up a quick response and got herself into the shower.

Any relaxation her kayak ride had brought her was quickly eclipsed by work stress. Her day was a flurry of meetings and covert texts and subtle looks between a handful of coworkers. There had been rumors of a merger for nearly a year. Rumors that her company was going to be taken over by a much larger conglomeration. Those rumors had solidified into truth about three months ago, but the company poised to take over was reputable and successful and *known*. Suddenly, the merger details had shifted, it seemed.

"Harbinger?" she whispered quietly to Ian, hand in front of her mouth, as they sat in yet another meeting. "Seriously? What happened to Curtis and Company?"

"Harbinger came in with a better offer, apparently," Ian said, just as quietly. Like Piper, he was young to be in the upper management position he occupied. But also like Piper, he worked his ass off and was excellent at his job.

"Let's hope we don't have to take their name literally."

"We could get lucky. Curtis could up their offer."

Piper spared a glance at Ian and quirked an eyebrow.

He sighed. "I know. I know."

The hardest part of all of this for Piper, aside from the not knowing anything for sure, was that her people most likely didn't know at all. She had over a dozen beneath her and, though they may have heard an occasional whisper of a rumor, they most likely had no idea their workplace was going to be purchased by another. Upper management had been sworn to secrecy.

The day was a whirlwind. It also felt like it lasted for a week. Piper didn't understand it, but thanked God it was Friday. When she finally turned her office lights off and closed the door, it was nearly seven, and she wanted a glass of wine. She had a lovely Sauvignon Blanc at home, already chilled, but she found herself driving to the lake path instead. Took her a while to find a parking spot—not unusual for a Friday in late May—but it was a nice night and she didn't mind walking a bit.

She'd thought about calling Matthew. She'd toyed with texting Gina. In the end, she did neither, deciding to go by herself. Why, she wasn't quite sure, but by the time she reached for the handle of Vineyard's door, she felt almost content. This was always where she'd go when she had work issues: to see her father and talk them through. The fact that he wasn't here—and never would be again—slapped at her like a toddler trying to get her attention, but she was getting used to it. She ignored it and pulled the door open.

Vineyard was about half-full. Good for Vineyard in general, but should be better for a Friday night. The last stool near the wall was open at the bar, and Piper took it. She hung her purse on the hook underneath, shed her spring rain coat, and made herself comfortable.

The Pandora station on the sound system filled the space with soft jazz as Kevin Short bustled around, a black apron tied around his waist and a smile on his face. He was of average height, despite what his name announced, and a little husky. He kept his dark hair cropped close because, Piper once overheard him explain to her dad, his hair didn't get long, it got big. The memory made her grin. Her father had liked Kevin a lot.

"Hey, what are you doing here?"

Lindsay's voice pulled Piper's attention and she turned to look at the face of a person who was, if Piper was reading it correctly, happy to see her. She'd worn the same expression this morning at the lake, though now, there was a shadow of hesitation.

"We said Monday, right? Did I screw up?"

"You didn't. I had a rough day at work and decided I wanted a glass of wine."

"You're in luck. We have that here. Lots of it." Lindsay tucked some hair behind her ear, leaned on her forearms so she was closer to Piper, and Piper was pretty sure nobody could hear but her. "Tell me what you want."

Piper was woefully out of practice when it came to the art of seduction. She was pretty sure she wouldn't know somebody was flirting with her even if they came right out and said, "Hey, you. I'm flirting with you." But the little tightening low in her body told her that flirting might be exactly what Lindsay was doing. She was close. Her eye contact was intense. She wet her lips, and that was all Piper needed.

All of a sudden, it was like riding a bike, something you never really forgot how to do. So she held that green-eyed gaze of Lindsay's, leaned a bit closer, and cocked her head ever so slightly before answering, "Surprise me."

The little mischievous half-grin and eyebrow quirk Lindsay sent back at her as she left to get the wine was so damn sexy right then, that Piper decided yeah, she was totally flirting.

Right?

This was so weird.

You don't like her, remember? her brain scolded her, and she tried hard to recall why. Weirdly, she drew a complete blank.

"Okay, try this." Lindsay set a glass of white wine in front of her, then rested her elbows on the bar and her chin in her hands as she waited.

"You're going to watch me drink?" Piper asked, amused.

"Yep."

"Well, okay then. Enjoy." Piper lifted her glass in a salute, then took a sip. The wine was chilled and danced on her tongue immediately. She glanced up and her gaze was caught, Lindsay's eyes sparkling as she watched. "It's got some zip," Piper said, as she focused on the taste left in her mouth. "But then it smooths out on the finish."

Lindsay was nodding, her face open and interested. "What do you taste?"

Piper squinted, took another sip, let it roll around before swallowing. "Peaches."

Lindsay's smile grew wide. "I got apricots, yes. Similar."

"Is this a blend?" Piper asked.

"Maybe it is, maybe it's not."

Piper shook her head with a chuckle. "Where's it from? Can you at least tell me that?"

"Sonoma." A couple entered the door and Lindsay held up a finger to Piper. "Be right back."

Piper could literally feel herself relax. She wasn't sure what to do with that, so she chose to tuck it away and not deal with it at the moment. Instead, she picked up her wine and spun a bit on her stool so she could look at the expanse of the wine bar. There were six occupied tables, and a couple of the parties were more than three people. Kevin was making a table of three couples laugh as Lindsay passed him with the couple trailing behind her. She got them seated, left them the menu of wines and cheeses, and returned behind the bar. Catching Piper's eye as she went by, she gave her a wink.

Piper's stomach fluttered. She closed her eyes and gave her head an almost imperceptible shake, then took another sip of the delicious California probably-blend as Lindsay delivered water to the new customers and took their order. Piper watched her return, watched the back of her as she poured wine. She was wearing her usual jeans. These were light rather than dark, and looked soft and worn, a few spots of near white telling Piper holes were imminent. One at the bottom corner of a back pocket held her attention for a beat.

She's got a great ass.

Piper's eyes flew open wide as the thought blasted through her head, and she had difficulty pulling her eyes away from said ass. Lindsay chose that moment to turn around, and Piper was pretty sure she failed to yank her own gaze up fast enough. Lindsay had a funky metal flight carrier in each hand. One held three glasses of red, the other, two whites and a rosé. Again, Lindsay quirked one eyebrow and Piper was pretty sure she'd been busted. Once Lindsay left with her flights, Piper let out a low groan and dropped her chin to her chest.

A few moments later, Lindsay was back. She resumed her previous position of leaning her forearms on the bar and focusing her attention directly on Piper. "So, why was your workday a rough one?"

Piper waved her off. "You don't want to hear about that." When she glanced up, Lindsay's gaze was intent on her.

"Tell me."

Something about her tone—something about the open kindness in her eyes—they made Piper feel oddly safe in Lindsay's presence. A brief thought of *what is happening here?* ran through her brain before she took a big breath in, then let it out. A sip of wine. A meeting of eyes once more, and Piper spilled like she had no choice. "I've been at my company for nearly ten years, and I've been a manager for almost four of those. As a manager in a corporation, you're privy to certain information that the rest of the employees may not be."

Lindsay nodded and seemed riveted by Piper's story.

"There's been a merger happening behind the scenes for a few months now. We're supposed to be bought by a place called Curtis and Company."

"And what happens to you? To your people?" Lindsay asked, zeroing right in on the important part.

"Well, Curtis and Company has a great reputation, and they've promised to do their best to keep everything as is. It would be a merger in appearance only. No firings."

Lindsay nodded, still engrossed.

"Today, we found out that a company called Harbinger put in a better offer."

"Harbinger? Like, Harbinger of Doom?"

"Right?" Piper said with a bitter chuckle. "I thought the same thing. Anyway, Harbinger's reputation is quite the opposite of Curtis's."

"And you're worried about your job."

"Not mine, no. I'll be fine. I'm worried about my people."

Lindsay's expression softened even more. "I bet."

Piper finished her wine. Lindsay reached for the bottle without taking her eyes off Piper and refilled it wordlessly.

"I mean, with Curtis and Company, there was the promise of no employee turnover, like I said." Piper sipped the wine, took a beat to savor the taste before she went on. "Not right away, at least. Obviously, there's no way to guarantee that, and my people aren't stupid. Curtis has their own people they'd bring in, but they promised the current owner that the staff would remain, as would their benefits."

"And that made you feel okay about the merger."

"Yes. But Harbinger…" Piper shook her head and let a rumble come up from her throat.

"Doesn't offer the same assurances."

"None. I did some research on them today." She stopped her glass halfway to her lips. "It wasn't pretty."

Lindsay reached out and closed a warm hand over Piper's forearm. "I'm so sorry you're having to deal with this."

It was exactly the right thing to say, and Piper felt whatever tension remained slowly drain from her shoulders. Lindsay didn't try to fix anything. She didn't try to tell Piper what to do or how to solve her issues. She didn't present solutions. She simply listened and offered her sympathy. It was just what Piper needed.

"Thanks," she said. "It's…stressful."

"I can imagine. Stress is why God made wine. I'm sure of it."

"Amen to that."

Lindsay squeezed her forearm. "I'll be right back."

A realization hit Piper right then. As she sat, sipping delicious wine and watching others doing the same while laughing and conversing, the thought entered her mind, made itself at home, and sat there.

I like it here.

It might not last. She knew that. It had been a long time since she'd been able to say that about Vineyard, and the feeling might be temporary. But for now? She'd take it. Hell, she *needed* it. Today had been a hell of a day, nerve-wracking and a little sad, so Piper decided she'd hold on to this feeling for as long as she could.

Lindsay was talking with a table of customers. One of them laughed heartily and Lindsay looked up, met Piper's gaze across the room.

Piper lifted her glass in a subtle salute.

I like her *here.*

CHAPTER NINE

"No. Absolutely not." Lindsay shook her head as she refilled Maya's coffee mug. "And I cannot stress that enough, so let me say it one more time. Ab. Solutely. Not."

"Told you," Bert said as she sipped from her cup of tea.

Maya made a face and her shoulders dropped in defeat. "But why not?"

Lindsay took a seat at her kitchen table with her two best friends in the world besides Angela and met Maya's deep brown gaze. She reached out and clasped Maya's hand. "I love you. I do. Very much. But nothing good has ever come out of you saying to me, 'we have somebody we want you to meet.'"

Maya pulled her hand away and pressed it to her chest as she let out a little mock-gasp of hurt. "That's not true."

Lindsay gave her a look that said, *Really?* "The barista with seventeen cats in her apartment? *Literally* seventeen?"

"The cop with mommy issues?" Bert added.

"Not helping," Maya shot back at her wife. Bert pretended to cower, but her grin said otherwise.

"Your architect friend who wanted to use whips on me?" Lindsay raised her eyebrows to punctuate.

Maya grimaced. "Yeah, that was unexpected."

Lindsay snorted. "You should've been there."

Bert chuckled into her coffee mug and Maya pretended to pout. Lindsay smiled as she looked at the two of them. They tried to do Sunday brunch at least once a month, and today had been Lindsay's turn to host. She'd known the couple for about five years now and they were her lifeline. They kept her grounded, especially when Angela was away. They smacked her when she needed it. They had big shoulders to help her carry a burden or to let her cry on. She loved them with all her heart.

"I just want what you guys have, you know?" Lindsay said, a serious note inching into her voice.

"Two student loan payments and not enough sex?" Bert asked. She was unable to duck away before Maya's napkin hit her in the face.

"Roberta!"

"I'm teasing, baby. You know I am." Bert leaned over and kissed her wife.

"That," Lindsay said, pointing to the kiss. "That right there is what I want."

"And you'll have it," Maya said. At Lindsay's sigh, she said, "You will. I promise." There was a beat of silence that wasn't totally uncomfortable before Maya went on with, "How's being the Wine Bar Boss? Going okay?"

Happy for the change of subject, Lindsay smiled and nodded. "It is, actually. We have our first band on Friday, so that'll be fun. You guys should come."

Maya looked to Bert. "I think we could. Yes?"

Bert had her phone out and was scrolling. "I think we're clear."

"Awesome," Lindsay said. "I could use extra bodies in there, just in case. It's a jazz duo. They just call themselves Smooth. Keyboards and bass. Should be pretty cool."

Bert finished punching info into her phone. "There. You're officially in the calendar. We'll be there."

"Great." Rocket took that opportunity to remind Lindsay he was there by setting his head on her thigh and whining softly.

"Somebody wants bacon," Bert said.

Lindsay grabbed half a strip off a plate and took it to Rocket's dish.

"How has the owner's daughter been with the changes?" Maya asked, picking up half a donut from the decimated plate on the table.

"It started off a little rocky," Lindsay told her. "But I feel like she's coming around. I'm meeting with her tomorrow night about the patio."

"What's her name again?" Maya furrowed her brow.

"Piper. She's some bigwig manager type at a big company that does...I have no idea what."

"Wow. You are full of helpful information," Bert commented.

"I know, right?" Lindsay said.

"Will she be there on Friday?" Maya asked, grabbing the last strip of bacon.

With a shrug, Lindsay said, "Not a clue. She seems to pop in when I least expect her to."

It was true, and a thought that came back to her a bit later when she let herself into Vineyard and locked the door behind her just as fat drops of rain began to fall. When Mrs. B. had initially told Lindsay of her plans, Lindsay hadn't expected to see much of Piper. She got the impression Mrs. B. had the same idea, that Piper would be a partner in name only, but she'd proven them both wrong. This wine bar seemed to be—and it sounded totally corny, Lindsay knew—changing people. Mrs. B. loved the place, but she'd obviously lost her passion after Mr. B. had died, no longer had the desire to put in the effort needed to increase sales, was fine with just keeping it afloat. Totally understandable, but hard to watch. Piper had rarely made an appearance at Vineyard in the entire time Lindsay had worked there. And now? She popped in a couple times a week, mostly unannounced and without a specific reason. Completely unexpected behavior as far as Lindsay was concerned. And Lindsay herself had been changed by the place, arriving as an untethered soul looking for something temporary to grab onto and ending up never wanting to leave.

How could one place—and a place of business to boot; it wasn't like Vineyard was a church or a park or a mountaintop—have such an effect on so many people? It was weird and strangely comforting.

Aside from when it was full of customers, this was Lindsay's favorite time being in Vineyard: when it was quiet and empty and the day was laid out before her. The chairs were all up on the tabletops, the floor was clean, the marble bar gleamed under the small pendulum lighting. The wine coolers behind the bar hummed steadily. Bottles of unopened wine were lined up with the precision of a marching band on black shelving and stacked on their sides in the diamond-shape spaces next to them. On the wall, a square painting hung. It was canvas-colored, and in black lettering, different wine varietals were listed in fonts of varying sizes and styles. It looked fantastic on the newly painted wall, and one of Lindsay's things to do today was to search the internet for a few similar pieces. They were fun and stylish, and while everything in Vineyard was tidy and organized, Lindsay also thought it was important to have that element of fun, of playfulness. Wine was no longer stuffy. She wanted to help crush that myth. Wine was hip and cool and trendy and she wanted to run with those things in this small town. She wanted people to walk into Vineyard and relax, not worry about ordering the wrong thing. She wanted them to try all different kinds of wine, test all the varietals and decide for themselves what they liked and what they didn't, not what they were *supposed* to like. The residents around Black Cherry Lake could get stuck in their ways. Lindsay wanted to unstick them.

She'd been in the office for about half an hour answering emails and getting ready to open when she heard rapping on the door. A glance at the clock on the wall told her she had another forty-five minutes before she needed to open, and she sighed. A customer who wanted her to open early, most likely. The office led into the back area of Vineyard where the cheeses and supplies were stored, and a small window looked out over the square parking lot. It was pouring now, and when Lindsay saw the tip of a bright green kayak, she stopped in her tracks.

Piper was here.

The butterflies that suddenly formed in her stomach annoyed her. Why was she there? They weren't scheduled to meet until tomorrow. Was there something wrong? Something she wanted to bitch about? Though they'd been good on Friday night, so Lindsay couldn't come up with anything.

"Maybe you need to let her in and find out, Linds," she muttered as she headed out toward the front door.

Piper was visible through the window, dressed in her kayaking gear, hair in that damn ponytail, and soaking wet. Lindsay unlocked the door.

"Hey," she said, ushering Piper in. "Oh, my god, you're soaked. Get in here."

Piper entered and stopped inside the door.

"Let me get you a towel," Lindsay said. She found two in the back room and also grabbed the sweatshirt she kept in the office for when the air-conditioning got too cold for her. Piper hadn't moved but was looking around Vineyard with an expression Lindsay couldn't identify. "Here," she said, and wrapped one towel around Piper's shoulders. A shiver went through her body; Lindsay felt it under her hands and pulled away quickly. She handed Piper the other towel and took a subtle step back. "What were you doing out in this?"

Piper shook her head. "I had this weird urge to kayak. It's much later than I normally go, but I just…needed to. Like an idiot, I never checked the weather."

Lindsay looked out at the sky. "It's not lightning, is it?" The thought of Piper out in the middle of the lake in a rainstorm was enough to make her a little nervous, but thunder and lightning on top of that...

"No, thank God."

"Has that ever happened?" Lindsay asked, turning back to her. She watched as a rivulet of water left a trail down the side of Piper's neck, from her ear down to where the towel lay across her shoulder.

"What? Have I been caught in a storm?" Piper toweled herself off, patted her face dry. "Once."

"Were you scared?"

"Terrified. I didn't go back out again for more than a month." Her grin was sheepish as she looked at Lindsay. Then her teeth chattered and they both laughed.

"Here." Lindsay handed over the sweatshirt. Piper took it gratefully and pulled it over her head, and there was something inexplicably sexy about Piper wearing Lindsay's clothes. She swallowed hard and glanced away. "It's starting to ease up," she said for no reason.

They stood side by side, no words, for a long moment, just watching the rain subside as the sun did its best to break through the clouds.

"Do you have to open soon?" Piper asked, and though her voice was low, it felt loud in the silence.

Lindsay glanced at her watch. "In about twenty minutes, yeah."

"Well, the least I can do is help you take the chairs down, right?" Piper smiled and Lindsay had to take a moment because it was so weird to have Piper not scowling at her.

"How come you came here?" The question was out of Lindsay's mouth before she even realized she was going to ask it. Piper gave her a quizzical look, and at that point, Lindsay had to press on. "I mean, you were in your car. You could've just gone home." She did her best to keep her voice gentle, light, non-accusatory. "But you came here. How come?"

Piper rolled her lips in, bit down on them, moved her gaze to the window, before finally meeting Lindsay's eyes. She looked away quickly before answering, very softly, "I'm not sure."

Before they could say more, there was a knock on the window that caused them both to jump. A familiar-looking bearded man waved like crazy, a big smile on his face.

"Matthew?" Piper laughed and went to the door to let him in.

"I thought I saw you pull in here," Matthew said as he wrapped

Piper in a big hug. "I was across the street getting some yarn for Shane and his new project."

"Lindsay, you remember my good friend, Matthew?"

Lindsay nodded. "From the night we sat down with your mom, yes. Hi, good to see you again." Lindsay shook the man's hand, remembering how much she'd liked him.

"What are you doing here like this," Matthew ran a hand up and down in front of Piper. "Did you get caught in the rain? Nice sweatshirt, by the way."

Piper sent a small smile her way. "I did get caught. I was soaked, so I came here to dry off and Lindsay was nice enough to lend me her shirt."

"You came here instead of going home?" Matthew actually sounded like he was thinking out loud rather than asking a question he expected an answer to. Piper had a weird look on her face, so Lindsay jumped in.

"We were just talking about that. I mean, it's her family's place, so maybe it's natural that she just wanted to come here. Old habits or…" She let her voice trail off, turned over a chair.

"I guess that could be it." Piper joined in, turning chairs over.

"Mm-hmm," was what Matthew said.

"It's family. I get it," Lindsay said.

"Do you have family here?" Matthew asked her as she cleared another table of chairs.

"I do. My dad and his wife live on the east side of town. My mom and her husband live at the other end of the lake."

"Ah, so you have two families. Siblings?"

"Only steps," Lindsay said. "Three stepsisters and two stepbrothers."

"Wow. So there are six of you altogether."

"Well…" Lindsay hesitated, as she always did when talking about her family dynamics. "Yeah, sort of."

Piper set a chair down and looked at her. "Sort of?"

Lindsay scratched her forehead and stared at her feet for a beat, acutely aware that Piper was listening and unsure why she felt a mix of excitement and hesitation about that. "I'm not really much of a part of either side. To be honest."

"No?" Piper asked, and the sympathy on her face seemed genuine. "Don't you get invited to gatherings and stuff?"

"Oh, yeah. I totally do. It's just…it's always a little weird and uncomfortable. I'm kind of the black sheep." The fact that Lindsay didn't really talk about this stuff to anybody floated through her mind, but like a small child caught in a lie, she just kept talking. "Like, I have to go to my stepsister's college graduation party on Saturday and I'm dreading it."

"Why?" Matthew asked. Piper's curious expression mirrored his.

Lindsay dropped into the last chair and pursed her lips as she thought. "Because while I will know a lot of the people there, I'll mostly hang by myself. It's always like that. I end up being the wallflower in the corner, people-watching." She added a chuckle so she didn't sound quite as pathetic as she suspected she did, her eyes on her feet. "Which is fine."

"You should go with her."

Lindsay heard Matthew say it and looked up. He was looking at Piper.

"What?" Piper said, her dark brows in a V above her nose.

"You're great at those things; small talk is your jam. You could keep Lindsay company, give her somebody to talk to, somebody to people watch with." Matthew was gesturing with his hands now, as if this was the single greatest idea in all of mankind. "I'm sure there will be alcohol, right?" He glanced at Lindsay, who nodded. "So, free drinks and a day out of the house. Get to know each other. You're partners in a business." He shrugged, and Lindsay got the odd sensation that his act of innocence was just that: an act. "Could be fun."

Piper was staring at Matthew with an unreadable expression on her face (Lindsay was beginning to realize this was a talent of hers). Matthew was staring back at her, a large grin on his face, his eyes dancing with what almost seemed like challenge. Lindsay looked from one of them to the other as the door opened and a trio of customers looked in hesitantly.

"Are you open?" one of them asked.

"Yes, absolutely." Lindsay gestured them in. "Grab a table and I'll be right with you."

"What time is this shindig, Lindsay?" Matthew asked as she headed toward the bar for menus.

"Two o'clock." She gave the trio their menus and returned to where Matthew and Piper still stood, and the weirdest thing happened in that moment. Lindsay couldn't explain it. At all. Not even a little bit. But suddenly, the idea of hanging at a party with Piper seemed…not frightening. Not strange or nonsensical. It seemed…enticing. It seemed like…a very good idea. And much to her own astonishment, she turned to Piper and said, very simply, "Wanna go with me?"

Maybe the weird was contagious. Anything was possible in that second because Piper said, just as simply, "Okay."

"Perfect," Matthew said, and clapped his hands together in elation, like he'd just accomplished something huge. "It's a date."

Piper's uncertain and hesitant smile seemed to say exactly what Lindsay was thinking. *What the hell just happened?*

❖

Zack was working with Lindsay on Monday, and for that, she was extremely grateful. She was meeting with Piper soon and she'd decided to do whatever she needed to not be alone with her today. She knew the reasons. Didn't want to analyze them, but knew them. One was because she was finding herself alarmingly attracted to Piper, and that made her entire world feel precariously tilted, like she needed to hold on to things as she moved through her day or she'd slide right off and into oblivion. The attraction wasn't really a surprise. It had been brewing for over a month now. But there wasn't any need for her to focus on it. There was work to be done.

The other reason—and the one Lindsay really didn't want to analyze—was that she didn't want to give Piper an opening to bail on Saturday's party. Her assumption was, if another person was in the room with them—Zack—Piper would feel uncomfortable bringing it up.

Lindsay refused to think about how much she wanted that assumption to be correct.

A couple tables were occupied when Piper walked in just after five.

Lindsay looked up and Piper's smile made her literally weak in the knees. She reached a hand out to the bar to steady herself. "Hi," she said, smiling back and hoping it wasn't so wide it made her look creepy. "You're earlier than I expected."

Piper crossed toward her, blew out a breath that made her lips motor. "Yeah, I needed to get out of my office today. It's just going to leave me extra to do tomorrow, but I couldn't take it anymore." She shrugged and they stood looking at each other for several seconds before Lindsay shook herself.

"Ready to see my ideas?"

Piper gave one nod. "Lead the way."

"Awesome. Zack? Could you join us?"

Piper's brow furrowed slightly, but Lindsay ignored it as she grabbed a manila folder from under the bar. Zack caught up with them and they all went through the door leading to the patio.

For the next fifteen minutes—with the door propped open so they could keep track of the customers—Lindsay went over the idea she had for the patio, ways to make it work to Vineyard's advantage. She talked layout, reinforcing the fencing around it to keep customers from walking to the water, décor, everything she'd researched to create a money-making space.

"I printed out info on the furniture I think would work best." Lindsay opened the manila folder. "I got a couple estimates for the fence repairs as well as a couple of heat lamps for cooler nights." She flipped through several sheets of paper as she stood next to Piper, who seemed to be following her with diligence. "I've emailed this all to you as well. I know paper is a bit old school, but I got used to printing things out for your mom. She says it's easier for her." Lindsay looked up and into those hazel eyes of Piper's and almost let herself drift away.

"I think it's all sick," Zack said, surprising Lindsay, as she hadn't realized he was looking at the information over her shoulder, and hauling her back to reality. "Super sick." He was nodding his approval, as he meandered around the patio, picturing it all, Lindsay assumed, just as she'd done.

"Right?" Lindsay said, grateful for the interruption. "Me, too." She turned back to the folder. "I've added everything up, so you have a bottom line." She indicated the number at the bottom of all her calculations. "I think it's reasonable."

Lindsay held her breath as Piper took the numbers sheet out of the folder and stood close as she looked it over. Her eyebrows made a gentle V above her nose, her lips pursed in concentration, and Lindsay tried not to stare, but couldn't help herself.

"You're right," she finally said, lifting her gaze to meet Lindsay's. "Seems reasonable."

Lindsay let out a breath, then covered her mouth in embarrassed humor.

Piper laughed. "Were you worried?"

"Absolutely."

"Well. You did your research. You said you emailed me? I'll take a closer look in the next couple of days, but I see no reason we shouldn't be able to do this. Seems like it'd be worth it down the road." She looked up and gazed out at the water. "It's definitely a great view."

"It is." They stood quietly for a moment before Zack walked in front of them, disrupting their line of sight. "All right then. Zack, why don't we head back in. Get to work."

With a nod, he went inside, Lindsay close behind him. At the door, she held it open and gestured for Piper to go in first.

"Wine?" Lindsay asked once they were back inside and the patio door was locked.

"I'd love to, but I've got some things I need to take care of at home." Piper seemed slightly disappointed, and Lindsay tried not to be happy about that.

"I understand. Saturday, then." Lindsay held her breath.

"Saturday." Piper smiled at her, turned, and left the wine bar.

Lindsay's eyes stayed on her until she could no longer see her.

Saturday...

Lindsay tried not to grin like an idiot over the idea of Saturday. She was pretty sure she failed.

CHAPTER TEN

The jazz duo Smooth lived up to their name, with tinkling keyboards and a deep, thrumming bass that was both inviting and warm, and Lindsay stood behind the bar sporting a huge grin at the nearly full house before her.

"These guys are good," Bert said to her, as she leaned over the bar.

"Right?" Lindsay nodded along to the beat as she surveyed the room.

The music was not too loud, not too soft, and customers were able to listen, as well as carry on conversations. Bridget and Kevin were working steadily, filling and refilling glasses, bringing Lindsay orders for cheese boards to arrange. There were two empty tables for two, but that was about it. It was after eight and nobody seemed in a hurry to leave.

Maya sat on a barstool, Bert standing next to her, both absorbed in the music, each holding a glass of wine. Maya turned to Lindsay and grinned widely, nodded her approval, her dreads bouncing. Lindsay wished Mrs. B. was there to see Vineyard this full, but she'd taken a few photos to text to her later.

In the back room, Lindsay put together a cheese board, which Kevin came in and scooped up. "The band idea was a good one, Linds," he said, with a smile.

She gave him a nod of thanks, followed him out and reclaimed her spot behind the bar. The band finished their tune and the customers applauded. As they launched into the next one, Lindsay's attention was on a trio of customers who were leaving. The door was held open for them and once they were out, the holder entered.

She must have gone home after work, because though she was still what Lindsay would consider "dressed up," she wasn't businessy.

Dark jeans and black ankle boots. A coral lightweight sweater with the sleeves pushed up. A scarf in solid navy blue. Her hair was down, wavy and fun, more casual than Lindsay had seen it. As she smiled at Bridget, those dimples made themselves known.

"Who's that?" Bert asked, then brought her glass to her lips as if she hadn't meant to say it out loud. Her eyes were focused on the same thing Lindsay's were. "I think she's looking for you."

"Yeah, that's Piper," Lindsay said, her voice low. Piper met her eyes and she gave a little wave.

Maya's head whipped around to look directly at Lindsay. "*That's* Piper?"

Lindsay nodded and sucked on the straw in the glass of water she kept under the bar as Piper approached. "Hey," Lindsay said, sidling up next to her so she was close enough to hear. "I didn't expect to see you tonight. What do you think?"

"I've been here for thirty-seven seconds," Piper said. "Let me listen."

Lindsay resisted the urge to roll her eyes at Piper's typical negative-comment-first behavior, and bumped her with a shoulder instead. "I meant the crowd, smart-ass."

"Oh. Oh, the crowd." Piper made a show of looking around, taking her time doing so. Lindsay could smell her perfume, something with a little spice to it. She liked it, inhaled quietly. "Not bad." There was an unspoken *could be better* attached to it, but Lindsay wasn't about to let that spoil her mood. Besides, it was about the answer she expected from Piper. Nothing was immediately positive. No compliments or kudos were given until she was 100 percent sure she wanted to give them. Lindsay was learning her.

They stood and listened as the band finished their number, then announced they were taking a fifteen-minute break.

Lindsay touched Piper on the arm. "Wine?"

"I'll have one. I can't stay long; I just wanted to come see how things were going."

You wanted to check up on me. Lindsay didn't say it, but the thought zipped through her mind. Weirdly, though, it didn't rankle. At all. She simply shrugged it off, admitted to herself that it made sense. Piper had approved an outlay of cash and she was checking to see if it had been worth it. "Piper, these are my very good friends, Maya and Roberta. Guys, this is Piper Bradshaw, Mrs. B.'s daughter."

Handshakes and "nice to meet yous" went around the group as

Lindsay poured Piper a glass of Zinfandel she was sure she'd like. No trying to ply her with blends tonight. Didn't seem like she was in the mood.

Lindsay handed her the wine. "I'm surprised to see you here tonight."

Piper shrugged, sipped the wine without asking what it was, which Lindsay found interesting. Did that indicate some level of trust? Doubtful, but a nice thought. "Like I said, I wanted to see how things were going. Check out the music." She sipped again. With a glance at Maya and Bert, who were in a conversation of their own, Piper lowered her voice. "I also wanted to check on details about tomorrow."

"Tomorrow?" Lindsay asked, momentarily lost. Then she remembered the graduation party. "Oh! Oh, right. Tomorrow."

Piper studied her for a beat. "Listen, if you'd rather I not go, I totally get that. Matthew sort of forced this on you."

So many responses went through Lindsay's head in the moment, even as she kept one eye on the room to make sure her employees didn't need her. The strange thing was, though, that she'd sort of been looking forward to not attending the party alone. Maya and Bert had other plans or she'd have asked them. "Oh, no, it's fine. It's great. I'm glad you're coming. Unless *you* don't want to…"

"No, I do. I do." Piper looked off into the wine bar.

"Okay. Good."

"Good."

Lindsay was suddenly aware that both Maya and Bert were now watching, and she would have questions to answer.

"What time shall I pick you up?" Piper asked.

"One forty-five?" Lindsay liked that Piper wanted to drive, though she wasn't sure why.

"Text me your address."

Lindsay pulled out her phone and scrolled to Piper's number, which she'd entered the night she'd met with her and Mrs. B. She typed in her address, hit Send. "There."

Piper checked her own phone, gave one nod, and put it back into her purse. "So, Maya. Roberta. What do you guys do?"

Apparently, that was the end of the party discussion, and Lindsay was somewhat relieved. A table of five left just before the band returned, so Lindsay crossed the room to bus it. As she gathered empty glasses and trash, a glance up told her Piper had moved to a vacated stool and was sitting closer to Maya and Bert, and she wasn't sure what to do with that. Bert said something that made Piper laugh loudly, and Lindsay smiled when she realized that it was the first time she'd ever heard Piper full-out laugh like that. It was a very pleasing sound, she had to admit.

Smooth started up again, playing a tune Lindsay recognized but couldn't remember the name of, and the front door opened to a trio of women looking for a table. Lindsay, her arms full of the mess from the table she'd cleared, welcomed them as Bridget took over and led them to a table.

Once Lindsay had dumped everything off in the back, she returned to her friends to find Piper finishing up her wine. She raised her eyebrows at Piper, who nodded with a grin. "One more. Your friends are funny." She turned back to Maya—who was a doctor and was telling a story about the mother of a patient, never discussing names or anything personal about her, of course—and Lindsay tried in vain to figure out how she felt about this. Piper Bradshaw, a.k.a. Princess Elsa, was sitting in the wine bar, enjoying a glass of wine and laughing at stories told by two of Lindsay's best friends. It was like being in the *Twilight Zone*. Surreal.

But in a good way.

That was the weird part. It was good. It felt…kind of perfect, actually.

Smooth finished their set at ten on the dot to a nice burst of applause. When Lindsay paid them, she asked if they'd be willing to play again. They agreed with enthusiasm and she mentally put the entire evening into the win column. She couldn't wait to tell Mrs. B.

Back at the bar, Piper had slid off her stool and was gathering her things.

"We're open for another hour," Lindsay told her, only aware of the slight plea in her voice after she'd heard it.

"I know," Piper told her. "It's been a very long day, though. I'm beat."

"Plus, she's got to rest up for tomorrow," Maya said, looking at Lindsay. "Big day."

"It was so nice to meet you both," Piper said, with a little wave.

"Same here," Bert said. "I suspect we'll see you again soon."

Lindsay watched as the door closed behind Piper.

"Well," Maya said, then set her empty glass in front of Lindsay with a determined firmness. "That was interesting."

"Tell me something, Linds." Bert took Piper's vacated stool, made a show of making herself comfortable as Lindsay filled Maya's glass.

Lindsay looked at her, knowing what was coming. "Okay."

"How is it that this woman," Bert waved a hand toward the door, "is your date to a family party tomorrow and we—your best friends in life—had no idea?" She tilted her head in confusion. "How is that possible? Hmm?" She propped an elbow on the bar and her chin in her hand.

Lindsay glanced around the wine bar, silently hoping somebody needed her help with something, but she was out of luck. Evidently, the Universe wanted her to explain herself to her friends. With a sigh, she told them about Sunday, how she'd been innocently talking about her dread around the family gathering, how Matthew had volunteered Piper to go with her, how neither she nor Piper could manage to get out of it. Nor did they seem to want to.

"At least I didn't," she finished up, being totally honest.

"You like her, huh?" Maya asked, and Bert chucked Lindsay in the shoulder.

"I don't know," Lindsay said, a little flustered. "And that's the truth." She took a moment to think about it. She'd never not been honest with Maya and Bert, and she wasn't about to start. "I find her intriguing. Maybe that's a better word for it." With a scoff, she added, "I mean, she hasn't been easy to like."

Maya shrugged. "I liked her right away."

"Me, too," Bert agreed.

Lindsay made a face at both of them. "Fine. *I* haven't found it easy to like her, and I don't think she liked me right away."

"Because of this place," Maya said, understanding.

"I thought she didn't ever come here," Bert commented. "Didn't you tell us that when your boss first said she was leaving?"

Lindsay nodded. "At that point, she hadn't. Now? She's been showing up a couple times a week."

"Maybe she's feeling extra responsible with her mom gone?" Maya asked, her expression one of searching for a solution.

"That would make sense," Bert agreed.

Lindsay shrugged. She really wasn't sure of the reasoning, but Maya's suggestion was as good as any she'd come up with. "I feel like I've been pretty good about giving her the benefit of the doubt around it." She had, hadn't she? "She doesn't seem to like change, so

I'm trying to slip my changes in slowly. I just want her to understand that I'm only trying to increase business. There are new restaurants and bars cropping up around here all the time. We have to stay fresh and unique in order to compete. You know?"

Her friends nodded their agreement, even though as a pediatrician and a history teacher, neither of them worked in any kind of sales capacity.

Maya gestured around the wine bar. "Well, I'd say your music idea was a success."

"Me, too." Lindsay grinned, a feeling of satisfaction washing over her.

A few moments later, Maya and Bert had finished their wine and gathered their belongings.

"This was great, Linds," Bert told her. "We need to come here more often."

"I will second that," Lindsay said. "And thank you. It was great to have you here for support. I know you guys are busy. I appreciate you coming." She moved around the bar to hug each of them goodbye.

"We expect a full report about tomorrow," Maya said quietly in her ear.

"It's just a graduation party," Lindsay said.

"Still."

"Fine." Lindsay shook her head with a chuckle.

"Don't make me hunt you down," Bert said, pointing a finger at her.

"Go home," Lindsay said, laughing, and shooed them out the door.

Things were winding down in the wine bar, and Lindsay began bussing the tables that had emptied. The success of the evening combined with the anticipation of tomorrow and made for a very weird, good-and-bad, happy-and-nervous, mixture in Lindsay's stomach. Satisfaction over the success of the evening plus butterflies about the party tomorrow equaled a very unsettled sensation in her body, like she was totally confident she knew all her lines, but was super nervous about stepping out onstage.

Only time would tell if she got a positive review...

❖

Saturday dawned bright and sunny, a lovely early-June day, and Piper was on the water first thing. These were the mornings she loved most: the temperature comfortable enough that she didn't need to tough it out until the paddling helped her body warm up; quiet and serene with only a few fishermen out in their boats; the water like glass, smooth and reflective. She could see the blue sky, the clouds in the water as if looking into a mirror. Her paddle cut into the lake silently, pulled her kayak along with almost no sound at all.

To her right, on the shore, a deer lifted its head and watched her as she glided by. "Hi, beautiful," she whispered. A hawk circled nearby and a fish jumped about fifty feet ahead of her, landing with a splash, sending circular ripples across the water.

Piper was a city girl at heart. She'd be the first one to tell you. She had no desire to camp. Hiking was okay, but wasn't her go-to activity. She loved animals, but in her house, not on a farm. She needed to know there was a grocery store or coffee shop or movie theatre within a few minutes' drive. But these mornings in her kayak, on the water, with nature, they grounded her. They helped her to breathe easier, to center herself. She supposed it was her own form of meditation, and though she wasn't able to kayak every morning, if she went too long during the summer without doing so, she got cranky, felt unbalanced. It was a need for her, something necessary for her sanity.

It was odd to her that she was actually looking forward to today. Well, somewhat. Parties full of people she didn't know weren't really her favorite thing (were they anybody's?), but she'd been to enough business meetings and mixers and conferences for work that she knew how to navigate a room full of strangers with maximum ease and minimum stress. The week had seen her cycle through several emotions over it: irritation at Matthew for butting in, annoyance at herself for *letting* him butt in and then being unable to just say no, thinking up and then discarding excuses to bow out. More than that, though, was the strange realization that she was finding Lindsay…intriguing. That was the only word she could come up with that seemed to fit how she'd been feeling lately. She was a big enough person to admit that she'd maybe jumped the gun on her judgment of Lindsay, assuming her to be flighty and flaky and not at all somebody who could run a business. So far, Lindsay had proven her wrong. And while part of her was embarrassed by that fact, another part was glad. Glad to have been mistaken—though she wasn't quite ready to admit that fully to herself. Or to Matthew. God, she'd never hear the end of it, a thought that actually brought a grin to her face.

Back home, she moved the kayak off her car and into the garage.

No need to show up at Lindsay's with it still strapped to the roof. She sipped coffee while scrambling herself some eggs and doing her best not to think about work. Of course, she failed, and for about the thousandth time in the past few days, wished her father was around so she could bounce some things off him, get his take. Things were looking good for the Harbinger deal, which meant things were looking not-so-good for Piper's staff. She and Ian had texted back and forth when Piper had gotten home from Vineyard last night, and that had gone on until well after midnight. He was as worried about his people as she was hers.

She spent the rest of the morning cleaning the bathroom, vacuuming, and doing various household chores that she always vowed she'd stop saving for her weekends, but she'd never been able to follow through on the promise. By 1:00, she was standing in her underwear in front of her closet trying to decide what to wear to a graduation party for somebody she didn't know. With a temperature in the mid-seventies, she decided it was time to break out the sundresses. She chose a black one with a yellow paisley design on it. It was sleeveless and soft and she paired it with some strappy black sandals with a slight heel. She clipped her hair back, added some jewelry and makeup, and was ready to go by 1:30.

On her way through the dining room, she snagged a bottle of wine off her wine rack. While she thought getting a card and giving money to a girl she'd never met in her life might be awkward and even a little creepy, she refused to show up with nothing at all. The wine would be for Lindsay's mother, the hostess.

At exactly 1:45, Piper pulled to a stop in front of the address Lindsay had texted her. It was a cute little Cape Cod with tan siding and navy blue shutters. A large pot of pink petunias stood to the right of the front door and a birdfeeder on a black shepherd's hook to the left. Several chickadees were lunching away. Before Piper could get out of her car or even beep, Lindsay was jogging up the driveway, a small black bag draped over her, cross-body style, a light blue envelope in hand. She wore her usual attire of jeans, but these were black and almost dressy. Her top was a pale yellow button-down, the sleeves rolled up her forearms and held there by buttoned fasteners. Black flats were on her feet. Her blond hair sparkled in the sunlight as she reached the car and pulled the door open.

"Hi there," she said, and for some reason, Piper wondered if the cheer in her tone was forced.

"Hey." Piper squinted at her for a moment. "You okay?"

Lindsay gave something between a grin and a grimace and waved her off with a sigh. "Yeah. I'm just never thrilled to go to my mom's house for things like this. I'd rather be one-on-one with her, you know?"

Piper nodded and shifted the car into gear. "Well, it's good that you're going. I imagine you get points for that. Where are we headed?"

Lindsay gave her the address and directions as they drove.

"Are you close to your mom?" Piper asked her after they'd driven for a few minutes.

"That is an interesting question," was Lindsay's reply, and Piper glanced at her. "Sometimes, I think yes. Other times, I think we used to be. Still other times, I think we're not at all."

"Complicated."

"Understatement."

Piper waited, but Lindsay didn't say more. "I'm going to need some details, please."

Lindsay was looking out the passenger side window, but Piper caught the corner of her mouth when it quirked up. "My parents were very young when they had me. Probably shouldn't have gotten married, but they did. They struggled for several years before deciding to get a divorce. They had joint custody, so I went back and forth. It could be great for things like Christmas or your birthday, when you get double the presents. But it was tough at times, like if Dad had something he really wanted to go to when it was his weekend to have me."

Piper nodded, but kept her eyes on the road. "I imagine that could leave you feeling a bit unwanted."

"Exactly. And it happened on both ends. Don't get me wrong; my parents were good to me and they did the best they could. I know that. But it wasn't the ideal childhood."

"They're both remarried?"

"Yeah, in the same year I turned eighteen. Isn't that weird? And my mom married a guy with two girls and my dad married a woman with two boys and a girl."

"Wow. That's a lot of instant family." Piper couldn't imagine how jarring that must have been for teenage Lindsay.

"You have no idea. And they're all younger than me. Josh is on my dad's side and Maddie is on my mom's side and they're both twenty-four. They're the oldest."

"And you're...?"

"Thirty-five."

"So you were eighteen and your parents each married people with kids that were seven and younger?"

"Yup."

Piper saw the likely path things took. "Let me guess. They each ended up with cute, new families that were intact, for all intents and purposes, and you ended up being an add-on."

Lindsay turned and looked at her, her expression registering slight surprise. "Yes. Exactly. I headed off to college and lived in an apartment with a friend, so it's not like I was even around most of the time."

"That had to be tough."

Lindsay lifted one shoulder in a half shrug. "I did okay."

"You did."

Piper glanced at her and their gazes met and held for a beat. Lindsay finally turned away and pointed. "It's that house on the left, the blue one. See the red car? You can park right behind that."

Piper did as instructed, and they both got out.

"You didn't have to do that," Lindsay said as she gestured to the wine bottle.

"I don't like to show up empty-handed," Piper said with a shrug, and something about the look that zipped across Lindsay's face made her think Lindsay liked that she'd brought a hostess gift.

"Um...did you notice that we match?" Lindsay pointed at Piper's black and yellow dress, then to her own black pants and yellow top.

Piper grinned. "If people ask, tell them there was a memo."

"Got it."

Lindsay didn't move, simply stood next to the car and Piper waited with her for a moment. "You gearing up?"

"Exactly." Then Lindsay made a little punching move with her fist and gave one determined nod. "Okay. I'm good. Ready?"

Piper held out an arm. "Lead the way."

Though Piper was reasonably sure the party couldn't yet be in full swing—it was still early—there was a significant number of people milling around, both inside and out. The house was gorgeous and spacious, open concept. Once she and Lindsay walked through the front door, they could see almost the entirety of the first floor, straight through to the sliding glass doors that led out to the backyard where part of a white party tent was visible, along with the sparkling blue of an in-ground pool. Piper looked around slowly, impressed with the style, the décor. All the trim was painted a creamy ivory, and in each room, the walls were a different color, but they all blended seamlessly into each other. The sage green in the front great room led to a melted-chocolate-ice-cream brown in the dining area, which led to a muted orange in the kitchen…an orange Piper would never choose in a million years, but that worked perfectly in this design. Light oak hardwood floors ran throughout, and Piper followed Lindsay into the kitchen, where more than a dozen people chatted and munched hors d'oeuvres.

"Lindsay!" a voice said cheerfully, and Piper observed a woman who had to be Lindsay's mother as she moved quickly toward them and wrapped Lindsay in a hug. It was almost eerie, how much alike they looked. They had a very similar haircut. Lindsay's mother's was a little bit brassier, indicating she probably had it colored regularly. Her eyes were the same startling green as Lindsay's, and they were built alike, both tall and lean, their smiles almost identical. Piper was certain this was exactly what Lindsay would look like in twenty years. Not a bad future. Not a bad future at all.

"Mom, this is my friend, Piper Bradshaw. Piper, my mom, Darcy Taylor."

Piper reached out a hand and shook Darcy's. "It's very nice to meet you. This is for you." She handed over the wine.

"Well, isn't that nice? You didn't have to do that, but I thank you." Darcy took a moment, looked back and forth between them, then asked Lindsay, "Are you two…?"

Lindsay's eyes widened in horror. "God, Mom. No. No, Piper is my boss's daughter."

"Oh! Bradshaw. I thought that name was familiar." Darcy lowered her voice a tiny bit before saying, "Too bad. She's very pretty."

Lindsay groaned. "Ma. Seriously. Enough."

Piper grinned and kept on grinning, finding the entire exchange very entertaining.

"Come outside and see Emma," Darcy said, grabbing Lindsay's hand and tugging her along.

Tossing a glance over her shoulder as Piper followed, Lindsay said, "My mother has no filters. I'm sorry."

"Don't be. She said I was pretty."

Lindsay scoffed, then caught Piper's raised eyebrows. "Not that you aren't. You are. Very. I mean, not that I think…God. Never mind. I'm going to stop talking now." Lindsay turned back to her mom as they went through the back door, but not before Piper noticed how red her face had gotten.

Oh, yeah. Very, very entertaining.

Lindsay's stepsister, Emma, threw herself at Lindsay, wrapped her in a hug. "I'm so glad you came." She, unlike Darcy, looked nothing at all like Lindsay. Red hair and freckles, blue eyes that sat close together on her face, small frame. Piper pegged her at about five-three. But she was full of energy and smiles and was instantly likeable. For a brief moment, Piper wondered what that was like.

Lindsay handed over the blue envelope she'd been carrying, then introduced Piper.

Emma shook her hand. "It's nice to meet you."

"Same here." Piper noted the firm handshake, the eye contact. "Congratulations on graduating. What are your plans?"

"Well, I've been doing an internship at an architectural firm for almost six months and they've offered me a job. I'm leaning that way, but I'm not positive yet."

"And that was your major?"

Lindsay jumped in for Emma. "Architectural design and business administration."

"Wow. Dual major, huh?" Piper was impressed. "That's tough. I did the same thing."

"Yeah? What was yours?"

"Economics and business administration."

Emma nodded, then lowered her voice. "I'm really glad it's over."

Piper laughed. "I was, too."

An older couple was coming out the back door and called Emma's name. "Gotta go meet my public," she said with a grin. "I'll see you later on, probs." And she was off.

"She's really nice," Piper commented.

Lindsay nodded, watching Emma go. "She's a good kid. I should spend more time with her." Piper wasn't sure if that last comment was meant for her or if Lindsay was talking more to herself, so she didn't comment. After a beat, Lindsay shook herself slightly and turned to Piper. "Something to drink?"

A few minutes later, each of them had a clear plastic cup of wine. Lindsay took a sip, made a face. "Ugh. I bet Ed bought this in bulk."

"Ed's your stepdad?"

"Mm-hmm." Lindsay nodded in the direction of the back deck where a stocky guy with thinning red hair stood chatting up two other men. Piper watched as the threesome was joined by Lindsay's mother and two other girls, one another redhead and one with long, dark hair and arms so thin, she looked like she'd stepped out of a Tim Burton film. Then Lindsay's mother gestured their way. The girls hesitated, then began walking in their direction.

"We're about to be visited," Piper whispered.

"Terrific," Lindsay said as she followed Piper's gaze.

"Hey, Linds," the redhead said. "Long time, no see." Her voice wasn't pleasant. In fact, it seemed to Piper that it was more accusatory. And also kind of grating.

"Yeah, well." Lindsay tipped her head toward Piper. "This is Piper Bradshaw. Piper, this is Maddie Taylor. Emma's sister."

Piper noticed Lindsay didn't say Maddie was her stepsister. She reached out a hand and Maddie shook it. "Nice to meet you."

"And this is my friend Ash." She turned to Ash and explained, "This is my stepsister, Lindsay. The one I told you about."

"Oh," Ash said, and her dark eyes lit up with recognition. "The bartender."

"Right," Maddie said.

Ash gave a wave rather than offer a hand. "Hey."

"I'm not a bartender," Lindsay said, her voice low with annoyance, telling Piper this wasn't the first time she'd stated that to Maddie.

"Well, you work in a place with a bar and you pour wine, right?" Maddie turned to Ash, her expression one of exaggerated confusion. "That sounds like a bartender, doesn't it?"

Ash nodded.

"Actually," Piper said, stepping in because the misery that was blooming on Lindsay's face was too much to watch, "Lindsay's so much more than a bartender. She's actually in the process of becoming a sommelier." She focused her eyes on Maddie. "Do you know what that is?" she asked, lacing her voice with obviously false innocence.

"I don't," Ash said, apparently not getting what was actually happening.

"Yeah, it's a wine expert," Piper explained. "It takes a lot of time and study and knowledge to become a sommelier, and there aren't that many in the state. Sommeliers are sought after by magazines and wineries and they judge contests, many that are international." At this point, the two were just blinking at her, and Piper focused her gaze on Maddie. "Are *you* an expert at anything?"

Maddie's freckled skin gave her hair a run for its money in redness as she stammered, "Um…no. Not really."

"Huh. That's too bad. Maybe, if you work really hard, you can be as amazing as Lindsay one day." Piper sipped her wine and then smiled at the girls as the conversation stalled. She let the silence hang as Maddie toed the grass and Ash looked around the yard as if trying to find an escape route.

"Hey, is that Jake and the guys?" she asked, poking Maddie in the shoulder.

"Oh. Yeah. It is." With a quick glance at Piper and Lindsay—but no eye contact—Maddie said, "We need to go see them." And without another word, they skittered away.

Piper watched them go over the rim of her glass as she sipped her wine. Maddie threw one look over her shoulder, but that was it. When Piper looked back at Lindsay, she was sure she saw wetness in her eyes. A hand on Lindsay's upper arm, she asked, "Hey, you okay? Look, I didn't mean to—" She was stopped by Lindsay's upheld hand, her grin.

"No. Don't apologize. Just let me bask in this moment."

"Okay…" Piper furrowed her brow and gave Lindsay some time, but kept her eyes on her.

Finally, Lindsay took a deep breath. "Thank you," she said, very quietly. "I've never been able to stand up to her like that."

"No? Well, you should start. I paved the way for you. You're welcome."

Lindsay chuckled, then leaned closer and whispered, "Also, I'm not studying to be a sommelier."

"I know. But…why not? There are classes. You just have to sign up." Piper fixed on those green eyes, was close enough to see the black circle around the outside that set them off so perfectly. "I think that's a business cost that's a no-brainer. My mother would agree. In fact, I don't know why she hasn't suggested it by now. Sign yourself up and use the business account."

Lindsay blinked at her for a full ten seconds before saying, "Seriously?"

Piper snorted like that was the most ridiculous thing ever. "Yes. Seriously. You run the place and you already know so much about wine. Why shouldn't you go all the way?" Lindsay's expression then was a mix that Piper couldn't quite pinpoint. Surprise. Happiness. Uncertainty. Excitement. And more. Lindsay held up her cup and Piper tapped it with her own. "Yeah, I'm going to need help with food pairings down the line. I stink at those."

"You got it."

That whole exchange, that fifteen minutes of the party, seemed to somehow bolster Lindsay and her confidence. Suddenly, she wasn't the wallflower she'd warned Piper she'd be. Rather, she grasped Piper by the hand and led her around the party to various corners of the yard and into the house, introducing her to so many people that they eventually just blurred together in Piper's brain, despite her efforts to remember them all. They refilled their glasses with the less-than-stellar wine and continued to mingle. Inside in the great room, Lindsay's stepdad was talking golf with a few buddies. As they approached, he said something that made them burst into laughter, and then his gaze landed on the two women.

"Hey, Linds. I thought I saw you earlier. How's it going?" Up close, his complexion was ruddy, his blue eyes set close together just like Emma's. He reached out a hand and awkwardly clapped Lindsay on the shoulder, like he wasn't sure if he should hug her, so he decided not to.

"It's going pretty well, Ed. How are you?"

Ed nodded and introduced Lindsay to the three men standing with him. Piper immediately forgot their names.

"This is my friend, Piper Bradshaw. Piper, my stepfather, Ed Taylor."

Piper shook his meaty hand, made sure her own grip was firm.

"Bradshaw," one of the men said. "You related to Tommy?"

Piper nodded, that uncomfortable feeling in the pit of her stomach that she'd come to expect whenever her father was mentioned rearing its ugly head and poking around in there. "He was my father."

"Good man, that one. I was sorry to hear."

"Thanks," Piper said, then sent a glance to Lindsay that she hoped wasn't too pleading.

"Well, we're going to go wander a bit more before we take off." Lindsay grinned at the men, then lowered her voice and leaned close to Ed. "Hey, next time you throw a party, ask me for wine advice, okay?" She held up her cup and grimaced, which caused the other three guys to burst into laughter.

And then Lindsay's hand was grabbing Piper's again and they were moving through the house some more. Piper tried not to notice how good it felt to hold somebody's hand. To have somebody hold her hand. She wasn't at all a touchy-feely person. In fact, she tended to avoid unnecessary physical contact because it was…slightly uncomfortable for her. But this? This was the opposite of uncomfortable. This was warm and pleasant and felt…right. Somehow. Piper blinked rapidly, trying to expel the train of thought from her head.

They meandered a bit more, said hi to a few people, and then found Darcy again, in the kitchen, fussing over dishes.

"Mom, why aren't you out there visiting with your guests?" Lindsay asked.

Darcy gave her a half-smile. "Because I needed to get away from the guests for a minute." She winked at them. "You doing okay, Piper? I'm sure attending a party where you don't know anybody isn't your idea of a fantastic time."

"I'm doing great," Piper said, and was surprised by how honest the statement was. Lindsay threw her a look then, one Piper *could* read. Clearly. It was joy.

"I think we're going to take off," Lindsay said. "Do you need anything before we do?"

Darcy shook her head. "Just make sure you say goodbye to your sister first." And then she hugged Lindsay, who looked like she'd been taken off guard by the contact. Piper was next. Darcy wrapped her in a hug as well and thanked her for coming.

Back out in the yard, they found Emma walking toward them. When she looked up and saw them waiting for her, she put on a cute little pout. "Aw, are you leaving?"

"We are," Lindsay said.

Emma hugged her and Piper heard her whisper in Lindsay's ear, "Take me with you."

Lindsay laughed. "Oh, no. You're the guest of honor. You have to stay until the bitter end."

"Fine," Emma said, injecting her tone with irritation.

"Do you ever come to Vineyard?" Piper asked her.

Emma looked stumped.

"The wine bar where Lindsay works."

"Oh! You know what? I've never been." Emma grimaced then, as if she realized how sad that was.

"Well," said Piper. "You should come. See her in action. You'd be impressed."

They finished up their goodbyes and, five minutes later, were seated in Piper's car. Both of them blew out huge breaths of relief, then their gazes met and they cracked up.

"You survived," Piper said.

"I did. You helped. In a big way." Lindsay reached across the center console and gave Piper a fist bump. "Thank you."

Piper had a smart-ass comment on her tongue, ready to go. But she looked into those green eyes, saw the genuine gratitude parked in them, and swallowed it down. "You're welcome," she said instead, her voice soft.

They sat quietly for a moment, and Piper was surprised by how easy is was to just…be with Lindsay. Not at all what she was expecting.

The ease was finally broken when Lindsay glanced at the clock on the dashboard. "Wow. It's after six? I had no idea we'd stayed so long."

"Me neither."

"I should probably look in on Vineyard, make sure everything's going okay."

Piper studied her for a few seconds before asking, "Who's there tonight?"

"Working? Bridget and Sharon."

"It's fine."

Lindsay squinted at her. "What do you mean?"

Piper turned the key in the ignition. "I mean that Bridget is more than capable of running the place for the night. You know it and I know it."

Lindsay opened her mouth as if to retort, but closed it again.

"Let's go grab a burger or something." Piper shifted the car into gear and pulled out into the street. "We didn't eat much at the party, despite all the food. What's wrong with us?"

"I can't speak for you, but I can't eat when I'm nervous." Lindsay shot her a quirky half-grin.

"Understandable. Are you nervous now?" Piper realized that question could be construed as loaded only after she'd asked it. She waited, breath held.

"Not at all."

"Good. Then let's eat."

❖

Lindsay was shocked by how much fun she was having. Despite her whole idea of finding Piper Bradshaw "intriguing," she'd still been a bit uneasy about how this day would go. She'd expected it would maybe be fine. She also wouldn't have been terribly surprised if it had been not fine, even a disaster. Some part of her had actually prepared for that.

What she had not prepared for—at all—was for it to be awesome.

It was a gorgeous night, the temperature had not cooled much, still hovering in the seventies, and they'd opted to sit at one of the half dozen picnic tables strewn around McDougal's to eat. The burger joint had both a dining room and a walk-up window where you could pick up your food and eat it outside. It was on the opposite end of the lake from Vineyard, so Lindsay didn't get here as often as she'd like to, which she scolded herself for every time she pulled into the parking lot and smelled the burgers grilling.

Lindsay stood alongside the pick-up window, waiting on their orders, while Piper saved their table. Once Lindsay looked in her direction, she had trouble tearing her eyes away. Piper sat on the bench, silhouetted by the sun as it slipped low in the sky and reflected its red-orange glow over the water. Her bare shoulders were visible against the black of her dress, her chestnut-colored hair still clipped back, but with many errant strands having escaped and now framing her face in gentle casualness. Her legs were crossed at the knee…those legs. God, had Lindsay ever seen a sexier pair of legs than Piper's? She was saved from rifling through the mental catalog of all the legs she'd seen in her life by the woman in McDougal's calling her number. A tray slid into view, piled high with two cheeseburgers, two orders of curly fries, two diet sodas, and a heaping stack of napkins.

Lindsay's mouth started to water.

Piper looked up as Lindsay approached with the tray. "Oh, my God, did we order all that?"

"Afraid so. I think there's a rule that you're not allowed to leave until you eat everything."

Piper snorted a laugh. "If that's the case, I'll be spending the night right here."

They dug in and conversation ceased for a few minutes as they chewed and looked out over the water.

"It's a gorgeous night," Lindsay said quietly, as a couple of toddlers ran past, their harried mother following closely behind them. She watched for several moments as the kids giggled and found something intensely interesting about blades of grass. Lindsay looked back at Piper, whose smile seemed…wistful. "You want kids?"

If the question surprised Piper, she didn't show it. "I think I do. I haven't really decided, but I also don't have a ton of time left, so I should probably figure it out."

"You're how old?"

"I'm thirty-eight."

Lindsay made a *pfft* sound and waved a hand. "Please. You've got plenty of time."

"What about you?" Piper popped a French fry into her mouth. "You want them?"

"I do." It was one of the few things in life Lindsay was certain of. "I've wanted to be a mom since I can remember. I was all about my dolls when I was little, and I loved to take care of them. I had a little crib and a little playpen and a little changing table. Changing diapers was my favorite. I also had a doll that burped."

"That is not at all how I would have pictured you as a child, but I have to admit, it's kind of adorable." Piper sipped from her straw.

"Well, I don't know about the adorable part, but yeah, that was me." Lindsay took a bite of her burger, then grabbed a napkin to wipe a drip of mustard off her chin. "What about you? What were you like as a kid?"

"Me?" Piper gave a scoff. "I was a total tomboy."

Lindsay couldn't hide her surprise. "You? Business suited, high-heeled you? Seriously?"

With a nod, Piper went on. "I chased any kind of ball. I loved to run around and climb trees. I was always outside. I used to drive my mother crazy with all the grass stains on my pants because I couldn't run the bases without sliding. I slid into every single base. Always."

Lindsay's laughter was genuine, the vision Piper painted beyond entertaining. "I so would have pegged you for a little girly-girl, with the dolls and the tea parties and stuff."

"You mean like you?" Piper smiled even as her straw was clamped in her teeth.

"Yes! Exactly like me." Lindsay was still laughing, and Piper finally joined her.

"No way. I knew I was gay way early on. At, like, twelve."

Lindsay stopped laughing then, for two reasons. One was a pleasant warmth at having Piper's sexuality confirmed (she'd suspected, but was never told explicitly). The second, because she was a little envious. "Twelve? Wow. I'm jealous."

"You are? How come?"

"Because I struggled for years. From the time I was about sixteen until my early twenties, I cycled around between confusion, fear, certainty, horror, and back to confusion again. I tried dating guys. Over and over, and I couldn't figure out why it didn't work for me. It sounds ridiculously naïve now, but with my parents both tucked snugly into their new families, I didn't feel like I had anybody to talk to about it. I just…floundered."

Piper had eaten a little more than half her burger, but now set it down and slashed her hand over the top of it in an "I'm done" gesture. "Well," she said, then dabbed at her mouth with a napkin. "Don't be jealous. I say I knew I was gay, but the more accurate statement is I knew I was different. I had very little exposure to anything sexual at that age, but I knew I'd rather be around the girls. And whenever a boy picked on a girl I liked, I'd punch him."

Lindsay snorted soda through her nose as the surprised laugh burst out of her, mid-swallow. "What? You punched people?"

"Boys. I punched boys." Piper handed her a couple of napkins, her grin wide. "I spent a lot of time in the principal's office. *A lot* of time."

"I can't even." Lindsay was still laughing. "I'm having trouble processing all this information. It's so…unexpected."

Piper shrugged, straw in her teeth. "What can I say? I like to keep people on their toes."

"I'm starting to get that about you."

They finished eating but sat and watched as the sun dropped down to the horizon, its red-orange color from earlier deepening to mostly red. When it was merely a sliver left peeking over the hills, Piper turned to her and rubbed her hands up and down her bare arms.

"I'm chilly."

"Yeah, me, too."

"Ready to go?"

"Yeah." Lindsay wasn't, if she was being honest. In fact, a big part of her didn't want the day to end. She'd had such an astonishingly good time and she wanted to hold on to it as long as she could. A glance at her watch, however, told her it was nearly nine. "My neighbor fed Rocket dinner, but I should get home to him." She stood and collected their garbage, took it to the trash can, and slid the empty tray back through the window.

Piper had the car running and the heat on by the time Lindsay pulled the door open and hopped in. The radio played softly, a pop song Lindsay vaguely recognized, but couldn't recall the artist's name, and they drove home in companionable silence. When Piper pulled up outside of Lindsay's house, she shifted into Park and turned those unique hazel eyes on Lindsay.

"There you go," she said, her face friendly and open. Lindsay realized it was a much different expression than she'd gotten used to with Piper.

"Listen," Lindsay said as she looked down at her hands, picked at a cuticle. "I can't thank you enough for coming with me today. I honestly wasn't sure how this was going to go." She looked up at Piper then, hoping her face was projecting a little humor. One corner of Piper's mouth lifted, so Lindsay went on. "But not only was it okay, it was so much more. I've never had that much fun at a family gathering."

"We did seem to mingle well together."

"Who knew?"

"Matthew, apparently."

Lindsay chuckled. "Yeah, I'd like to get to know that guy." A beat went by. "Anyway. Thank you, Piper. I had a great time today."

"Me, too."

And then, without taking time to analyze what she was doing, Lindsay leaned over the center console and kissed Piper on the cheek. The skin was soft under her lips, velvety, her perfume prominent. Then she pulled back, yanked on the door handle, and climbed out of the car without looking back. Once she got to the side door, she ventured a glance. Piper was still there, watching and waiting and Lindsay was kind of relieved she couldn't make out her expression from this distance. She slid the key in the lock, turned it, and sent a wave in Piper's direction.

Only then did the black Audi pull away.

Inside, Lindsay closed the door gently and leaned back against it, stood in the stairway without taking the four steps up to open the door into the kitchen. Instead, she exhaled slowly, gave herself time to regulate her racing heart. Rocket sniffed loudly along the bottom of the door, obviously sensing that Lindsay was home, probably wondering why she wasn't coming in. The sound became almost comical, loud inhale, loud exhale, another loud inhale, until Lindsay relaxed and smiled and started to feel like herself again.

"I hear you, buddy," she said as she climbed the steps and entered the kitchen.

Rocket acted like he hadn't seen her in days, spinning in a circle, tail wagging, howling with glee. Lindsay got right on the floor with him, lavished him with love, let him do the same. It helped her focus on something other than today, something other than the woman who, Lindsay knew, was about to start taking up a lot of brain space.

"So, today was interesting," she said, from her spot on the kitchen floor.

Rocket flopped down next to her like a giant sack of flour.

"Oh, you want to hear all about it, do you?" She took a moment, then opened her mouth, but no sound came out, and she shut it again. Maybe she wasn't quite ready to analyze any of it. Maybe it would be better if she just…sat with things for a while. After all, it was a lot to process. But then, it wasn't. Right? Nothing had happened. She'd had a great time with Piper Bradshaw, which was something she hadn't expected. That really was the long and short of it.

It was then that her brain decided to remind her how soft Piper's cheek was under her lips. How captivating her scent was. How she'd put that little bitch Maddie in her place without raising her voice or breaking a sweat. Lindsay tried to combat these thoughts by calling up the Princess Elsa persona she was used to associating with Piper, but it wouldn't come. All she could see was Piper sitting in the driver's seat, smiling gently at her, seeming only approachable and unassuming.

Rocket pawed at her gently, letting her know she wasn't giving him enough attention.

"I just need to not think about this, right, pal?" she asked him as she scratched his furry belly. With a turn of her head, she gazed into his kind brown eyes. "I mean, so she was nice today. Doesn't mean she won't go back to freezing cold tomorrow, right? I should just chalk this up to being a great day and leave it at that. Yes?"

Rocket's tail thumped the floor twice.

"That's my boy." She kissed him on his head and pushed herself to a standing position, then slid her palms together as if wiping something off them. "Okay. The nice day is over. Let's watch some TV. Wanna?" Lindsay plopped onto her couch and snatched up the remote. Rocket joined her, lying so half his body was actually in her lap. She groaned. "Dude, you weigh, like, ninety pounds." He didn't care; he never did. Instead, he rolled his body slightly to give her better access to his tummy. She shook her head with affection and dutifully scratched him while she channel surfed. Finding an episode of *Fixer Upper*, she tried to focus on the houses and the designs while not falling into a sugar coma from watching Chip Gaines fawn all over his gorgeous wife.

She failed at both, falling asleep on the couch and dreaming about a beautiful brunette with hazel eyes and dimples to die for.

CHAPTER ELEVEN

I feel like we need to tell them." Ian's suit was perfectly tailored to fit him, the jacket accentuating his broad shoulders, the lines clean, the red tie adding a nice splash of color to the black ensemble. He always looked fantastic, the consummate professional. Today, though, his hair was disheveled, and Piper imagined the cause was Ian agitatedly running his fingers through it in frustration. His face was marred by worry and stress. She wondered if she gave off a similar vibe.

"I know," Piper said on a sigh. "But we can't."

"No," Ian said, holding up a finger. "We're not supposed to. It was *suggested* that we don't. That's different than being forbidden."

"Splitting hairs, Ian. There was a directive. We could be fired."

He scratched at his forehead. "I know."

They sat in Piper's office, silent, for a long moment.

"Wouldn't you want someone to warn you?" Ian asked, finally. His voice was very quiet and he continued to gaze out the window as he spoke. "Wouldn't you want to at least be prepared for the worst?"

"Of course I would, but…" Piper didn't look at him either.

"I know you're not friends with your people, but I am with some." He didn't say it in anything other than a factual capacity, but Piper still felt a little accusatory sting at the words. He was right. She made it a point not to make friends with her staff. They got together often, met for Happy Hour or gathered at someone's house. Piper was always invited, but she always bowed out gracefully. She just didn't think it was the boss's place to fraternize with her subordinates, not to mention, it was safer. Something her father had taught her. Ian went on. "I can't imagine one of them getting laid off and then finding out that I knew it was probably going to happen. What kind of a friend does that make me?"

You're not their friend. You're their supervisor. Big difference. Piper could hear her father's voice as clearly as if he were standing in the room with them. "Look, Ian, you've got to do what you've got to do. I understand that."

Ian's face registered disappointment, defeat. "But you're going to sit tight."

Piper swallowed, took a second or two before answering. "I feel like I have to. You read the same thing I did. Leaking any information about the upcoming merger can and will result in termination."

"Yeah, I read it." Ian blew out a huge breath, pushed himself out of the chair and looked just this side of disgusted. "I don't agree with you, Piper."

"I know."

"But we've known each other a long time, and I respect you."

"I appreciate that. I respect you as well." It was true. Ian was a good guy. He and Piper had moved up the ranks together. But he was a lot softer than she was. Not necessarily a bad thing, just a difference between them.

"Good. Well." He nodded at her and left, closing the door behind him with a quiet click.

Piper sat back in her chair. She picked up a pen and went to work on its clicker, the sound weirdly comforting. A half spin in her chair gave her a view out the window, and she watched as puffy clouds floated by, their white popping against the deep blue of the sky. Her people were going to be laid off once this merger went through. She was sure of it. Why else send out a memo to all upper management warning them against leaked details about the merger? Which was, let's be honest, a buy-out. It was the only thing that made sense.

Piper looked off to her right at the shelves that lined the far wall. On it were books on marketing, managing, and other various business subjects. There were also several framed photos, her favorite being an 8x10 of her and her father on the day she graduated from college. He'd been so proud to have one of his girls following in his businessman footsteps. She stared wistfully before whispering into the empty office, "God, I wish you were here, Dad. I could really use some guidance."

Another framed photo caught her eye. It showed her parents, Piper, and Gina, standing in front of Vineyard on the day of its grand opening. Her father had been so happy, so proud of the place.

"But won't you miss work?" she'd asked him for the twenty-seventh time since he'd retired.

He'd smiled patiently at her as he slid wine glasses onto the overhead rack. "This *is* work, Pipsqueak." He'd called her that since she was born, a month early and weighing in at a mere four pounds, six ounces. "Just a different kind."

"You know what I mean. Won't you miss the business world?"

"Of course, I will. But times change. People change. Sometimes, you have to make change. You know?" He'd thrown out his arm to encompass the bar. "This is my change."

"But why?" she'd asked, feeling small in her inability to comprehend.

"Corporate America can take a toll, Pips. Not always. Not on everybody. Depends on where you are, where you work, what kind of values you have." He paused, seemed to search for the right words. "Sometimes, you *need* to make changes. For the people around you. For yourself."

"Are you being cryptic on purpose?" she'd asked him, laughing.

He joined her, his laugh deep and coming from his gut like it always did. "I don't want to sour your love of the business world," he said, reaching out to touch her cheek. "But whenever you need to talk something through, I'm here. Okay?"

She nodded, felt only a tiny bit better, but the joy in his eyes was unmistakable. "You're a wine guy now, huh?"

"Yes," he'd agreed with great conviction. "That's me. Wine Guy. I expect you to call me that now, you know."

Back in her office, Piper could feel the grin stretch across her face. Wine Guy. She'd taken that to heart and had referred to him— loudly—as Wine Guy every time she'd entered Vineyard. He'd adored that place...

Thinking about the wine bar brought another person to her thoughts. Unsurprisingly, her focus turned to Lindsay Kent.

They'd texted a bit since Saturday, but Piper had purposely kept contact to a minimum. She didn't want to analyze why. Now it was Wednesday afternoon, and once she let Lindsay into her head, there was no pushing her out, as her brain dragged her back to last Saturday night after she'd dropped Lindsay home.

That kiss.

Yes, it was just a chaste peck on the cheek, a thank you for a nice day, but it had surprised Piper. It had surprised Lindsay as well, judging from the shocked look on her face when she'd pulled back. But it had stayed with Piper all night. The sincerity and genuine emotion in Lindsay's eyes when she thanked Piper for accompanying her. The way she'd looked at her hands as she spoke. The softness of Lindsay's lips as she pressed them to Piper's skin. Piper had been a split second from turning her head to capture those lips with her own, and the mix of relief and disappointment when the opportunity passed was alarmingly heavy.

She'd watched Lindsay walk up the driveway to the door, watched that golden hair as it caught the glow from the streetlights. She'd watched her ass (God, she had a great ass). She'd waited until Lindsay had tossed a little wave telling her she was in, and then Piper had to force herself to drive away, to drive home to her cat and her cold, lonely bed where she'd crawled under the covers later and taken care of herself to the image of a free-spirited blond with haunting green eyes and a smile like no other.

Yeah. It had freaked her out a little bit.

Okay, a lot. It had freaked her out a lot.

The next morning, she'd vowed to ease up on the contact, responding politely to Lindsay's text that thanked her once again and said what a great time she'd had. There had been a couple more throughout Sunday and then another text on Monday telling Piper to stop by and try some of the wine that had come in from a new winemaker she'd fallen in love with.

There'd been nothing yesterday. Nothing today. And Piper was irritated to realize that she missed the contact…that she missed Lindsay.

Unexpected, to say the least.

Piper tried to push that out of her mind, did a commendable job for the remainder of Wednesday, but Wednesday night, an idea blossomed in her head and would not leave her alone. It sprouted like a weed, its vines wrapping themselves as they grew, winding around her brain, around all of her thoughts, even invading her sleep. By the time she woke up Thursday morning, she'd decided to stop fighting it.

It was 5:45 a.m. when she pulled into Lindsay's driveway, got out of the car, and pushed on the doorbell. She'd seen Lindsay in the woods often enough at this hour, so she wasn't really worried about her being awake. What she was going to say once the door was opened…well, that was a different story.

The surprise on Lindsay's face when she did open the door was kind of priceless, and Piper felt herself grin.

"Good morning."

"Hi," Lindsay said, confusion apparent, but Piper was fairly certain there was also a level of happy-to-see-you there.

Piper handed over a small bag. "Here. Go put these on and come get in the car."

"Wow, you're bossy in the morning."

"I'm bossy all the time. Now, get to it." With that, Piper turned and got back in the car, trying to hide the fact that she was stupidly nervous. She could feel Lindsay study her for a moment, then she disappeared into the house.

No more than five or six minutes went by before the door opened and Lindsay came out, locked it behind her, and walked around the front of the car.

Piper's mouth went dry.

"This shirt's kinda tight," Lindsay said as she hopped into the passenger seat. "But I squished myself in. Does it look ridiculous?"

Piper turned to look at Lindsay, dressed in one of her black, skintight tops. The sleeves stopped at her elbows, and the nylon fabric hugged every single curve Lindsay had in the best of ways. Piper had to make a conscious effort not to stare at her chest.

"No," she said, then had to clear her throat. "No," she said again. "You look great."

"Okay, good. I was worried."

"No need." Piper put the car in reverse and backed out of the driveway.

"I notice there are two kayaks on your roof."

"You're observant."

"I can assume I'm in for an unexpected lesson?"

For the first time since she'd hoisted Kat's old kayak into the rack, Piper faltered just a hair. "Is that okay? I mean, if you don't want to, I totally get it. It was probably dumb that I didn't check first. Maybe you're afraid of water or something. I just thought—" Mercifully, her rambling stopped when Lindsay laid a hand on her thigh.

"It's great. I'm really glad we're doing this. I *am* surprised. In a good way."

"Okay. Good." Piper hoped she didn't sound quite as relieved as she felt. This was very unlike her. Flying by the seat of her pants? Walking a tightrope with no net? Yeah, not in Piper's bag of tricks. At all. This was totally new for her. And to be honest, it was exhilarating. As was Lindsay's hand on her thigh, which was warm and solid and something Piper *really* needed to ignore if she planned on not driving them into a telephone pole.

The parking lot at the end of Black Cherry Lake was empty, save for Gil Shankman's pickup. He'd be out on the water fishing in his canoe. Piper paddled past him almost every morning.

"I love the quiet," Lindsay said, her voice barely above a whisper, as if she didn't want to disturb the peace she spoke of.

"Me, too." Piper began to loosen the straps holding the kayaks.

"I think even if I didn't work evening hours, I'd still walk Rocket here at this time of day. It's so peaceful." When she saw the kayak was free, she helped Piper lift it off the roof and carry it to the water's edge. "How come you have two?"

Piper nodded at the orange kayak they'd just set down. "This one was my ex's."

"Oh." Piper glanced at Lindsay as they went to retrieve the other kayak, watched her face as she obviously struggled with whether to ask for more info. "She didn't want it?"

Piper half shrugged. "She didn't really enjoy it like I do. I think she thought she would, so we bought them together, but she rarely came out with me. I'm actually glad it's about to get some use."

"I'll try not to sink it."

"I'm not worried." Once the green kayak was set next to the orange one, Piper opened the back door of the SUV and pulled out Kat's old life jacket. "Here."

Lindsay took it, slipped it on while Piper donned her own. When she glanced up at Lindsay, she had one end of the buckle and was craning her neck from side to side trying unsuccessfully to find the other. "What is happening? This does not bode well for the whole not sinking thing."

Piper laughed. "Come here." Lindsay stepped closer. Very close. Right into Piper's personal space. Piper took the end with the buckle from Lindsay's hand, then reached around behind her, feeling with her fingers and untwisting the strap as she went. Their faces were very close together, Lindsay's higher, as she was a couple inches taller. It crossed Piper's mind that, with a simple tipping up of her own chin, she could easily press her lips to Lindsay's. A hard swallow later, she found the other end of the strap—thank freaking God—and buckled it at Lindsay's stomach with a loud snap. "There. All set." Again, she hoped the relief she felt wasn't apparent in her voice, because that had been close.

Lindsay opened her mouth, presumably to speak, and made a croaking sound instead. She quickly cleared her throat and muttered a thank you as the two of them each took a quick step back.

Doing her best to busy herself with something other than staring at Lindsay Kent, Piper got the paddles out of the SUV, along with two waterproof bags.

"Put your phone in here if you need to have it with you. I brought a couple granola bars and some water." She handed one of the bags over, along with a bottle of water and the bars. Lindsay put everything in and closed it up, grabbed a paddle, then followed Piper to the kayaks. "Tuck your bag in here." She indicated a little compartment on her own kayak.

The water was still quite chilly, but not like it had been a month ago. Piper walked into it, gently pulling her kayak alongside, making sure not to let it grind against the bottom.

Lindsay mirrored her perfectly.

"Okay, getting in from standing in the water is a lot easier than getting in from a dock." Piper moved so she was on the other side of her own kayak, standing next to Lindsay. "Your feet go here," she said as she pointed to the foot rests inside. "Your butt goes here, obviously. And you paddle. It's really pretty intuitive."

Lindsay gave a nod. "I can do this."

"You can. Go ahead and get in. I'll hold it."

With only some minor hesitation and just a little bit of tipping, Lindsay got herself into the kayak and situated properly. Piper pushed her out toward the open water, then hopped into her own boat and paddled up alongside.

"So, I have sort of a set route I take each morning. We can do that or try something different."

Lindsay held out an arm. "Set route works. Lead the way."

For a while, the only sounds were the subtle splashes of paddles as they dipped into the water and the various birdcalls coming from the trees on the shore. Lindsay had no trouble keeping up, though paddling as quietly as Piper did took some effort. When they came to the spot where the shore sort of turned in and created a little makeshift cove, Piper steered her boat that way, Lindsay about ten yards behind her. Once in the cove, Piper lifted her paddle and laid it across the top of her kayak, just floated. Lindsay pulled up next to her and did the same. The canopy made by the trees created some shade, and the water lapped at the land gently from the ripples the kayaks made. Some small creature scurried through the woods, the rustling of leaves and sticks the only sign. The air smelled like nature, clean and honest.

"This is my favorite place in the world," Piper said quietly.

"I can see why," Lindsay whispered. "It's beautiful."

A honk came from their left, and two Canada geese floated a few feet off the shore, followed by six babies. Piper indicated them with her chin. "That's Fred and Daphne and their kids."

Lindsay's smile grew wide. "Fred and Daphne? Do they solve mysteries in their spare time?"

"Please. Fred and Daphne never solved anything. They were always off making out. Velma did all the work."

"Totally true." They floated quietly for a few more minutes, before Lindsay asked, "Do you come here every time you're out on the lake?"

Piper nodded. "Yeah. For some reason, it's one of the only places where I feel like I can clear my head, where I can shake off the stresses of work, especially lately."

Lindsay cocked her head, and the gesture made Piper's heart skip. "What's going on at work? Still the Harbinger merger stuff?"

"You remembered that?"

"Of course I did. Is it going through? I know you were worried about that last time we talked."

Piper just looked at her, blinked several times. And then the weirdest thing happened. She didn't even hesitate. She just opened her mouth and it all spilled out. Everything. The merger, the memo with the threat to her job, her discussion with Ian yesterday, her father's words, all of it.

"Wow," Lindsay said when Piper finally stopped talking. "That's a lot. Maybe you should just stay here all day and float."

"Don't think it hasn't crossed my mind."

A hawk flew over them, landed in a tree as Piper watched.

"What are you going to do?" Lindsay asked, her voice soft.

Piper inhaled very slowly, let it out, lifted her shoulders, dropped them. Finally, she turned to look at Lindsay. Lindsay, sitting there in Kat's kayak, in Kat's life jacket, but so *not* Kat. "What would you do?" she asked, surprising herself.

"I'd warn them." There was no hesitation, not a falter, not one second of debate.

"Just like that?"

"Hell, yes."

"But you'd get fired."

"Yeah, but why would I want to work for a company that would put me in such a position? They obviously suck."

Piper couldn't help the laugh that snorted out of her. "Sure seems like it." She did her best to remind herself that this was Lindsay, though. Lindsay, who was experienced in retail but not corporate business, where things were completely different. Still…her words stuck.

"So, you come here in the early morning and you float."

"I do. Like I said, I find peace here, for some reason."

"For lots of reasons. It's beautiful. It's calm and serene. It feels… almost restorative to me somehow." Lindsay turned to her, and her smile was radiant. "Thank you so much for bringing me here. I feel…" She squinched up her face, seeming to search for the right description. "Honored. If that makes any sense." Then she shrugged and looked away, obviously embarrassed, and Piper had the sudden need to make her feel better.

"It does. Perfect sense." Piper swallowed, looked off into the trees. "I've never brought anybody here with me before," she said, softly.

"Well, then, I am most definitely honored."

Their gazes held and something passed between them, something Piper felt as it sizzled through her body and wondered if Lindsay felt it as well.

"Let's go," Piper said suddenly, needing to break whatever spell she suddenly felt had a hold on her. "We're not getting any exercise floating."

"Oh, this is about exercise?" Lindsay asked with gentle laughter. "I thought we were relaxing."

"We were. Now we're not." Piper dug her paddle in deep and took off, leaving Lindsay in her wake—and feeling like she needed to. At least for a moment. When she felt a little more like herself, she eased up on the paddling and let Lindsay catch up.

"Wow, you're strong," Lindsay said as she finally pulled up next to Piper. "I was paddling my ass off and couldn't catch you. I'm impressed."

Piper smiled. "I've been doing this for a long time." She waved at Gil Shankman as they passed his canoe, and he waved back.

"How long?"

Piper inhaled as she thought about it, then exhaled slowly. "Let's see, well, I tried out for crew in college."

"Yeah? I always wondered what that sport was like."

"I made the team, but I didn't enjoy it."

"Why not?"

"First of all, it's brutal. When you think of crew and all the people in the scull working together, it looks easy. Trust me, it's not. Every person in the boat is working his or her ass off. Training was constant. There was bitching within the team. Every girl wanted to be the best, but it doesn't matter if you're the best because you have to work together to be successful." Piper shook her head. "It just wasn't what I was looking for. So I quit the team." She stopped paddling and looked off in the distance, at the serene water of Black Cherry Lake. "But I missed the water. I missed the calming motion of paddling. One morning, I rented a kayak and took it out, and I was hooked. The exercise, the fact that I could challenge myself but didn't have to worry about others, the peace on the water. I realized right away *that* was what I'd been hoping to get from crew." She turned to Lindsay with a shrug. "And I've been kayaking ever since."

"I wish I had something like that," Lindsay said, her voice slightly wistful.

"You have Rocket," Piper said, feeling the weird urge to make her feel better. "And wine. You know more about wine than anybody I know."

Lindsay turned to look at her then, and her expression…Piper swallowed hard, yanked her gaze away, and cleared her throat. "Thanks, Piper."

"We'd probably better head back. I have to get to work."

Lindsay nodded, but said no more. Piper turned her kayak and they paddled wordlessly back to shore, where they packed up the kayaks and equipment like they'd been doing so together for years. It wasn't until they were both in the SUV and pulling out of the lot that Lindsay spoke.

"That was great. Thank you so much for bringing me."

"Thanks for being open to it." Piper glanced over, but then back at the road. She couldn't look at Lindsay for long. Couldn't look at those mesmerizing green eyes, that warm and inviting smile, that blond hair Piper had thought about running her fingers through. Things were stirring within her. Things she wasn't sure what to do with, wasn't sure what she *wanted* to do with.

Thank God, the drive back to Lindsay's was quick. She pulled into the driveway and slid the gearshift into Park, but didn't turn off the engine or attempt to get out, making it clear this was a drop-off and nothing else.

A beat of silence went by.

Two beats.

Lindsay cleared her throat—she'd done that a lot this morning, Piper noticed. "So, this was great. Truly. Thank you so much." She reached across the console and closed her hand over Piper's bare forearm and it was as though an electric current ran through her.

"You're welcome."

"If you ever want company again, just say the word."

"I will."

That sat there for another long moment, Lindsay's hand still on Piper's arm.

"Okay," Lindsay said.

"Okay."

"You should come by Vineyard tonight." Lindsay seemed to blurt it, like it came out before she'd had time to think about it.

"Yeah?"

"Definitely. We can talk." Those green eyes snared hers. "About the wine bar, I mean."

"Oh. Of course. Sure."

"I mean…other stuff, too. We can talk about other stuff. Maybe."

"Yeah, okay." *God, we sound like two junior high kids with crushes.*

Lindsay looked straight ahead out the windshield, still holding Piper's arm. "All right. I'm off." She didn't move, though. Instead, she looked down at her lap, and Piper watched her. It was as if Lindsay was contemplating something. When it seemed like she'd made up her mind, she lifted her gaze, and moved so quickly, Piper wasn't even sure what had happened until Lindsay's mouth was pressed to hers.

Lindsay's soft, warm mouth.

And Piper was lost.

There was nothing else then. She couldn't hear the car's engine running. Work was nowhere in her mind. The only thing that existed was that kiss and Piper closed her eyes, sank into it without thought. Without hesitation. Lindsay tasted so surprisingly sweet, and Piper felt herself leaning in, leaning closer, as if her body had taken over separately from her brain. Lindsay's fingers slid along Piper's face and gripped the back of her head, pulling her in as she pressed her tongue into Piper's mouth and a moan escaped—Piper wasn't sure from which of them. The only thing she *was* sure of was that she never wanted to stop. Ever. She could stay right here, in her car, leaning over the center console and kissing Lindsay Kent, for the rest of her life. It was the moment when she lifted her hands, intent on grasping Lindsay's head, intent on keeping her mouth pressed to Lindsay's, that Lindsay pulled away. Piper almost fell forward, but caught herself.

When she finally opened her eyes and looked at Lindsay, the expression on her face was one of surprised wonder.

"Oh, wow." Lindsay brought her fingers to her lips in one of the sexiest gestures Piper had ever seen, her eyes wide, her chest heaving, and for a moment, Piper wasn't sure if Lindsay was about to apologize or kiss her again.

"Yeah," Piper said, because no other words would form and come out of her mouth.

"Wow."

Piper nodded.

"Um…" Lindsay looked around. "Okay then." A tug on the door handle later and she was sliding out of the car.

Piper watched as she walked to the side door of her house, then turned back to look at Piper. Before Piper could get a read on what Lindsay might be thinking, Lindsay unlocked the door and went inside. Piper had the sudden urge to chase her but forced herself to be calm and rational, to keep her ass in the driver's seat, both literally and figuratively. She jammed the car into reverse before she could change her mind.

Once on the road, a glance in the rearview mirror had her squinting at the woman in the reflection, who was apparently a complete stranger to her.

What the hell just happened? And what do I do now?

CHAPTER TWELVE

Lindsay looked at the screen on her phone, set it down without responding. Again. She'd been texting with Maya early this morning when Piper had shown up, and Lindsay had made the mistake of telling her who, with two kayaks strapped to her roof, had just pulled into the driveway. Maya had demanded a full report and Lindsay had promised and now Maya was looking for details.

But Lindsay wasn't ready to share what had happened this morning.

Mostly because Lindsay wasn't sure what had happened this morning.

Well. That was a lie. She'd made out with Piper Bradshaw in the front seat of her Audi SUV, that's what had happened. What she wasn't sure of was *how* it had happened. Or why. Or what she was supposed to do now.

You made the move, the little jeering voice in her head reminded her. Not her smartest idea, not at all, because she had to work with Piper. She *needed* Piper. Jesus, Mary, and Joseph, Piper was the boss's daughter.

"Oh, God, what was I thinking?" She'd asked this question out loud about thirty-seven times already today, and it was always followed by the dramatic dropping of her face into her hands, and *that* was always followed by a groan.

Lindsay had taken Rocket for a walk around the neighborhood in the hopes of clearing her head. When that hadn't worked, she'd scrubbed her bathroom until she could see herself in every surface. When that didn't work, she moved on to the kitchen. After that, she'd decided to come into work a bit early, focus on some paperwork, some ordering, maybe set up a few meetings with vendors. Anything to force her concentration onto something that wasn't a hot brunette in skintight nylon with dimples that made her go weak in the knees.

Didn't work.

Nothing worked.

Now it was early afternoon, and she still felt as if Piper followed her around as she tried to do her job. Two customers sat at a table in the far corner of Vineyard, a man and a woman, their heads close together as they spoke in hushed tones. Lindsay had taken notice of them before. He was a bit older, maybe in his mid-fifties. She didn't look any older than her early forties. Both wore business attire and they always came in around lunchtime or early in the afternoon. Never at night when there were more people, and Lindsay had never seen them on a weekend. She and Bridget often wondered if they were having an affair, had started creating little imaginary scenarios to represent their lives.

Bridget came in to allow Lindsay to take care of some managerial things and do the payroll, and she stood behind the bar next to Lindsay, refilling the couple's glasses. "The Clandestines," she whispered, and Lindsay grinned.

The door opened and they both turned; Lindsay suspected Bridget's face held the same guilty expression hers did, as if the person coming in knew exactly what they'd been whispering about.

But the person coming in was Piper Bradshaw.

Gone was Kayak Piper. In her place was Business Piper. Black suit and skirt, candy apple red top underneath the jacket, hair in waves hanging around her shoulders. She radiated determination and seriousness as she marched right up to the bar. Bridget took the two glasses of wine and headed for the Clandestines.

"Can I talk to you?" Piper asked quietly, her hazel gaze boring into Lindsay's, something in them that she couldn't quite put a finger on.

"Sure. What's up?" Lindsay set aside the tablet in her hand and gave Piper her full attention. "You're early. I didn't expect you until tonight."

"Not here." Piper swallowed audibly. "In your office?"

"Oh. Okay. Sure." Lindsay turned and led the way into the back. Mentally, she prepared herself to be scolded or reamed out or at least get a good talking to about the morning. *This is probably good. We'll get it out there, laugh it off, and it'll be done. Good. Necessary.*

Once in the office, she waited for Piper, who was closing the door behind them. When she turned and they faced each other,

Lindsay actually caught her breath. Piper's expression had changed. Dramatically.

Gone was Business Piper.

In her place was...

Piper's hands grasped Lindsay's head and spun her quickly until her back hit the door and she let out a soft "oof." And before Lindsay could even begin to process what was happening, Piper's mouth was on hers. The kiss was deep. Thorough. Demanding. There was no question who was running this show, and it wasn't Lindsay.

Yeah, this was Takes What She Wants Piper.

Lindsay's brain seemed to short-circuit. She could focus on nothing other than Piper's mouth, Piper's tongue, Piper's hands as they cradled her face. Lindsay felt herself floating, her entire existence in Piper's (obviously) very capable hands and then—all contact was suddenly gone.

Lindsay opened her eyes to see Piper, who had taken a very small step back from her, looking a strange combination of horrified, angry and...Lindsay squinted. Aroused. Yes. Definitely aroused.

"What the hell?" Piper whispered.

Lindsay could only shake her head.

Piper brought her hand to her lips. "I don't understand what's happening. I can't..." She gestured between their two bodies, still only a few inches apart. "This isn't a good idea."

"No." Lindsay shook her head again, apparently unable to do anything else.

"I mean, people who have to work together shouldn't do this."

"No." More shaking.

"People who get on each other's nerves shouldn't do this."

"No." Another shake, but with a ghost of a smile.

"It's a terrible idea. This."

And before Lindsay could lamely shake her head one more time like a damn bobblehead doll, Piper had grabbed her face and was kissing her again.

This kiss was raw.

Almost animalistic.

And desperate.

That's the descriptor that fit best in the moment, and Lindsay latched onto it. It felt desperate, like they couldn't not kiss, like it was as necessary as breathing. Before Lindsay realized what she was doing, her hands came up to Piper's waist and pulled her closer so Piper leaned into her body. Lindsay ran one hand all the way up and slid her fingers into that soft, bouncy hair on Piper's head, held her close, pushed her tongue into Piper's mouth as deeply as she could.

This time, when Piper pulled away, she stayed close, her forehead against Lindsay's as she whispered one more time, "It's a terrible idea."

This time, Lindsay nodded, whispered back, "It so is."

"You're kind of a pain in my ass."

"Right back atcha."

"Okay. Good. I'm glad we settled that."

And Piper kissed her once more. Softly this time. Quickly.

Then she moved Lindsay out of the way, opened the office door, and left before Lindsay could even register that it was done.

Lindsay watched her go, watched the way her body moved as she walked. The broad shoulders. That gorgeous ass that Lindsay now chastised herself for not getting her hands on. Those ridiculous legs. When Piper was out of sight, Lindsay closed the office door quietly so she could collect herself.

If that was even possible.

Fingertips against her own swollen lips, Lindsay forced herself to breathe slowly and easily, to calm her hammering heart. There was a gentle but insistent throbbing between her legs, a throbbing she hadn't felt in a very long time, and her blood seemed to be racing through her system at warp speed. She closed her eyes, inhaled slowly, and held it before letting it out.

Had she ever been ambushed like that?

More importantly, had she ever been this turned on?

Slowly, she shook her head, back and forth, back and forth.

No. No, she had not. Of that she was certain. And the sheer truth of it was almost frightening because it had only been a kiss. Piper had done nothing more than kiss her, and yet Lindsay's body had prepared itself in anticipation of more.

She was so ready for more.

It was more of a flop backward than an actual sit when she settled into the desk chair, like her bones had liquefied and her body simply… fell. Then she dropped her head to the desk with a thump, lifted it an inch or two, dropped it again. Four times.

Two simple words kept running through her head on a continuous loop. Just two. The same two, over and over.

Now what?

❖

What was happening to her?

Piper didn't like this. Not one bit. She was always in control. Always. No questions asked. She'd been like that since she was a kid. Gina said she was a control freak, and Piper could never argue with her, because it was absolutely true. Piper didn't like feeling untethered. She didn't like to drift. She wasn't a raft. She wasn't a kite. She was the mistress of her own destiny. Things didn't happen to her. She made them happen.

Why was Lindsay so different? Why did she find herself so physically drawn to her recently? Why now? Granted, she hadn't spent a lot of time with her in the past, but she'd met her. She'd seen her. And not once in the past had Piper wondered what she'd look like naked, what her skin would feel like under Piper's fingers, what she'd sound like when she came.

"For God's sake," Piper muttered, scrubbing a hand over her face as she sat at her desk in her office and faced the windows. She had barely any recollection of her drive to Vineyard an hour ago. A few glimpses of a traffic light or a right turn popped into her brain, but she'd mostly been on autopilot. The next thing she was aware of was turning Lindsay and backing her into the door with a thump.

And then they made out like two kids on prom night.

It wasn't the kissing that had Piper freaking out. She knew that. Not that the kissing wasn't something that warranted scrutiny, because it absolutely did. But at the moment, Piper was more shocked by her own inability to control herself. It was true that Lindsay had opened the door by kissing Piper that morning in her car, but in normal life, Piper would have easily waved that off, chalked it up to a fun few minutes and nothing more, never given it another thought. The fact that she hadn't been able to wipe it from her brain all morning had nearly driven her insane. She replayed it over and over as her body thrummed. She'd sat through a two-hour meeting with nine other people and could barely recall what they'd talked about because all she did was fantasize about kissing Lindsay again. About doing more with Lindsay.

So, the instant she had a free half hour, she'd hopped in her car, driven to Vineyard, and kissed Lindsay senseless in her mother's office.

"What the fuck," she whispered, in disbelief. Not one to swear, the surprise appearance of the F-bomb was a pretty good indicator that Piper was no longer in control.

What was happening to her?

A light knock on her door pulled Piper back to the reality of her job and she almost jumped up with joy to say thank you. Instead, she simply called out, "Come in."

"Hey there." It was Ian. He looked only slightly less frazzled than the last time they'd talked.

"Hey," she greeted as he entered.

Ian was almost always impeccably dressed. Perfectly pressed suits, power ties, shined shoes. He took the role of office professional very seriously. Today, though, it was as though he'd slipped down a couple rungs on the ladder of Look the Part. His jacket was missing; Piper envisioned it tossed haphazardly somewhere in his office down the hall. The sleeves of his white shirt were rolled up to reveal forearms covered in dark hair. His striped tie was askew, as if he didn't want to take it completely off, but couldn't stand it around his neck. He crossed the office and dropped into one of her extra chairs.

"I emailed you that report."

"I got it." Piper studied him. "You okay?"

He shrugged, coupled it with a shake of his head. "I just hate this, you know? I realize we're of different schools of thought here, but I can't sleep. I can't eat. I just feel awful."

Piper flashed back to her conversation with Lindsay about Piper and Ian knowing their staffs were most likely going to be let go.

"I'd warn them."

"Just like that?"

"Hell, yes."

"But you'd get fired."

"Yeah, but why would I want to work for a company that would put me in such a position? They obviously suck."

Lindsay and Ian would get along really well.

Piper managed to redirect her focus and listen to Ian, who thankfully did not continue on his path of *this is driving me crazy* but instead veered into more business-related things. Piper felt a surge of relief, because she was doing enough wavering in her own head. She didn't need Ian tipping any scales for her. But after a few moments of discussion on another project, when Ian stood to leave, Piper stopped him.

"Are you...?" She let the sentence dangle, scratched the back of her head. When she looked up at Ian, he was waiting expectantly, openly, his expression friendly. He really was a good guy. "Are you going to tell your people?"

He nodded. "I have to. I won't be able to look at myself in the mirror if I don't."

"When?"

He hesitated then, the openness dimming a bit.

Piper held up a hand. "I'd never tell anybody. I promise. I was just curious if you had a timeline."

"I haven't decided on an actual day, but I want to give them enough notice before the actual merger is announced. I want them to have time to go looking if they want."

Piper nodded. "Makes sense."

They stood for several beats, looking at each other, then glancing away, then meeting gazes again. Finally, with a nod, Ian took his leave.

He'd left Piper with a lot to think about.

Just what she needed.

She let her head drop back along the top of her chair and groaned.

CHAPTER THIRTEEN

I don't love this one. It tastes a bit...musty."

It took every bit of energy Lindsay had not to roll her eyes at this man as he sat at the bar in front of her and finished the sample she'd poured him of the French Syrah/Grenache blend. The staff had dubbed him Mr. Can I Taste That. He wasn't a regular, thank goodness, but he'd been in enough times and gone through the same ritual enough times for the staff to see him coming and run to get Lindsay to wait on him. None of them wanted to deal with him and his finicky ways. The man was probably in his mid to late fifties, rail-thin and balding. His clothes were nicely tailored and he gave off an air of good education and an upper-class upbringing. Lindsay could almost hear Mrs. B.'s voice saying, "Just because somebody has money doesn't mean he intends to spend it."

"I'd like to try the Malbec," Mr. Can I Taste That said, pointing at the Argentinian wine in the menu and pronouncing it *male-beck* rather than *mall-beck*.

Lindsay heard Bridget cough behind her, knew that was code for a snort of laughter. "Sure," she said, and turned to pour him a taste. She knew from experience that by the time he decided on a wine, he would have sampled maybe four or five—which would pretty much add up to an entire glass of wine he would end up drinking for free.

Gotta choose your battles, Mrs. B. would say.

It was after six, and the crowd was fairly steady. Not big, but not tiny, and Lindsay tried not to focus on the fact that business was definitely picking up. She had a woman named Patrice Dymond lined up for the weekend—a jazz singer in her fifties who brought her own keyboard player and a voice as velvety as a good Merlot, if her YouTube clips were any indication. Lindsay had begun running a contest on the

Vineyard Facebook page, getting people to show up for a free glass of wine if they brought a friend who'd never been. It obviously wasn't something they could enforce, so she played it kind of fast and loose, but Lindsay was sure she'd brought in some new customers via social media.

Mr. Can I Taste That was making a face at the Malbec (but drinking it all) when the door opened and Piper walked through. Lindsay's body betrayed her the instant their eyes met. Her heart rate kicked up. Her stomach muscles tightened. Her underwear dampened.

Goddamn it, how does she do that?

Piper must have come from work, as she wore the same suit she had on earlier that day, but her expression was different. Lindsay studied her from across the wooden floor, trying to decide which Piper she was getting this time.

Mr. Can I Taste That pulled her attention away from watching Piper cross the room toward her by sliding his (empty) glass to her. "How about the Shiraz? Let me give that one a whirl."

Lindsay forced her eyes off Piper and poured the wine, giving him as little as she could get away with. When she looked up, Piper was standing next to him.

"Hey," Lindsay said, as she slid the glass back to her customer. When she made eye contact with Piper, the heat rose up through her body so fast she was surprised she didn't break into an immediate sweat.

"Hi."

Piper seemed…serious. It was the only word that fit. But not serious in a, "I'm about to kiss your face off" way like earlier. Serious in a "I'm about to tell you something you probably won't like" kind of way instead. Lindsay felt herself automatically bracing. "Wine?" she asked Piper.

With a shake of her head, Piper declined as she was reaching into her bag. "I went over those numbers regarding the patio."

"Okay." Lindsay watched as Piper pulled out an envelope and slid it across the bar top.

"This is what I'm willing to allow for the changes you want to make. If you have any questions, feel free to call me." With that, Piper turned on her high heel and clicked her way back to the door and out of the wine bar. Lindsay stared after her, brow furrowed.

What the hell?

A large party entered Vineyard after holding the door for Piper, so Lindsay stuffed the envelope into the back pocket of her jeans and did her best to focus on her job. Not on the woman who had kissed her senseless that afternoon and pretty much blown her off this evening.

It wasn't easy.

Later that night, Lindsay was home on the couch, Rocket with his head in her lap, and Angela on FaceTime.

"So, wait." Angela was squinting into the screen, obviously trying to sort out the order of events Lindsay had reported. "She came right into the office and kissed you?"

"She asked if we could go into the office," Lindsay corrected her. "And then, yes, she was just…on me." The pang in her lower body then reminded her of how sexy that had been. "I didn't see it coming. She just took over. It was amazing."

"Wow." Angela propped her chin in her hand and let out a dreamy sigh.

"Yeah, but then tonight, everything was different. I think she's freaked."

"What happened tonight?"

Lindsay thought back and the expression on Piper's face came shooting back to her. "She came in all stern and businesslike."

"Not like she'd had her tongue in your mouth a few hours earlier?"

"No. Not like that at all. She was all firm and professional-ish and told me she'd gone over the numbers for the changes we'd talked about for the patio. Then she slipped me an envelope and left. She barely looked at me."

"Mm-hmm," Angela said. "Definitely sounds like a woman freaking out. Silently."

Lindsay nodded into the screen at the accuracy of the statement. "That's her." Piper would definitely be the kind of woman that nobody would realize was panicking because she was so stoic. So in control. It hadn't take Lindsay long to learn this fact about her.

"Did you look in the envelope?"

"I did." Lindsay glanced at the paper she'd tossed on the coffee table.

"And?"

"She cut the number we'd talked about pretty much in half. The number we'd *agreed* on."

"That girl of yours is a control freak, Linds."

Lindsay snorted. "First of all, she's not my girl. She's my boss's daughter and it would do me good to remember that. Second, tell me something I *don't* know."

"Watch yourself, okay?" Angela's voice had softened with concern. "I know you and I know that tender heart of yours."

Lindsay nodded into the screen. "I will."

They talked about a few more things and promised to get together soon, then hung up. Lindsay stayed on the couch, petting Rocket's fuzzy head and thinking about Piper. She'd tried to banish her from her thoughts, but that wasn't working, so she decided maybe she needed to let her in fully, focus on her for a bit. Maybe then she'd be allowed to sleep.

Lindsay was pretty sure she knew what was going on with Piper: she was freaked about what had occurred between them, and she was probably feeling a bit out of control. So she looked around to see what she *could* control and decided it was the money. The purse strings. Piper had been totally on board with the suggestions Lindsay had made and the cost of those suggestions. Now, suddenly, it was too much? No, she needed to feel like she had a handle on something, like she was fully in charge of at least one thing.

"What do you think she'd do if I called her on it?" Lindsay asked aloud. Rocket cocked his head in her lap so he could focus his big brown eyes on her. "I mean, besides be pissed off at me. Because you *know* she'd be pissed off at somebody holding a mirror in front of her face." She stared at the ceiling, stroked her dog's fur, and her voice got quiet. "I don't think she enjoys when somebody knows her. Like, *really knows* her. I think she keeps everything closed off so that doesn't happen." She looked down at Rocket with a shrug of nonchalance. "Problem is, she's not all that hard to read."

Yeah. She and Piper were going to have a little chat.

❖

Piper had hoped the rain would hold off long enough for her to get her morning paddle in, but she was cutting it close. A gentle mist had begun to fall as she pointed her kayak toward the shore, and she dug deeper, the muscles in her shoulders protesting slightly. She'd worked hard this morning, paddling faster, punishing her body for reasons of which she was uncertain.

She'd hardly slept. That was part of it. Lack of sleep made her cranky. Angry. She had no choice but to do what she could to work through it—physical exertion worked best for her—or she'd carry it around all day, taking her frustrations out on friends and colleagues alike. She had lunch scheduled with Gina today, and her poor sister would get the brunt of it, as usual.

So, paddling it was.

The gentle mist changed to a steady rain as Piper glided toward shore. And when she glanced up and saw Lindsay standing there, leaning back against her silver Camry, arms folded across her chest, a duo of emotions hit her, one and then the other. Arousal was first and foremost because Lindsay looked so cute in her yoga pants and sneakers and hot pink hat. But the arousal took Piper by surprise and that pissed her off, which only served to accentuate the anger she'd been trying to paddle away from.

"Son of a bitch," she muttered, as she reached a spot where she could hop out of her kayak and walk it the rest of the way in.

The rain fell steadily now, soaking but warm, and Piper felt her ponytail flatten against her neck and her clothes begin to stick to her as she reached the shore.

"Good morning," Lindsay said as she met Piper at the edge of the water and grasped the front of the kayak.

"I can do it," Piper said, her voice testier than she'd intended.

"I didn't say you couldn't."

Piper would never admit to being grateful for the assistance—lifting a wet kayak in the rain all by herself wasn't an easy task—but she allowed it, and together they hauled the boat out of the water, to Piper's SUV, and up into the rack.

"I looked at the numbers you left for me last night." Lindsay's voice was casual. Breezy.

"Good."

"Yeah, I don't agree with them. I think you should take another look."

Piper stopped, her hands on the kayak strap in mid-tie, and gaped at Lindsay. "I'm sorry. What?"

Lindsay shrugged, her nonchalant demeanor not slipping a millimeter. "They're not accurate."

Piper felt her blood begin to boil. She yanked on the strap, hard, and clenched her jaw tightly to keep from blowing up at Lindsay. When she couldn't make the straps any tighter, she parked her hands on her hips and turned to face Lindsay, both of them nearly soaked at this point. "What the hell does that mean?" she asked.

"What do you mean, 'what does that mean?' It means they're not accurate. They're incorrect. They're not what we agreed on and you came up with them for all the wrong reasons." Lindsay walked closer, her green eyes seeming to spark a bit, but the rest of her just as relaxed as could be. Meanwhile, Piper felt like every muscle in her body was as taut as a bowstring ready to launch its weapon.

"I don't appreciate being second-guessed."

"I'm aware."

Lindsay was dangerously close now. Too close. It did things to Piper, this proximity, and she didn't like it. Except that she did. Lindsay stood only a few inches away, and Piper found herself with her back against the SUV. Piper swallowed hard but stood tall, determined not to be intimidated by this woman. And failing. With Piper not in heels, Lindsay's two-inch advantage in the height department was obvious, and Piper lifted her chin in a useless effort to make up for it. "Exactly what wrong reasons are you talking about?" There was a subtle crack in her voice she hoped Lindsay didn't hear, but she wasn't optimistic, as she suspected Lindsay could probably also hear the pounding of her heart and the whooshing of her blood in her veins.

Lindsay's answer was to place a hand on either side of Piper, effectively trapping her between the car and Lindsay's body. Which was so alarmingly close now that Piper had trouble breathing. That turned out to be fine, though, because in the next second, Lindsay's mouth was on hers and breathing became secondary to the kiss.

The deep, explorative, warm, wet kiss.

Piper's mind screamed at her. Shrieked for her to put a stop to this, that she was giving up all of her precious control to this woman with the soft lips and the magnetic eyes, but Piper felt completely helpless. She couldn't do anything but kiss Lindsay back. Because damn it if this wasn't the most amazing kiss she'd ever shared with another human ever in her entire life. She felt Lindsay's hand cup the side of her face, felt Lindsay's fingertips grasp her ponytail and give it a gentle tug, felt Lindsay's lips, Lindsay's tongue run a hot path along the side of her neck, heard a soft moan and wasn't sure which of them had produced it. The back of her head thumped against the car window and the rain had soaked them completely, as Lindsay's mouth covered hers again and they kissed while Piper waged an internal battle with herself, wanting—needing—so much to put a stop to this, but unable to. She felt adrift, again, as if she kept grasping at something solid to stop her from floating away but couldn't reach anything, her fingertips slashing at empty air.

But Lindsay kept kissing her.

And just when Piper was about to give up, about to give in, to let herself sink fully into the kiss, it was over. Ended. Just like that. Lindsay took a step back, her palm still resting against Piper's cheek, and she ran her thumb across Piper's bottom lip in a move so possessive it sent a hot surge of arousal blasting through Piper's body.

"For *those* wrong reasons," Lindsay said quietly.

Piper blinked at her in confusion, needing several moments to remember that she'd actually asked Lindsay a question and this was Lindsay's answer.

"Look at those numbers again, okay?"

Piper watched as Lindsay took a few more steps backward, then got into her car, keyed the engine, and pulled out of the parking lot. The whole time, Piper stood there in the rain, soaked to the skin, her entire body thrumming with unfulfilled desire. Her breathing was still a bit ragged as she watched Lindsay's taillights disappear into the wet morning, and it took her a few moments before she felt like her legs would hold her if she moved. With some effort, she pushed herself off the SUV and stood on her own, brought her fingertips up to her swollen lips, and swallowed hard.

Yeah, it was pretty clear who had the control now, and it wasn't Piper.

❖

"What is wrong with you?" Gina's voice was quietly firm as she leaned toward the table between them and fixed her gaze on Piper.

Piper cleared her throat and avoided eye contact. "What do you mean?"

Gina arched one eyebrow. "Seriously? You're going to play this game with me, the person who's known you your entire life?" When Piper didn't respond, she continued. "Okay. Fine." She ticked off each example on a finger. "You ordered wine at lunch. You're being a jerk to the waiter, who is doing his best. You haven't made eye contact with me once since we sat down. And I'm doing all the talking. You're cranky and you're either mad or upset about something. So spill, because I'm tired of this."

Gina knew her better than anybody. That was true. And trying to lie to her or pull one over on her was an exercise in futility—Piper had learned that the hard way more than once. Still, she wasn't sure how much she was ready to share with her sister.

"Lindsay's been trying to make a lot of changes at the wine bar." She started there, wanted to see how Gina responded.

"Okay." Gina forked some salad into her mouth and chewed. "Bad changes?"

"I…" Piper did her best to think about it and answer honestly. "No, I guess not."

"Like, she's trying to improve business, right?"

Piper inhaled and let the breath out, already seeing that this would get her nowhere. "I suppose so."

"I see the Facebook page has been updated."

"Dad was so inept when it came to social media."

"Yeah, he was. But this is good. Social media is the best way to reach customers, don't you think? She also created a Twitter account and one on Instagram. I don't know if it's her or Bridget, but somebody's been posting some great shots. This is all good, right?"

"Yeah. It is." Piper's nod was reluctant. "We also went over some numbers regarding fixing up the patio a bit."

"That's a great idea." Gina grinned with excitement. "I told Dad for months he wasn't using that space like he should."

"Lindsay didn't like the numbers. Said I should look again." Piper didn't tell Gina that she'd verbally agreed to one number, then changed her mind later. After kissing had ensued.

Gina lifted her shoulders. "So look again. Can't hurt, can it?"

Piper sighed. "Why do you always have to be so agreeable?"

Gina chuckled. "Look, all I'm saying is, Mom always said Lindsay had a ton of ideas and she should let her try some out. You and I both know that. Looks like that's exactly what Lindsay's doing." Gina studied her. "So, if it's good for Vineyard, what's the problem?"

Piper shook her head, giving up on this tack. "Nothing."

"P. Come on. Something's on your mind." Gina's voice had softened. "I'm worried about you."

It was on the tip of her tongue to just spew it all out onto the table, to tell Gina everything, including the ridiculous chemistry she'd suddenly developed with Lindsay and the three steamy make-out sessions that Piper couldn't get out of her head. It was like Lindsay was taking over every aspect of her life, and it had Piper freaking out a bit. She came so close to saying exactly that to Gina, so close, but chickened out at the last minute, veering in another direction.

"The changes are hard," she said, and gazed out the window next to their booth.

Gina nodded, and Piper knew she got it. She didn't have to say anything; Piper knew she understood. "I know. But he's gone, P. And he liked Lindsay. Don't you think he'd be happy to see that she's got Vineyard making money? Being successful?"

Piper nodded, working as hard as she could to keep her eyes from welling up. She needed desperately to change the subject. "I think I'm just frustrated with work. That's all. It's coloring everything else in my life right now, and my coping skills are in the toilet."

It had exactly the effect Piper hoped, and Gina turned her focus, thank God. "Oh, man. Still the merger stuff?"

Piper waved a hand. "Yeah, but you won't want to hear all about my corporate crap."

Again, Gina arched an eyebrow at her as her face hardened a bit. "Yeah, don't do that. Don't talk down to me, okay?"

Piper looked down at her plate, shame tinting her cheeks with pink. "You're right. I'm sorry."

From that point on, things shifted to work talk. For a woman who had never been in the corporate world, Gina was surprisingly wise about all things regarding office politics, and in the past, she'd given Piper excellent advice. Piper would do well to remember that. For the next half hour, they went back and forth between discussing Piper's office merger and some of the annoying faculty at the community college where Gina taught. Throughout the conversation, Piper felt herself relax at least a little bit.

When they'd paid the bill and stood to leave, Gina grasped Piper's arm. "Hey," she said, and her expression was gentle and loving. "If you ever need to talk about Dad—I mean, aside from Vineyard—I'm here. You know that, right?"

Piper nodded, forced a smile. Gina always wanted to talk about him. Piper almost never did. She knew that bothered both Gina and their mother, but she couldn't seem to change it.

❖

Patrice Dymond blew the roof off Vineyard. Lindsay couldn't have been happier with her talent or with the turnout. It was Friday night, the tables were all full, and Lindsay stood behind the bar with a huge smile on her face. Mrs. B. would be so proud of her right now.

Zack and Kevin were both waiting tables. Lindsay was currently taking a breather from arranging cheese boards but knew she'd be back at it any moment, given the two new parties that had just sat.

"I don't remember ever seeing this place so busy," Angela said to her from her seat at the bar. She'd come by after work and surprised Lindsay, saying she couldn't stay long. Ms. Dymond had changed her mind. She sat on the barstool, still in her work attire, her legs crossed, one foot swinging to the beat. "She's amazing." She used the hand holding her wine glass to point toward the band.

"Right? I'm going to see if I can book her next weekend, too." Lindsay hesitated. "Do you think I should do that?"

Angela furrowed her brow and squinted her dark brown eyes at Lindsay. "Do what?"

"Book the same singer two weekends in a row."

"Oh, like, will customers get bored of her? That kind of thing?"

"Exactly."

Angela shook her head. "I don't think so. I mean, look at this place." She indicated the crowd, Lindsay's bustling waiters. Angela's positive attitude helped and Lindsay decided not to second-guess herself.

Her tablet beeped and she saw Zack's order for a cheese board, so she excused herself from Angela and went in the back to put it together.

The first time Mrs. B. had taught Lindsay the ins and outs of arranging the cheese boards, Lindsay had focused like crazy, cutting the cheese wedges precisely, scooping olives and honey into the small serving dishes just so, making sure the baguettes were sliced evenly and the presentation was perfect. Now it was old hat for her and she was able to let her mind drift while she cut.

She was disappointed Piper hadn't come by. Lindsay didn't want to admit that but finally realized she had to. She hadn't seen or heard from Piper since yesterday morning, when they'd had that rain-drenched kiss that had kept Lindsay's insides aflame all day long. No texts. No calls. No surprise appearances at Vineyard.

It could mean a lot of things. It could mean Piper was simply busy. With work. With life. She was a busy woman.

Lindsay sliced a wedge of brie, set it at an angle on the slate tray.

It could mean that she was freaking out. Lindsay had taken her by surprise. With her appearance. With the kiss. That much was obvious to anybody who had two eyes and half a brain. *But*—and this was important, as far as Lindsay was concerned—also obvious to anybody with two eyes and half a brain was how open Piper was to that kiss. Lindsay had pretty much ambushed her. It was risky, but turnabout is fair play. Piper might have pushed her away. Piper might have punched her in the throat. Lindsay had prepared herself for those possibilities, and Piper had done neither. Piper had kissed her back. In a big way. After the kiss in Lindsay's office, after the way Piper seemed to be a little discombobulated by it, Lindsay was taking a risk Thursday morning, and she knew it. But she had honestly never felt such immediate chemistry with somebody before. Was it because of the friction between them? Or was the friction because of the chemistry?

Lindsay shook her head as she arranged the baguette on the tray. She wasn't sure. All she did know was that kissing Piper Bradshaw was something else. Something unlike anything she'd ever experienced. Yeah, she wanted more of *that*.

This train of thought taking her nowhere but careening toward *I'll need to excuse myself to the bathroom* land, Lindsay did her best to shake her mind free of all things Piper. At least for now. Cheese board in hand, she headed back out to the bar and delivered it to Zack.

Angela's wine glass was nearly empty and Lindsay raised her eyebrows. Angela waved her off. "No, but thank you. I've got to scoot." Still, she sat, her foot moving to the beat Patrice Dymond's keyboardist had set. When the number was over, she applauded with the rest of the crowd, then turned to look Lindsay in the eye. "So? What are you going to do?"

Lindsay had filled Angela in on everything, every last bit of what had transpired between her and Piper. She'd listened quietly while Lindsay spoke, concluding with the ridiculously low re-estimate for the patio update. When she finished, Angela had only one comment. "That girl is so into you, it's making her a little crazy."

Now Lindsay shook her head as she came around the bar. "I haven't decided yet."

Angela slid off her stool, gathered her purse. "Keep me posted. This is like a soap opera, and I need to know where it goes."

Lindsay pushed at her playfully before wrapping her in a hug. "Thanks for coming. Thanks for everything."

"I'm serious," Angela said in her ear. "You keep me in the loop. And call me any time you need to. I'm here even when I'm not."

Lindsay tightened her hold before letting Angela go, then followed her with her gaze as she turned at the door and gave Lindsay a little wave.

The truth was, she had no idea what she was going to do, and that made her a little nuts.

CHAPTER FOURTEEN

W hy don't you just ask her on a date?" Matthew was completely serious as he swigged his beer from his comfy spot on his chocolate brown leather couch. He plopped his feet up on the coffee table and crossed them at the ankle.

Piper slapped at his loafers as she went by. "What, were you brought up in a barn?"

"You sound like my grandma when you say that."

"Hey, I bought you that table and it wasn't cheap, thank you very much."

Matthew removed his feet and looked like it was a struggle for him not to roll his eyes. "Man, you're cranky."

Piper dropped into the chair across from him and swigged her own beer. "I know," she said with a sigh. "I'm sorry."

"I'm telling you, ask her out. You obviously want to."

Piper wanted to argue. She wanted to snap at Matthew, tell him to shut the hell up because he didn't know what he was talking about. Instead, she gazed out the sliding glass door where Shane stood at the grill.

He turned to her and grinned through the screen, gave a small shrug. "He's right, you know."

"I hate both of you right now."

It was Sunday afternoon and the sky was filled with clouds that looked like they were made of steel wool. Rain had come and gone and come back, and Shane had an umbrella within reach, just in case. Piper loved having dinner with these two. Their home was gorgeous, but not ostentatious. The decorating was flawless, of course, the muted, earthy colors blending seamlessly from dining room to living room, set off by gleaming dark oak hardwoods. (Why did gay men seem to automatically get that amazing interior decorating gene? So unfair.) She always felt welcome here. She felt safe with them, insulated from her everyday life.

Except for now. Now she felt cornered.

"Seriously, Pipes, what's the worst that could happen?" Matthew sat forward on the couch so his backside was perched on the edge, and he propped his elbows on his knees. "You've both already attacked each other, for God's sake. Going on an actual date seems like the next logical step. You could actually get to know each other. I know, crazy, right? I mean, what have you got to lose?"

Shane saved her from answering by moving to the screen door, his hands filled with two plates of food—one with burgers and one with grilled veggies. "Help?" he said through the screen.

Once they settled around the table, passed around dishes and filled their plates, and started eating, Matthew circled back around. This time, though, he was gentler. "Lately, you've seemed...unsettled. Like you need to move forward, but aren't sure where to step. You know?"

Piper nodded because he was right. That was exactly how she'd been feeling.

"It's very rare." He gave her a pointed look.

Piper furrowed her brow. "What's rare?"

Matthew looked to Shane, seemingly for help, but Shane only shrugged and said, "I'm right there with you, but this is all you, babe."

Matthew set down his fork, folded his hands together, and set them on the table.

"Uh-oh," Piper said with a nervous chuckle. "We're getting serious here with the folded hands."

"When friends ask me to describe you, I tell them you're steady."

"Gee, thanks."

"Shut up and let me finish. Steady, intelligent, levelheaded, even-keeled, people feel safe with you, like they don't have to worry because you've got it all under control."

Piper shot him a smile. "Better."

Matthew held up a finger that said *not so fast*. "Lately, though, you've been different."

"Different how?" She looked at Shane, who took an enormous bite of his burger and made no comment.

"You've seemed...frazzled. Emotional. Quick to anger. A little snappy."

"A little snappy?"

"Not in a good way."

Piper grimaced. She wanted to leap to her own defense. But she couldn't. Because again, he was right. Instead, she blew out a breath and sat back against her chair like she'd been deflated. "I know. You're right. You're totally right. It's because of my mom leaving and work being crazy and…"

"And because you're super attracted to somebody you didn't expect to be attracted to, and you don't know what to do with that."

The table fell silent, save for the sound of utensils on plates and people chewing. Matthew held Piper's gaze like his was a tractor beam, wouldn't let it go, daring her to argue with him.

Long moments went by before Piper gave up. Pulling herself from the strength of Matthew's gaze, she turned to look out the window. "I don't know what to do with that," she agreed, very softly.

Matthew leaned forward, his face open and loving. "Ask her out. Go to a movie. Take her to dinner. Make a move, my friend. You've got 'em."

"You think?"

"Hell, yes." Matthew stabbed a mushroom with his fork.

"I don't know. She makes me kind of crazy."

Shane scoffed. "Yeah, that's what our brains make us do. She drives me a little nuts, so now I like her. Congratulations, you're a perfectly normal human being."

Piper closed her eyes and shook her head. Was it really that simple? Could it be? *She makes me crazy, so now I want to sleep with her all the time?* Seemed awfully basic and not a little bit silly. "I don't know."

"Okay, answer me this." Matthew had picked up his fork and was eating again. His voice almost too nonchalant, he said, "Why did you revamp the numbers for the patio cost?" He stabbed a piece of grilled zucchini, popped it into his mouth, and raised his eyebrows expectantly as he chewed.

Piper poked at the inside of her cheek with her tongue. "I wanted to show who was in charge," she ground out.

"Mm-hmm. Why?"

"Because I didn't want her to think she'd get special treatment."

"Mm-hmm. Why would she get special treatment?"

Piper groaned.

"Just say it." Matthew cocked his head as Shane looked back and forth between them like a spectator at a Ping-Pong match.

"Because I'm attracted to her."

Matthew sat back in his chair, looking far too self-satisfied. "Finally. Was that so hard?"

"I want to slap you right now."

"I know." Matthew drained his beer. "But only because I've been right all along. Now, do us all a favor and take the poor girl out on a proper date. Please, so we can stop watching this train wreck you're creating." He got up to retrieve another beer, but called from the kitchen, "And let her do what she wants with the damn patio."

Piper snorted a laugh. "I'm sorry, have you met me?"

Shane coughed, camouflaging the words "control freak" within it.

Piper pointed at him. "Exactly. At least I can admit it."

Matthew returned to the dining room with three fresh beers, kissed Piper on the top of her head, and handed the bottles around. "It's a good thing we love you, you emotionally stunted specimen of a woman."

"Where will you take her?" Shane asked.

"Ooh, good question," Matthew commented. "Let's think about that."

Piper held up a hand. "No way. No. We're not doing that."

"Aww." Matthew pouted.

"Oh, my God," Piper said as she pointed at him. "That's exactly the face you made when we were kids whenever you didn't get your way."

After that, the conversation lightened up in a big way, but Lindsay still seemed to be hanging out in the back of Piper's mind. Taking up space, smiling at her, keeping Piper feeling off balance somehow. It had been so long since she'd been so affected by a woman. Since Kat. And even then, it hadn't been like this. It had been logical to ask Kat out. Practical. There was nothing logical about this. Practicality had no place. Kat and Piper had been so much alike. Friends joked that they were almost the same person. But Lindsay? No. Lindsay was *so* different from Piper. Well, what she knew of her.

Maybe Matthew was right.

Not that she'd ever tell him that.

Maybe it was time to take the bull by the horns here and really get to know her.

❖

Vineyard wasn't busy. Piper counted six customers when she walked in just before nine that Sunday night. A table of two, a table of three, and a single gentleman sitting at the bar. Lindsay was waiting on him—it looked like she was the only staff member working—and though her expression was pleasant enough, Piper got the distinct feeling she was not happy with this man.

And when Lindsay glanced up at her...Piper felt suddenly warm, deep down inside. Lindsay's face shifted. Not a lot, but enough for Piper to see it. Her expression relaxed and a small smile lifted the corners of her mouth, and it was obvious, at least to Piper, that Lindsay was glad to see her. She waved her toward the bar. Piper obeyed.

"I'd like to try the petite Syrah," the man was saying as Piper took one of the empty stools. He slid his glass toward Lindsay.

"Of course," she said and turned to pull the bottle from the rack on the wall.

Piper took the time to study Lindsay from the back. She wore those same light-colored jeans with the small fray at the corner of one back pocket and Piper had the inexplicable urge to grasp the threads there and tug on them, see what would be revealed. Her top was black, the sleeves rolled up to her elbows, and when she turned back around, Piper saw the buttons at the top were open to reveal an enticing collarbone and skin that begged for fingertips.

Piper shook her head. Literally.

The man sipped from what Piper now saw was just a sample taste, and she realized that Lindsay'd had to open a new bottle just so he could taste a wine that he—judging from the grimace he made—didn't care for. He glanced back down at the menu in front of him. "Let me try the Beaujolais." He finished all the Syrah first, which Piper raised an eyebrow at.

Lindsay glanced at her and gave a quick eye roll that the man didn't see but Piper did. Piper bit down on her bottom lip to keep from laughing.

Two more samples were downed (completely) by the man before he settled on a Chianti. He paid, took his glass, and moved to a table where he sat and pulled out a paperback.

Piper finally had all of Lindsay's attention. She looked at her and grinned, then felt silly and schoolgirlish.

"Hi, you," Lindsay said. "I didn't expect to see you tonight."

"I had dinner over at Matthew and Shane's and had to drive by on my way home, so..." Piper let the sentence dangle, not wanting to offer up any more information at the risk of giving herself away. Lowering her voice to barely a whisper, she added, "Wow, you were so patient with that guy."

"That's Mr. Can I Taste That."

"Fitting name."

"Bridget named him that. Right after she told me she refused to wait on him anymore."

Piper chuckled. "I'm with Bridget."

"I don't blame her. Or you. He's a pain, but I suspect he also has lots of money and possibly some influence. So I'm always careful to take good care of him, no matter how ridiculous he gets. I don't ever want him to be able to trash Vineyard, you know?"

Piper nodded, suddenly realizing something about the way she viewed Lindsay. It was almost as if Lindsay was walking around with a life-size cardboard cutout in front of her that depicted what Piper initially thought of her. Hippy-like. Irresponsible. Flighty. And each time Lindsay squashed one of those descriptors, a piece of the cutout fell away. Pretty soon, it would all be gone and what would be left standing in front of her would be the real Lindsay.

Piper was stunned to understand that she looked forward to that day.

"Oh!" Lindsay held up a finger. "I want you to try something."

"Okay…" Piper drew out the word, a smile in her voice. "Should I be worried?"

Lindsay arched an eyebrow at her. "Maybe," she said in a teasing tone as she turned back to the bottles. Piper watched her hands as she took two glasses down, pulled two bottles of white wine from the small wine cooler, and poured a couple swallows into each glass. Then she turned to face Piper, a glass in each hand. She set one down. "Angelina Jolie." She set down the other one. "Jennifer Aniston."

Piper cocked her head in curiosity.

Lindsay glanced over Piper's shoulder. "Taste them and think about it. I'll be right back."

Piper watched her go, then turned back to the wines. Angelina was on the left. Jennifer on the right. "Hmm." She picked up Angelina. Sipped. It had an immediate sharpness to it on the front, a bite of sorts. Notes of pine, citrus, a little floral. Then it smoothed out with a long finish that lasted. She sat with that for a moment before picking up the other glass and giving Jennifer a try. No bite, just a mellowness that coated her mouth. Notes of pear and vanilla were prominent, a completely different flavor combination from Angelina, but that lingered on the finish in a similar way.

Lindsay returned behind the bar only long enough to grab her little tablet, which told Piper the party was checking out. Lindsay gave her a wink, but said nothing, and Piper's insides went all mushy anyway.

I've become officially ridiculous.

She sipped each wine again, paid even closer attention to the flavors, and then the lightbulb went off. By the time Lindsay held the door for the departing customers and returned to the bar, Piper was grinning from ear to ear.

Lindsay returned the grin, tenfold, as she gestured to the now empty glasses. "Tell me."

Piper made a show of clearing her throat and sitting up straight on her stool. Indicating the glass on her left, she said, "This wine, while clean and crisp, starts off very strong, like a bit of a slap to your taste buds. It gets itself noticed. Once you're on board, it evens out and takes you on a lengthy ride, with you for a long time. Angelina Jolie." She gestured to the other wine. "This wine is subtler in its approach, it gently taps your shoulder to let you know it's there and when you actually focus on it, you're captured by its beauty. It stays gentle, but noticeable, and it sticks around. It has staying power. Jennifer Aniston." Piper inclined her head in a small bow. "Ta-da!"

"Yes!" Lindsay clapped her hands together once and beamed with happiness. "You nailed it exactly."

"So, tell me what *it* is."

"It's an additional way we want to describe the wines. We'll keep all the regular descriptors on there, but Bridget is great at this, so I'm going to have her assign celebrities to each wine to give customers a fun way to understand what they're getting."

"Thereby staying traditional *and* being more modern. At the same time."

"Exactly." Lindsay pointed at her. "I knew you'd get it."

And then they had what Piper could only describe as "a moment." Their gazes held. Lindsay's green eyes sparked with excitement, with a love for her job, but also with something else. There was a connection here, between them. A connection Piper suspected neither of them saw coming. She certainly didn't. But it was there. In that second, there was no place else in the world Piper would've rather been. She just wanted to sit there and stare into those eyes and feel no pressure, no worry, just…comfort. Just contentedness. Just desire.

"Have dinner with me." The words pushed from her lips without her permission, as if her heart had overridden the rest of her.

Lindsay's light eyebrows rose in surprise, though Piper noticed, not shock. Just gentle surprise. She gave one nod. "I'd like that. A lot."

"Good."

Their eyes were still locked as Lindsay hunkered down, put her elbows on the bar and propped her chin in her hands. "When? Where? What time?"

"So many questions," Piper teased. She didn't actually have answers, as she hadn't exactly planned it up front, despite what Matthew and Shane had told her. "How about Tuesday? Have somebody close for you. I'll pick you up at seven. Should I get you from here?"

"I think that sounds perfect." Lindsay didn't move. Piper absently wondered how long they could sit there making eye contact with one another before one of them gave in. "Where are you taking me?"

"It's a surprise," Piper told her, but didn't add that it would be a surprise to her as well since she had no idea.

"I do like surprises."

They were flirting now. Not that they hadn't been, but Piper had never been good at picking up on such things. Therefore, she knew, if it was blatantly obvious to her, there was definite flirting going on. "I'll make a note," she said, and then something told her it was the perfect time to make her exit. She slid off the stool. "Thanks for the samples."

"You can have a sample any time you want."

Oh, yeah. Absolutely flirting.

"I'll see you Tuesday."

Lindsay gave her an adorable little wave, and Piper made her way to the door and out. Once she was at her car, she stood completely still for a second. Two seconds.

And then she broke into a quick little dance, shuffling her feet and fisting her hands.

She'd done it. She'd asked Lindsay out.

She had a date.

Matthew wasn't going to believe it.

CHAPTER FIFTEEN

*S**he's nervous.*

That thought came into Lindsay's head the moment she settled into the passenger seat of Piper's SUV and turned to look at her. Piper's smile seemed a tad forced and her knuckles were white on the steering wheel.

"Oh, good," Lindsay said, with a chuckle. "You're nervous, too. That'll make it easier."

"You're nervous?"

"God, yes."

Piper gave a nod, seemed to file that away. "Well, still. It's good to see you." This smile was genuine, wider and open. "Hi."

Lindsay felt her entire body relax. "Hi yourself."

"Ready?" Piper shifted the car into gear and pulled out of the Vineyard parking lot.

"Where are you taking me?" Lindsay took in Piper's outfit. She was very casual for Piper, sporting denim capris and an emerald green tank top that left an enticing expanse of skin bare.

"Someplace a little different."

"Excellent. I'm in."

Piper glanced at her with a grin, her sunglasses disguising her eyes, but making her look no less sexy. "Because you weren't if I was taking you someplace not different?"

"You don't know. I might have jumped out, right here, while we're moving."

"Yeah, don't do that."

Lindsay returned the grin, then looked out the window as they drove alongside Black Cherry Lake. Everything was in its full summer bloom. The trees were green and lush, the lake water blue and serene. It had been a gorgeously warm day full of sunshine and puffy clouds, and the evening was turning out to be perfect. Warm, but not too warm, the sun taking its sweet time moving toward the horizon. "I love it here," she said on a little sigh.

"Me, too." Piper turned onto an unmarked road that Lindsay wasn't sure she'd ever noticed before, and it went from asphalt to dirt fairly quickly.

As the SUV bounced over a hole, Lindsay let out a nervous chuckle. "Are you taking me into the woods to kill me? Because the theme from *Deliverance* is running through my head right now."

Piper glanced at her, her expression completely stone-like, and for a split second, Lindsay felt a small surge of worry. Then Piper's face split into a grin. "Not today," she said with a wink.

The road seemed to smooth out a bit, and in another minute or two, Piper pulled the SUV to a stop. There was a small cabin in front of them. No, cabin was actually too ornate a word. A shack was closer to accurate. Piper turned off the engine, opened her door, and slid to the ground.

Lindsay followed suit, slammed her door closed, and looked at the shack. The water wasn't far—maybe twenty-five yards away. She turned to see Piper rifling through the back seat of the SUV and went to her. "Can I help?"

Piper gave her a cooler bag with a chilled bottle of Rosé in it, then handed her a folded blanket. She pulled out a large wicker basket, slammed the door shut, and turned to Lindsay. "Ready?"

Lindsay knew her smile was wide. "Did you put together a picnic for us?"

Piper gave a shrug of nonchalance. "I might have..." And then she was off on a small path that Lindsay hadn't seen right away, heading toward the water. Lindsay skipped to catch up with her.

When they reached the water's edge, Lindsay's eyes widened in surprise. Not only was there a very nice dock that reached out many yards into the lake, but there was a large expanse of wooden deck attached to it on the shore, complete with tiki torches and four sturdy Adirondack chairs, each in a different primary color. The water lapped gently at the edges of the wood, the sound peaceful and inviting.

"What is this place?" Lindsay had the inexplicable urge to whisper, as if making any sound would break the spell that seemed to be cast.

Piper stepped up onto the deck. "My parents own this land. It's my dad's fishing spot. He came here all the time. That shack has all of his tackle and gear. It really needs to be cleaned out, but…" She gave a small frown. "I haven't been able to bring myself to do that yet."

"This is beautiful," Lindsay said as she walked to the edge of the deck and looked into the crystal clear water, followed the tiny minnows as they flitted around just below the surface.

"Thanks."

"You come here a lot?"

Piper spread the blanket out on the deck, set the basket on it. "I used to. I came here as a kid with my dad, but I never really caught the fishing bug. My sister Gina was more into that. But I started to come by myself in high school, once I had my driver's license. I'd bring a book and just sit here and stare at the water." She did that now, standing there looking beautiful, facing the water. Several sails dotted the water. A distant buzz could be heard and a small motorboat sped by in the center of the lake. "I stopped coming after my dad died."

Lindsay stepped toward her and set the wine bottle down on the blanket. "And then started again?"

Piper looked at her then, and something unreadable passed over her eyes. "Yes. Today."

Lindsay cocked her head and stared for a beat. "Today? You mean, you haven't been here since your father died?" She said it quietly, gently, completely understanding the importance of what she'd just learned, and trying not to let her surprise show.

Piper shrugged and gave a nod. "Right."

Lindsay watched as Piper busied herself with the picnic. She opened the basket and began removing small Tupperware containers. She handed two plastic wine glasses to Lindsay, and then a corkscrew, and Lindsay took her cue and opened the wine. They worked wordlessly, as if they'd been a team for years, and within about ten minutes, there was an amazing spread laid out on the blanket. Piper looked up at Lindsay with those unique hazel eyes, and this time, Lindsay could see everything. They were filled with hesitation and uncertainty and excitement and just a touch of sadness, and Lindsay was lost.

"Hungry?" Piper asked quietly.

All Lindsay could do was nod.

Piper waved a hand at the empty space next to her and Lindsay sat, handed one glass to Piper. She held up her own in a toast. "To your dad," she said and knew by Piper's soft smile that she'd chosen correctly. They touched glasses, sipped.

"Wow," Lindsay said, looking at the food and hoping to break the spell of melancholy that had fallen over them. "This is amazing." There was cheese, crackers, stuffed grape leaves, three different varieties of olives, sliced baguette, bruschetta. She dug in, popping an olive into her mouth while she decided what to eat first. "How are things at work?"

Piper gave another shrug—which Lindsay was beginning to understand was Piper's nonchalant mannerism, for when she wanted to portray that a topic was no big deal—as she arranged four crackers on her paper plate, then put a square of cheese on each one. "Stressful. Worrisome. Frustrating."

Lindsay chuckled. "Okay. Next subject."

Piper laughed, popped a cracker into her mouth. "When was your last relationship?"

"Oh, perfect. A much more comfortable topic." Lindsay gave a good-natured roll of her eyes, then looked toward the sky. "Let's see…" It was a personal question and she could have joked it away, changed the subject. But there was something about Piper Bradshaw, something about the trust she'd shown in Lindsay simply by bringing her here, by sharing this place that obviously meant so much to her, and she just couldn't lie. She couldn't be anything but honest with Piper. "Three years ago? Three and a half, maybe?"

"What happened?" Piper was gazing out at the water, but she turned quickly to face Lindsay. "I mean, if it's okay to ask."

"It's totally okay." And she meant it. Lindsay had no idea when this shift had taken place, but somewhere over the last week, she'd gone from feeling uncertain and irritated around Piper to completely comfortable. And more than a little bit turned on, which seemed to now be a regular aspect of being around Piper. And today, given Piper's arms and that tank top, arousal was in full force—even though she'd promised herself she'd let Piper make the next move. If there was to be one. "I guess it depends on who you ask, but I've had lots of time to think about it, to go over things in my head."

"And the conclusion you've come to is?"

"I was emotionally unavailable, which is a phrase I hate and think is way overused, but in the case of me and Crystal, it fits." Lindsay sipped her wine, recalling several of the loud arguments they'd had, she and Crystal. Well, loud on Crystal's part. "When we fought, it was mostly Crystal yelling at me, listing all the things I was doing wrong or wasn't doing at all and I would just sit there and take it. Pretend to listen. Nod and agree."

"Well, that sounds like a perfectly lovely partnership."

A laugh burst out of Lindsay. "Doesn't it, though? For many months after we split, I blamed her for being too demanding, for being too critical. It took me a while to understand that I just wasn't invested. In her. In our relationship. In life. All her yelling was simply born of frustration because she felt she wasn't being heard, and she was right. I wasn't listening. To anybody. I was really floundering." She looked at Piper then, and went completely, utterly serious. "Your mom and dad saved me."

Piper's brow furrowed. "From what?"

"From myself." Lindsay looked into her glass of Rosé and gathered her thoughts. "It sounds dramatic and I don't mean it to be. I just…I was floundering. There's no better way to describe it. I didn't know what I wanted to do with my life. I was working three jobs, none of which I enjoyed even a little bit. I felt useless and small and unimportant and like I didn't know who I was or who I wanted to be. And when Crystal left, it all was amplified."

When she lifted her eyes to Piper's face, she seemed riveted, every bit of her attention focused on Lindsay. It made Lindsay's heart pound a little bit harder.

"I drank too much for a while. I got fired from one of my jobs. My best friends seemed to disappear, though I think they just got sick of my bullshit." She chuckled, but there was an edge of self-deprecation to it, as there always was when she was dealing with this subject. "And one day, I wandered into Vineyard, hoping to find a bartending job. I didn't realize it was a wine bar. I was looking for a regular bar, and my first thought was that I was totally out of place, that Vineyard was way too snooty and uppity for me. But your dad was there, doing a tasting with a distributor, and your mom was behind the bar and…" Lindsay shook her head as she recalled the moment. "There was something in your mom's eyes, something about the way she looked at me. I have no idea how, but I knew in that second that everything was going to be okay, that these people were safe, that I was meant to walk through *that* door at *that* moment. I was certain of it. I still am."

Piper inhaled slowly, let it out the same way before speaking. "Wow," she finally said, her voice very quiet. "I had no idea. I mean, I knew my parents were fond of you, but I didn't know any details." She sipped her wine, seemed to sift through words in her head. "I guess I wasn't around that much, though, if I'm being honest. Not after my dad died. So I wouldn't have known anyway."

"He was a really great guy. I liked him a lot." Lindsay looked up at the sky. "I wish I'd had more time with him."

"Me, too."

"Is it weird for you to be here? I mean…" Lindsay let her voice trail off, worried she'd maybe stepped on Piper's feelings, so when Piper turned to her with a small smile, she returned it.

"Not at all. Which kind of surprises me. It feels…right to be here."

Lindsay's smile was wide; she could feel it split across her face. "Good." It was when she shifted her gaze back to the water that she realized yet another gorgeous aspect of this spot Piper had brought them. "Oh, my God, we're going to see the sunset, aren't we?"

Piper's face was radiant just then. The deep dimples on either side of her face burst into view. "Did I forget to mention that?"

"You know, Piper," Lindsay said, her voice suddenly low and husky, "this might be the most romantic dinner I've ever had. With anyone. Ever."

"Yeah?"

"Yeah."

"Good." Piper leaned toward her, pressed their lips together in a gentle kiss, tentative and soft. They parted slowly but stayed with their faces close together, and Lindsay gazed at Piper.

"God, I love your eyes."

The corner of Piper's mouth tugged up. "Thanks," she whispered, then moved in for another kiss.

This one was also tentative and soft, just a gentle melding of lips. Piper slid her hand along the side of Lindsay's face, tugged her head a bit closer, deepened the kiss just a tad. Lindsay wasn't a woman who needed to be led in any aspect of making out, but she found herself perfectly content to let Piper choreograph this dance. Piper's mouth was warm, and the taste of wine clung to her tongue. The softness of her lips astounded Lindsay, though she wasn't sure why. She'd kissed her share of women. But something about Piper…was it her taste? Her method? The slow drawing out of this connection? Whatever it was, Lindsay was crazy about it. She could sit on that blanket near the water and make out with Piper until the end of time. She was positive.

Lindsay had no idea how long they'd been kissing before Piper pulled away and whispered, "We're going to miss the sunset."

Lindsay blinked several times and fought to reorient herself with reality. "Oh. Um, okay."

Piper grinned and brushed some hair off Lindsay's forehead. "You okay?"

"Mm-hmm." Lindsay swallowed, forced her eyes to focus. "I just..." After a clearing of her throat, she looked at Piper and said quietly, "You're a really, really good kisser."

Piper's face was tinted a soft orange by the setting sun, but Lindsay was almost certain she could see subtle bursts of pink forming on her cheeks. "You're not so bad yourself." And as if by unspoken agreement, they scooted a little closer together, moving some of the dishes out of the way. Piper refilled their glasses with the remaining wine, and they sat in silence, their bodies touching, content in each other's company, and watched the beauty of nature as she put on a show for them.

It felt perfectly right to sit there in the quiet with Piper, and Lindsay wasn't quite sure what to do with that. It was natural for her to keep her guard up, at least a little bit, especially when the physical pull was so strong for her. She had a tendency to let that arousal blind her to other things. But this? This felt completely different, completely unfamiliar, completely perfect. She knew she could drive herself crazy if she sat here and analyzed it. *Please, that's exactly what I'll be doing tomorrow.* So instead, she forced herself to shelve her worries, to box up all her concerns and put them away, at least for now, at least for this moment. Her head against Piper's shoulder, she watched the gorgeous ball of orange/red disappear behind the trees.

They stayed like that for a long while after the sun had gone down, propped together, listening to the cicadas and the occasional burp-like sound from a random frog.

"Look," Lindsay said quietly, pointing. "Lightning bug."

"We always called them fireflies." Piper followed Lindsay's finger, then pointed to another. "There's one."

"I remember when I was a kid, I thought they were the coolest thing. And I'd catch them and put them in a jar in my room so I could watch them as I fell asleep." Lindsay sighed. "I could never understand why they were all dead in the morning."

Piper's chuckle made no sound, but Lindsay felt her shoulder move. "Aww, poor little Lindsay, unknowingly destroying the lightning bug population, three or four at a time."

Lindsay pushed against her and let out a mock gasp. "Shut up." But she was laughing.

Piper slapped at her own arm, the sound exorbitantly loud in the quiet of the woods. "And that's my cue," she said. At Lindsay's raised eyebrows, she explained. "Mosquitoes. They love me. Apparently, I'm delicious." She started packing up the picnic.

Lindsay followed suit. "The mosquitoes obviously have great taste."

The smile Piper shot her then pretty much made her night.

Well. Almost.

❖

Half an hour later, Piper glided her SUV to a stop in front of Lindsay's house and put the gearshift into Park. They sat for a moment in the dark, the engine idling quietly. Lindsay was nervous. She didn't understand why; she simply recognized the thumping of her heart and the thrumming of her body, the slight tremble in her hands. She knew what she wanted. It wasn't unusual for her to ask for it, to be bold, to set the pace. But Piper threw her off for some weird reason, made her feel unsteady. A beat went by before Lindsay cleared her throat, deciding to bite the bullet. "Want to come in? I'm sure Rocket would love to see you."

Piper's half-grin was knowing. "Sure. I'd like to see Rocket, too." She emphasized his name, making Lindsay wonder if she knew exactly what was going on in her head.

As they exited the SUV and headed up the driveway, Lindsay did a quick scan in her brain of exactly how messy her house might be. Too late now, she thought as she slid her key into the lock and opened the side door.

They were met with eighty-five pounds of excited, wiggling, woofing yellow Lab. Rocket bypassed Lindsay immediately and went right to Piper, who got down on the floor with him. Barely a minute passed before he was lying in her lap, his head lolled over her thigh, her hand scratching his belly.

"Oh, for God's sake, Rocket," Lindsay playfully scolded. "Don't be so easy. At least play a *little* hard to get. Have some self-respect."

"The boy obviously knows what he wants," Piper said, and when she looked up and met Lindsay's eyes with her own, her meaning was clear. *So do you. So do I.*

Lindsay swallowed hard. "Come on, Rocket. Outside."

Rocket jumped up and trotted to the back door, Lindsay right behind him. She turned on the back light, let him out, and rested her forehead against the cool glass of the door's window for a moment. She felt like her blood was on fire, and she inhaled quietly through her nose, doing her best to steady herself.

In the living room, Piper was looking at the handful of framed photos on the bookshelf in the corner. She held one up, eyebrows raised.

"That's Angela. One of my best friends. She actually came to Vineyard on Friday night."

With a nod, Piper set it back down, then picked up a baby picture of Rocket. "Oh, my God." She pressed a hand to her chest. "Look at him."

"He was ridiculous," Lindsay said, her chuckle filled with pride. "His head was so big, it was like it was on the wrong body." She poked at the thermostat, kicking up the a/c to cool the room.

"And those feet," Piper said, pointing.

"Huge head, huge feet. I was worried about what I was getting."

As if on cue, a bark sounded from the back. Before Lindsay could turn to go get him, Piper grasped her arm and kissed her. Just a quick, soft kiss. More than a peck. Then she smiled at Lindsay and reached to set the photo back where she'd found it.

"Something to drink?" Lindsay asked after she'd let Rocket in. "I have wine, coffee, Diet Pepsi, water, vodka, gin, rum..." She grinned at the last three.

"Wine would be great." Piper took a seat on Lindsay's worn couch and Rocket jumped up to join her. "Well, hello there, handsome," she said to him, and Lindsay's smile grew.

In the kitchen, Lindsay leaned her hands on the counter, braced herself there, and reminded her lungs to take in air. Slowly. Steadily. In. Out.

It's simple, right, this breathing thing? Supposed to be automatic, isn't it?

When she felt a touch calmer (though not much), she opened a bottle of the Malbec she'd been saving for the next time she went to dinner at Maya and Bert's, poured two glasses, and went back out to the living room...where her dog was making a move on the woman she'd brought home.

Rocket lay on his back, sprawled out completely, half-on, half-off Piper's lap, his tongue lolling in delight, his eyes gazing at this new person he'd discovered, so full of worship that Lindsay had to laugh.

"Really?" she said, her eyes on the dog. "Seriously with this?"

Rocket could barely be bothered to spare a glance in her direction.

Lindsay reached over him and handed a glass to Piper, who did spare her a glance. A very heated one, if Lindsay was reading it correctly. Which she was unsure of, because she was a little bit rusty at this. But Piper's eyes were dark and heavy and her gaze lingered on Lindsay's mouth as she thanked her quietly for the wine.

Still standing, Lindsay touched her glass to Piper's. "Cheers."

They sipped, holding that delicious eye contact, and a zap of arousal shot right down to Lindsay's center.

Yeah, this was going to happen. Tonight. She knew it; she could feel it.

With a tap to Rocket's back paw, she said, "Off."

He was up immediately and off the couch. Piper looked impressed. Lindsay shrugged and sat next to her.

"So," she said, painfully aware of their thighs pressed together.

"So," Piper said back.

Lindsay swallowed. "Is this too close?" She indicated their proximity with her eyes.

"Not close enough," was Piper's whispered reply.

Somehow, the wine glasses made it to the coffee table. Later, Lindsay would wonder how, as she'd have zero recollection of that. The next thing she knew, Piper was straddling her lap, their mouths fused together hotly. There was nothing soft or gentle or tentative about this kiss. This kiss was fire. It was flame. Blistering. Any other word that meant heat, it fit this kiss, and soon Lindsay could barely recall her own name. She couldn't recall anything because nothing else existed. Nothing in the world mattered except for this woman whose ass was cradled in Lindsay's palms, whose tongue was doing incredibly erotic things in Lindsay's mouth, whose fingers were dug deeply into Lindsay's hair, and she wondered how she'd managed to go this long in life without kissing Piper Bradshaw. Because she was obviously meant to. This was obviously her sole purpose in life: to kiss this woman senseless, to be kissed senseless by this woman.

Vaguely aware of fingers working the buttons of her shirt, Lindsay suddenly felt the coolness of the a/c from a nearby vent on her bare torso. Her shirt was completely open and before she could register anything beyond that, Piper used both hands to cup her breasts through her bra, kneading them firmly as she pressed her tongue more firmly into Lindsay's mouth.

A loud moan hummed through the room. It took a second or two for Lindsay to realize it came from her own throat, and she tightened her grip on Piper's ass, digging her fingers in, then sliding them up her back, beneath her tank top.

Snap decision made, Lindsay grasped the hem of the shirt and pulled it up, giving Piper no choice but to lift her arms to accommodate the movement. Lindsay tossed the fabric to the floor.

Piper Bradshaw sat in her lap, wearing denim capris, a white lace bra, and the sexiest expression Lindsay had ever seen on any face, anywhere, ever, in her entire life.

"Oh, my God," she whispered. "You are so fucking beautiful." There was a reverence in her voice and she knew it. She couldn't help it because it was true: Piper was the most beautiful thing she'd ever seen right then, in that moment.

Piper responded by grabbing her face with both hands and kissing her so deeply, Lindsay forgot what planet she was on. They made out for several more long, sensuous moments before Lindsay finally managed to come (somewhat) back to her senses. She was not a passive woman, especially when it came to sex, and she'd let Piper have control for long enough. Grasping Piper's hips, she shifted her off her lap, stood, and held out a hand.

❖

How had Piper never realized how amazingly sexy Lindsay Kent was? How was it possible that she'd met this woman, spoken to her on several occasions, and dismissed her? That that fact had simply slipped by? How had she not noticed? Now, as Lindsay stood before Piper, her black shirt hanging fully open, black bra cradling breasts that were surprisingly full, Piper knew she'd never see Lindsay any other way. She was holding out her hand to Piper and there was no way Piper wasn't going. She'd go anywhere with Lindsay right then. Up a mountain. Into a tunnel. Anywhere.

She put her hand in Lindsay's and was pulled to her feet.

Piper's mind was racing almost as fast as her blood, so she barely registered anything on the trip up the stairs. Lindsay's bedroom was a surprise, however. Piper wasn't sure what she was expecting, but it wasn't this. It wasn't…soft and inviting and feminine. The walls were a light blue-gray, cool enough, but not cold. The floor was hardwood, light oak if Piper was guessing correctly, with a large, oval, white rug in the center of the room. The queen-sized bed had a white fabric headboard, was covered in a thick, soft-looking comforter in a light gray, and was covered with throw pillows in varying shades of blue and white.

That was all she had time to take note of before Lindsay turned her, tilted her head up with a finger under her chin, and captured her mouth. They'd kicked their shoes off on the way into the house, so their two-inch height difference—which was almost never prominent given that Piper had heels on much of the time—was obvious now. As Lindsay slowly walked them toward the bed until the backs of Piper's legs hit, Piper felt deliciously surrounded by Lindsay and her body.

Like the trip up the stairs, Piper didn't recall falling back onto the bed. She was just...there. Suddenly. Lindsay's weight above her, Lindsay's tongue pressing into her mouth as she felt her breast freed from the cup of her bra, Lindsay's fingers zeroing in on an aching nipple. Piper tugged at Lindsay's shirt, pulled it off, was rewarded with a warm, smooth expanse of skin that felt indescribably wonderful beneath her palms, and she found she couldn't stop moving them, running them over Lindsay's shoulders, down her back, dipping into the waistband of her jeans as far as she could, then back up. Every inch of her felt like silk.

Try as she might to focus on each individual move, each individual sound, each individual touch, Piper couldn't. Everything blurred together. She couldn't differentiate between Lindsay's fingers, her mouth, her tongue. Every point of contact combined to form one indistinguishable wave of bliss. It wasn't until Lindsay's mouth touched Piper's center that her focus came screaming back and she found herself completely naked on her back on Lindsay's bed, her thighs spread wide, held open by Lindsay's hands as Lindsay's tongue danced through the wet flesh revealed there.

"Oh, God," Piper whispered, grabbing for something, anything to hold on to. "Oh, my God."

Lindsay increased the pressure. She pushed her tongue inside Piper, expelling all the air from her lungs. Piper wasn't one for being vocal in bed, but when Lindsay traded tongue for fingers and drove them confidently into Piper's body, she sucked in a loud breath and moaned like somebody she didn't recognize, gripping the comforter in her fingers. Her hips raised off the bed and colors danced behind her eyelids as the orgasm ripped through her body.

Piper was vaguely aware of Lindsay staying with her, holding tightly to her hips, keeping her mouth still, but pressed to Piper's center as she climaxed. Only once she'd come back down to the bed, her breath coming in ragged gasps, did Lindsay move. Gently, she took her mouth away and slipped her fingers out, then pressed a soft kiss to Piper's heated flesh, causing a small spasm to ripple through her legs. Lindsay laid her cheek against Piper's inner thigh and was still, except for her fingertips that ran lightly along Piper's hip. When she felt like she could breathe again without hyperventilating, Piper opened her eyes, lifted her head a bit, and sent a glance down her own body where she met those sparkling green eyes looking back at her.

"Hi," Lindsay said softly.

Piper dropped her head back down to the bed with a groan.

Lindsay chuckled and moved up her body, leading the way with soft kisses to Piper's knee, her hip, her stomach, each breast, and then her mouth, where Lindsay lingered and Piper could taste the salty-sweet still clinging to her lips.

"I'll say it again," Lindsay told her as she settled next to Piper. "You are so fucking beautiful."

Piper closed her eyes and gave her head a slight shake as she felt her cheeks flush even more than they'd already flushed.

"Why does that embarrass you?" Lindsay asked. "It's true."

"Thank you."

Lindsay cuddled closer, tucked her head on Piper's shoulder, up under her chin. She tossed a leg over Piper's and grabbed the edge of the comforter to pull it up over them. Piper's eyelids felt heavy and she let them drift closed even as she muttered, "You still have your pants on. They should be off." There was movement, the warmth of Lindsay's body disappeared, but Piper was too tired to force her eyes open, and she scolded herself for it. And then Lindsay was back, her warm flesh pressed against Piper's naked body, and all was right in the world again. "Oh, so much better," she mumbled, and felt rather than heard Lindsay's responding soft laugh as her shoulder moved under Piper's hand.

❖

Lindsay hadn't intended to fall asleep. She'd intended to watch Piper sleep. That was the plan and she was perfectly content. She had no issues with Piper not reciprocating her lovemaking; there'd be plenty of time for that and Lindsay didn't think that way anyhow. She was beyond happy to touch Piper's gorgeous body, to taste every inch of her, to be the one to coax those incredibly sexy sounds from her throat, and she was ecstatic to have been the one to give her an orgasm so intense it had wrecked her and put her to sleep.

Lindsay saw that as a win.

And then, apparently, she'd drifted off right behind Piper.

She only knew this because she was now being woken up by a gentle caress along the outside of her breast. As she slowly surfaced from slumber, she took stock of her situation. She was on her side, and Piper's warm body was pressed tightly up against her back, the smaller woman playing the bigger spoon. Lindsay could feel the tickle of Piper's breath against her hair, the soft press of her bare breasts into her back, and the path of her fingertips was causing gooseflesh to break out along Lindsay's arms.

She didn't move. Well, she did her best not to move. She wanted to relish the feeling, the quiet, the warmth. The sun hadn't come up; it was still dark in the room, so it wasn't yet morning. They were still covered by the comforter, wrapped sideways. Piper ran her fingertips around and around Lindsay's nipple…she could feel it tightening and had to consciously keep herself from squirming, from pushing her ass back into Piper's body for some kind of purchase. She was doing pretty well, she thought, but then Piper's thumb skimmed over her nipple and Lindsay sucked in a breath.

"I wondered if you were awake," Piper whispered in her ear as she continued her assault on Lindsay's breast.

"Oh, I am."

"Good. Because I literally fell asleep on the job earlier and I'd like to make it up to you."

"Well, who am I to protest?" Lindsay asked as she allowed herself to be turned onto her back. Piper slid a leg between hers and pressed her knee up, cluing both of them in to just how wet Lindsay already was. She swallowed hard as Piper's eyes widened.

"Wow," Piper said.

"Yeah, you're kind of a turn-on."

"Good to know." Piper lowered her head to pull Lindsay's nipple into her mouth, and all coherent words were pretty much obliterated for Lindsay after that.

For somebody who was such a control freak, somebody so determined, Piper took her time on Lindsay's body. Not at all what Lindsay had expected. She'd expected Piper to push toward the finish line, to want to get to the goal quickly and efficiently, to win the race.

Not so. She meandered. She wandered. She explored Lindsay's body like she had all the time in the world. She lavished attention on each breast, slowly, softly, one then the other, back and forth, reverently, then more firmly, then sucking hard enough to make Lindsay hiss in pained pleasure and arch her back. Piper's hands were everywhere, and she was the director of this show. She lifted Lindsay's arm over her head, then ran her tongue from Lindsay's elbow slowly down until she reached her breast, where she again took a nipple into her mouth. Then she repeated the process on the other arm until, for the first time in her life, Lindsay thought she might come just from the attention to her breasts.

Finally, Piper shifted her focus. Slipping her other leg between Lindsay's, she pushed herself up to all fours and moved her knees, forcing Lindsay's legs apart, giving her full access to the hot wetness of Lindsay's center. Lindsay's breaths were coming in short, ragged bursts now and she looked at Piper, propped above her, looking devastatingly sexy, and lifted her hand to Piper's face, touched her lips.

"Please," Lindsay whispered.

"Please what?" Piper ran her thumb over Lindsay's aching nipple, watched Lindsay's face.

Lindsay whimpered. "Please, Piper. Touch me. Please?"

Piper's expression in that second...Lindsay couldn't even describe it other than to say it was sensuous and erotic and so goddamn sexy. Their gazes held as Piper moved her hand and ran one finger through the wetness waiting for her. Lindsay sucked in a breath, her neck arching as she pushed her head back into the pillow.

It was like Piper had made love to her a hundred times before. She knew exactly where to touch. She knew when to increase the pressure and when to ease up. She slid her fingers inside Lindsay's body and Lindsay heard a small cry come from her own throat. Lindsay grasped the back of Piper's neck with one hand, Piper's hip with the other, and before she knew what was happening, Piper had spun them so she was on her back and Lindsay was on top. Electric arousal shot through her body as Lindsay pushed herself up to a sitting position and found a rhythm on Piper's hand, taking her fingers in as deeply as she could. Piper helped her by bending her own knees, and Lindsay braced herself with a hand on each one, rocking slowly, her eyes locked on Piper's. All Piper had to do was use her other hand, stroke Lindsay once with her thumb, twice...

Lindsay threw her head back and let out a cry she'd never heard herself make before as her entire body tightened in climax, Piper's fingers deep inside her, her muscles contracting around them.

Unlike Piper's slow coming down from her orgasm, Lindsay simply collapsed. She let her body fall forward so her face was buried against Piper's neck, their breasts pressed together, Piper still inside her. They lay that way for she had no idea how long, but the gentle stroking of Piper's fingertips up and down her back was about as close to perfect as she'd ever imagined getting and there was a large part of her that never wanted to move again. Ever.

When her legs started to tingle from being bent for too long, Lindsay surrendered and let herself roll to one side, hissing softly as Piper finally slid her fingers out. She couldn't think of a single thing that needed to be said, and strangely, that felt perfect. Piper tugged the covers so they fell over both of them, wrapped Lindsay in her arms, and in minutes, Lindsay could feel the even rise and fall of her chest beneath her ear.

That had been surreal.

Lindsay wasn't a pie-in-the-sky kind of person. She wasn't a dreamy fantasist. She was a realist. She was pragmatic. She tried in vain to ignore the voice in her head that reminded her how nobody had ever made love to her like that. Nobody had ever been such a perfect sexual match for her.

Because the truth was, she had no idea what this was. Where it was going. If it was going anywhere. She didn't really know Piper Bradshaw, and that was a fact. Maybe she did this all the time. Maybe she'd get up in the morning, be on her merry way, and that would be that.

It was possible, but she didn't think so.

She didn't want to think so.

She didn't want to think.

Doing her best to shove those thoughts away, Lindsay let herself bask in that pleasant, warm, muscles-like-jelly afterglow of sex and burrowed further into Piper.

She wouldn't think about tomorrow.

CHAPTER SIXTEEN

Piper had never been a fan of "the morning after." More times than not, it was awkward. Things that were said and done—*and let's not forget sounds that were made*—under cover of darkness tended to be embarrassing in the harsh light of day.

She'd entertained the idea of getting up early and sneaking out, which she knew was not a cool thing to do, but at least she could have some time to gather her thoughts. That plan went out the window, though, when she woke up to find Lindsay gazing sleepily at her with those eyes.

And then there was morning sex.

Piper couldn't remember the last time she'd had an orgasm to start her day, but she was pretty sure she could get used to it as she lay there in Lindsay's bed, breathless. Lindsay slid out from under the covers, donned an adorable pair of blue and white striped pajama pants and a matching blue tank, then bent over and kissed Piper on the forehead.

"I'll go make coffee."

Piper lifted a hand in a wave, but that was all she could muster. Lindsay's mouth had been on her before she was even fully awake and her orgasm must've been waiting right there in the wings because Piper had come inside of five minutes.

"Jesus," she whispered now, arm thrown over her eyes, body still thrumming.

Afraid she'd fall back to sleep—and doing so was so tempting—Piper forced herself to get up and out of bed. She donned all the clothes she found in the bedroom. Which left her in her pants and a bra. With a sigh, she vaguely recalled being divested of her tank top while on the couch in the living room.

She located the bathroom, washed her face and hands, squirted a blob of Lindsay's toothpaste on her finger, and did her best to freshen up her mouth. Then she marched downstairs a bit self-consciously, being topless and all, and found her tank on the floor. She was just pulling it over her head when Lindsay came into the room, a mug in one hand and a stainless steel travel mug in the other.

The smell of coffee was heavenly.

"Much as I'd love to have you stay so I can make you some breakfast, I'm pretty sure you're ready to be on your way." Lindsay's soft smile took any accusation out of the words.

Piper returned the smile. "I do have a meeting first thing."

Lindsay held out the travel mug. "For the road, then."

Piper took it. "Thank you." Their eye contact held and Piper lowered her voice. "I had a really good time last night."

"Me, too."

Locating her purse, Piper picked it up, crossed the room to peck Lindsay on the lips—quickly so as not to be overwhelmed by temptation—and said, "I'll call you later." Then she was out the door, walking quickly to her SUV.

Normal morning-after behavior for Piper was to wipe the previous evening from her mind, at least temporarily, so she could focus on the day ahead. And today was a busy one. She realized, in hindsight, that last night probably wasn't the best timing for a sexcapade that stretched into the wee hours. Today was a big meeting with some of the folks from Harbinger, and Piper needed to be on her game. Unfortunately, it became obvious very quickly that her mind had other ideas. Her mind wanted to reminisce. Her mind wanted to flash back. Her mind wanted to replay. Her mind was not at all interested in working.

It went on like that for much of the morning. While in the shower. While getting dressed and putting on her makeup. While driving to her office. The most prominent thing in Piper's head was the previous night. And not just the sex (though that *was* front and center), but the time near the water. She still wasn't sure what had possessed her to take Lindsay there, and it was true that she hadn't been there in more than two years. Gina and her husband and kids went often; Gina's husband was an avid fisherman. But Piper had just found it too hard. Taking Lindsay there with her had been risky, as she'd had no way of gauging her own reaction. She'd also had no way of knowing that something about Lindsay's solid, quiet presence would be exactly perfect.

In her office, she tossed down her purse and her laptop case, then braced her palms on the desk's surface and just closed her eyes. Breathed. In and out. She needed to focus.

A knock on her doorjamb startled her.

"Ready?" Ian asked, looking ridiculously entrepreneurial in his navy blue suit and red power tie.

"I am." She gave him a nod.

She'd think about Lindsay later.

❖

Lindsay couldn't get Piper out of her head, even after she'd gone. Piper's eyes. Piper's voice. Piper's body. Piper's hands on her body. Her hands on Piper's body.

Truth was, she hadn't really tried to get Piper out of her head. Why would she?

"That was, arguably, the best night of my life," she said now, to Bert, as they tromped through the woods along the lake, Rocket running ahead and then back like always.

"You mean the best *sex* of your life," Bert amended.

"That, too."

"Come on, Linds. You barely know this girl. There could be some crazy narcissist hiding inside. You have no idea yet."

"Piper's not a narcissist."

"You have no idea yet," Bert said again, enunciating each word.

Bert had texted just as Lindsay was loading Rocket into the car for their morning walk and asked if she could join them, as she did once in a while. Lindsay had told her the day before that she had a date with Piper, and this morning, she'd texted that Piper had just left. Now part of Lindsay was regretting telling Bert she could come along because she was killing Lindsay's buzz. "Can you just let me bask for a few minutes before you tear my fantasy apart? Please?"

"Sure. Sorry. Go ahead." Bert made a sweeping gesture with her arm. "Bask away."

"Thank you."

"I'm just looking out for you," Bert said almost immediately. "That's what friends do."

"Seriously? Four seconds of basking? That's all I get? Gee, thanks. You're a swell friend."

Bert at least had the good sense to look a tiny bit ashamed. "I'm sorry. But I promised my wife that I'd have this talk with you. That I'd make sure you knew what you were doing."

Lindsay shook her head. "I'm so glad to know that you guys think I'm an idiot."

Bert grabbed her arm, stopped her from walking. "We don't think you're an idiot," she said once Lindsay—reluctantly—met her gaze. "We just want to protect you. You've had exactly one date with this woman, you slept with her on it, and now you're all with the googly eyes and dreamy sighing."

Lindsay cocked her head, "I'm sorry. Forgive me if I've got this wrong, but…didn't you and Maya sleep together on your first date? And isn't she now your wife?"

They stood, staring each other down, Bert blinking at her in surprise.

"You know what?" Bert asked. "You're right. That's totally true. Carry on." Lindsay punched her playfully in the shoulder and they resumed their walking. They did so in silence for several moments before Bert asked, "So. It was that good, huh?"

Lindsay let her head fall back and bent her knees slightly as they walked. "Oh, my God, Roberta. So, *so* good."

Bert chuckled. "Wow."

"You ever have that kind of sex where there are all these weird sounds in the room? Like moans and gasps and things you've never heard before…and then you realize that *you* are the one making them?"

Bert glanced up at the sky and gave a dreamy sigh of her own. "Long, long ago, I seem to recall something of the sort…" They walked on. "She a control freak? Seems like she would be."

"Little bit."

"Only a little?" Bert's eyes were wide.

"Yeah, I was surprised, too. I ran the show as much as she did. I also ran it this morning, thank you very much."

Bert held up a hand for Lindsay to slap. "Nice. I do *not* have enough morning sex. I need to fix that."

"I highly recommend that you do."

"What now?"

Lindsay shrugged. "No idea. Just floating along, seeing what happens, I guess."

They walked some more, and Lindsay whistled when she didn't see Rocket. He came bounding back, looking like the happiest animal on earth. Lindsay wondered absently how awesome it would be to have so little to worry about. She'd never really envied her dog before, but she did right then. Because the truth was, she didn't feel nearly as breezy and nonchalant about things as she was leading Bert to believe. She simply didn't want her friends to worry about her. Or judge her. Or think she was stupid and naïve. The truth was, she had no idea at all what happened next. Piper had said she'd call later. Lindsay had to trust that she wasn't just feeding her a line so she could get away. Plus, it wasn't like they'd never run into each other again. They had no choice.

Lindsay may have seemed like a fly-by-the-seat-of-her-pants kind of person to a lot of people who didn't know her, but the truth was, she liked knowing what was coming. She liked to be prepared.

She was not prepared for Piper Bradshaw.

She'd thought she was. She thought she had been. A little kissing here and there was one thing. That had been a fun little teasing game, and Lindsay had enjoyed it immensely. Getting ambushed in her office by an unexpectedly sexy Piper had been the highlight of many weeks for Lindsay. And when Piper had asked her out, she'd been flattered. Excited. A little anxious, but in a good way. When Piper had taken her to her dad's fishing spot, Lindsay'd been surprised, but also flattered. Honored that Piper trusted her that way—though she wondered if Piper had surprised herself as much as she'd surprised Lindsay…it kind of seemed like she had. Still. It was an event Lindsay didn't take lightly. She understood, simply by watching Piper's face, by listening to her voice, that being there was a huge deal. Lindsay took that seriously, and things shifted a bit with that surprise.

And then last night.

"Hey, you okay?" Bert's voice yanked Lindsay harshly back to reality. Probably a good thing.

"Yeah." She nodded. "Fine. Just a little tired. You know." She lifted her eyebrows up twice so Bert would think she was being a frat brother rather than having an internal panic attack about what would happen next. Because the truth was, she hadn't a clue what would happen next. And Lindsay hated that.

❖

These people are horrible.

It was a thought she couldn't get out of her head no matter how hard she tried, and finally, Piper gave up. Because it was the truth and she needed to simply accept it.

She'd held out hope. She'd been banking on the fact that her current bosses gave a crap about their people, that even after they took the massive amount of money they'd each garner from the merger, they'd still make sure those who had worked for them for years, those who had helped them build their company from the ground up and make it into the successful, *buyable* company it was today, were taken care of.

It was rapidly becoming clear that this was not the case. Not even a little bit.

Piper looked around the large mahogany conference table, scanning the faces of her fellow managers as well as her three bosses who sat at one end of it. At least they had the good sense to stare at their own hands as the four executives from Harbinger went over their plan for slowly eliminating three unsuspecting departments, shaving the customer service department by nearly 40 percent, and bringing in six of their own upper-level managers to help the transitions run smoothly. Ian had stopped giving her looks and instead, had resorted to kicking her under the table every time more bad news was delivered. She was going to have a severely black-and-blue ankle when this meeting was over.

Why would I want to work for a company that would put me in such a position? They obviously suck.

Without warning, Lindsay's voice echoed through Piper's head. She'd been right all along, hadn't she? Slowly, Piper shook her head back and forth, then stopped abruptly as Ian kicked her again and she shot him a warning look. He shifted his gaze to the tabletop in front of him, gleaming with his reflection. Piper could feel the despair coming off him like heat, and she was both annoyed and relieved to feel it within herself as well.

The Harbinger guy speaking told them layoffs wouldn't begin for a month or so after the initial merger. Piper wanted to correct him with "why don't you just call it what it is: a takeover," but she stayed quiet. He was, unsurprisingly, a white man in his sixties with an impeccably tailored suit, a red power tie that somehow looked more expensive than Ian's, and a manicure. The first thing you thought when you saw him was that he was wealthy. His smile reminded her of the clown in the Stephen King movie *It*: no surprise it was there, but it was creepy and sinister, and Piper wanted to avoid it at all costs.

She managed to keep her ass in her chair and her mouth shut throughout the entire meeting. Even more impressive: Ian did the same.

When the gathering finally broke up and everybody was excused, she and Ian both blew out heavy breaths, then looked at each other with sad smiles.

"This sucks," Ian said quietly.

"Agreed."

They parted ways in the hall, each heading to their own office. Piper closed her office door, flopped into her chair, and blew out yet another large breath, surprised she had so many.

Why would I want to work for a company that would put me in such a position? They obviously suck.

There was Lindsay again, invading her head, seeping into her thoughts. Well. It wasn't like she'd ever left, not since last night. But Piper had done an admirable job shoving her to that back corner so she could deal with work stuff. And now here was Lindsay, chiming in on work stuff.

Piper opened her email program as she tried to remember whether Kat had taken up so much headspace after they'd first slept together. It had been good, there was no doubt, but it hadn't been earth-shattering or anything. Piper was a practical woman. She wasn't a hopeless romantic and she'd never expect sex with anybody to be earth-shattering. That was saved for romance novels and rom-com movies. As long as it was good, she was fine with that.

Sex with Lindsay had been beyond good. It had been pretty damn close to earth-shattering, and she wasn't sure what to do with that. Sure, she could throw herself into her work. She could focus on the business aspects of running Vineyard. But Lindsay would creep in. She already was, as evidenced by today, by just now. It seemed she was slowly invading all aspects of Piper's life: her kayaking, her parents' wine bar, her job, her bed. The weird thing was, Piper wasn't freaked out about it, even though she knew she should be. Her control was slipping right through her fingers, and *that* should have her panicking.

What is happening to me?

Doing her best to shake the thoughts away, Piper focused on her computer screen. Typing quickly and efficiently, she created a group email and sent it to each of her staff members. She asked them, if at all possible, to stay late tonight for an extra twenty minutes. Half an hour, tops. They'd meet in her office at 5:30.

She clicked Send before she could second-guess herself.

Yeah. Lindsay was invading everything.

CHAPTER SEVENTEEN

I sn't Zack scheduled tonight?"

Bridget's question startled Lindsay, who realized she'd been daydreaming while leaning on the bar.

"I'm sorry?" she asked, giving her head a slight shake and blinking several times.

Bridget squinted at her. "You've been looking awfully schmoopy lately. What's that about?"

"Schmoopy? Is that an actual word?"

"Yes. I'm sure it is." Bridget studied her for a moment, her dark eyes so intensely focused on Lindsay, it was difficult not to squirm.

"Stop that," Lindsay said, turning away and busying herself by rearranging glasses that didn't need rearranging.

After a beat, Bridget let it go and repeated her question. "Wasn't Zack supposed to be here at six?"

Lindsay squinted and looked at the ceiling. "Yeah, I think so." This was the third time in less than two weeks that he'd either been late or had called in at the last minute. "I'll have a talk with him."

"If he shows up," Bridget said, her tone conveying that she wasn't counting on it.

"Thursdays have gotten busy. I'm here. I'll help."

"More tips for us," Bridget said with a shrug, picked up her flights, and carried them to a table for two.

"You ready for a refill, Mr. R.?" Lindsay asked Paul Richardson as he slid his empty glass toward her.

"I think I'm good for tonight, Lindsay." He smiled warmly and pulled his wallet from his pocket.

"I'm surprised to see you here on a Thursday."

"I was told mixing things up is good for the soul," he told her with a wink, and dropped thirty dollars on the bar. "Keep the change."

Lindsay watched him leave, a soft smile on her face, and wished all her customers were half that pleasant.

Mixing things up is good for the soul, huh?

She thought about that. If it was true, she was in pretty good shape, because she'd certainly been mixing things up lately. And, just as it had for the past thirty hours or so, her brain tossed her an image of Piper Bradshaw. Take Charge Piper, boldly asking her on a date. Vulnerable Piper, smiling hesitantly as they sat on the dock. Naked Piper, above her. Beneath her. Touching her. Kissing her.

"God," she muttered as a pleasant shudder rippled through her body.

"You okay?"

Bridget's voice startled her; she hadn't heard her approach. "Yeah. Yeah, I'm good." Bridget was giving her that look again. "Seriously. Stop that."

Vineyard was fairly busy. As she'd said, Thursdays had picked up considerably, people blowing off steam from their week, preparing for the weekend, just looking to relax a bit. Four tables were full, a party of three were sitting in the mismatched chairs on the patio overlooking the lake. Two were seated at the bar, and a party of five had just come in the front door. She and Bridget would have their hands full tonight, and that was a good thing, because she needed her mind taken off Piper, at least for a little while.

She hadn't seen her yesterday, and that bummed Lindsay out more than she'd expected. There had been a couple texts during the day. Lindsay had been overtly flirtatious. Piper had been…not overtly flirtatious. Or flirtatious at all. She'd been pleasant. Light. But any attempts by Lindsay to reminisce about their night together had been gently sidestepped.

Lindsay didn't know what to make of that.

Setting up another time to meet seemed like the only way to address things. It made sense. She didn't like talking about serious matters over text. There was no tone of voice, no facial expressions, and she wanted Piper to see her, to understand what she was saying, where she was coming from. More importantly, she wanted to be able to see Piper, see her face, her eyes.

So why hadn't she done that yet? Why hadn't she set something up?

A beep on her tablet indicated an order for two cheese boards, so she headed to the back to arrange them as she continued to analyze her current situation.

A wheel of brie in hand, she asked herself again why she hadn't yet asked Piper to meet.

Because I'm afraid.

Yeah, not a surprise. She knew that already. And she supposed it was normal to feel that way, but talking about it was the only way to know where things were going. If anywhere.

What if they're not going anywhere?

It was a question that had been niggling at the back of her brain all day, but she'd refused to give it any energy. Now she forced herself to deal with it. What if Tuesday night was it? Piper had a good time. So had Lindsay. (No, Lindsay'd had an *amazing* time, but whatever.) And sometimes, that was all it was.

Lindsay refused to believe that. Whatever she'd felt that night, Piper had felt it, too. She knew it. She *knew* it.

Pulling her phone out of her back pocket, she typed out a text.

When can I see you again? Tomorrow?

Lindsay hit Send before she could second-guess herself, then set the phone on the counter where she could see it. Which was kind of pathetic and a little desperate, but she didn't care. She didn't want to miss a reply.

Bridget interrupted her worried thoughts as she blew into the back and snapped up the cheese boards. "Table seven is ready for their check and a party of two just came in," she said, not even a little bit frantic. Simply matter-of-fact.

"On it." Lindsay followed her out, and they went to work.

By nine thirty, things had finally started to slow down a bit, and they were left with four occupied tables and a couple at the bar. Zack had been a no-show, which was grounds for firing in Lindsay's book, though she knew that Mrs. B. gave everybody a second chance. She was going to have to think about that. Maybe Piper would have some insight, as she managed a staff of her own every day.

It was the first time in almost three hours that she'd thought about Piper. She found that to be both astonishing and also a relief. Sliding her phone from her back pocket, she found a text from her mother and one from Josh, who wanted to bring his work pals by again, but nothing from Piper. Trying not to let the dejection wash over her completely, she frowned and stuffed the phone away.

Lindsay sent Bridget home at ten, then she managed things until eleven, when she locked the door. Forty-five minutes of paperwork and she was ready to head home, but as she came out of the back, she was stopped by the giant metal Vineyard sign on the wall with its faded and cracking paint. Yeah, something needed to be done about that. She crossed to it, took it down—slowly and carefully, as it was heavier than she'd expected—and took it out of the wine bar with her. It just fit in her back seat along with the blanket she used for Rocket and his muddy feet. Then she drove home, vowing not to think about Piper Bradshaw for the rest of the night.

"Yeah, right."

At 1:17 a.m., Piper was wide awake in bed. Edgar purred loudly in the crook of her knees as she tried her best not to stare at the clock and guess when it would turn to 1:18. 1:19. 1:20.

She'd done it.

She'd told nobody. Not even Ian. But she'd done it.

She'd met with her entire staff, told them exactly what Harbinger intended to do when the merger took place in the very near future, and that if they wanted to start looking for new employment now, she'd do her best to cover for them if they needed to leave for interviews.

"Unfortunately, there's nothing I can do for you monetarily," she'd said, her voice laced with genuine regret. "I'm not even supposed to be warning you. I could lose my own job. But..." She let her voice trail off as an unexpected lump of emotion lodged itself in her throat and she had to swallow a couple times to clear it. "I thought it was only fair that you know. I'd prefer that you didn't share this information or tell anybody where you got it, but I know that I can't force you to follow my wishes. Just...do what you have to do to take care of yourselves and your families."

In the history of speeches, it hadn't been much. It had been quick. It had been quiet. It had been matter-of-fact. But it was so much more than her staff was going to get from anybody else at the company.

Did I do the right thing, Dad?

She'd asked the question so many times today. Out loud. In her head. Over and over. She never got an answer, other than to understand that she *felt* like it had been the right thing. And then no sooner would she feel that sentiment than the panic would set in. *They're going to fire me! What the hell was I thinking? Damn Lindsay and her do-gooder attitude! This is her fault.*

It was interesting that she blamed Lindsay. Why didn't she blame Ian? It had been his idea first. She'd told him, in no uncertain terms, that he was wrong. That she wasn't going to do what he was suggesting. And then Lindsay had come along with her beautiful green eyes and her pragmatic reasoning, and Piper had been lost.

When was the last time she was so easily flipped?

Never. That's when.

Piper Bradshaw wasn't a person who let others influence her decisions. She made them. *She* made them.

With a loud sigh, she turned onto her other side, annoyed at the clock for moving so slowly. Edgar never stopped purring; he simply readjusted his curled body so he was against her stomach. She was being unreasonable. Piper knew that. None of this was Lindsay's fault. All Lindsay had done was shine a light in a corner of Piper's mind that she'd been trying not to see. But the blame had to go somewhere.

When can I see you again? Tomorrow?

She hadn't responded to Lindsay's text, which was rude. She was aware. Her brain had been too full of worry, regret, self-flagellation, and second-guessing. She felt like she was losing control of everything. And *now* she'd begun to panic. Too much so to even entertain the idea of another date with Lindsay.

"Another date," she whispered softly, then scoffed. "Please." She knew exactly where another date would end them up: in bed. Or on the couch. Or hell, on the floor. Didn't matter where. Piper knew beyond a shadow of a doubt that she wouldn't be able to keep her hands to herself. She couldn't deal with that earlier, couldn't even make room in her overcrowded mind.

But now…

It was late, but she picked up her phone from the nightstand and typed out the text anyway.

I'll stop by after work.

She clicked Send and turned the phone to silent. And just like that, she felt her eyelids grow heavy as Edgar's purring faded.

She'd see Lindsay tomorrow.

A small smile tugged the corners of her mouth as she finally drifted off.

She'd see Lindsay tomorrow.

CHAPTER EIGHTEEN

Piper wandered into Lakeshore at 2:40 Friday afternoon feeling—and probably looking—completely stunned and very much like she'd been mentally beaten up. Ian held the door for her, and when she turned to look at him, he seemed fine. For a moment in time, she wanted to punch him in the throat.

There wasn't much left of a lunch crowd and only two people sat at the bar—two retirement-age men sipping Coors Lights and watching golf on the TV mounted on the wall. It was a gorgeous day outside, sunny and warm with a light breeze, and a sign to the left of the bar announced a new outdoor patio. Piper could see several customers seated out there. She and Ian took stools at the opposite end of the bar from the two men and made themselves comfortable. Then they smiled at each other, however wanly.

Ian signaled the bartender, a thirty-something guy with a full beard and kind eyes. "We'll take two vodka tonics and two shots of tequila."

Piper snapped her head around to gape at him.

"Oh, yeah, baby. Shots. We earned 'em." Ian scrubbed a hand over his face.

"One shot," Piper said. "That's it for me."

The bartender poured the shots first, slid a salt shaker their way, and handed them each a wedge of lemon on a napkin.

"It has been a day." Ian licked his hand and sprinkled salt on it. His grin was calm. Unworried.

"How is your head not exploding right now?" Piper asked him, her frustration coming through.

"My head is not exploding because I did the right thing," he said, matter-of-factly. Then he held up his shot. "And so did you. To doing the right thing."

Piper shook her head, but touched her shot glass to his. They licked, shot, and sucked in tandem. She felt the burn of the alcohol as it went down and she wished she felt better, wished she felt as sure as Ian did, wished she didn't feel like the rope anchoring her was frayed so badly, it was about to snap and send her drifting off into oblivion.

They exchanged their empty shot glasses for full-size ones of vodka tonic. Neither spoke as they sipped, but Piper wondered if a stranger could see their differences as they sat there at the bar; they seemed glaringly obvious to her. Ian was calm, relaxed, a confident man without a care in the world. He looked satisfied. Piper, on the other hand, felt jittery, nervous and jerky. Worried. Uncertain. She felt like her eyes were open a bit too wide, as if she was expecting something to jump out and surprise her and was already preparing to see it. Her sips of her drink were too big, but she couldn't seem to stop herself. She finished her cocktail quickly, ordered another.

She'd been let go.

Canned.

Kicked to the curb.

Fired.

She'd been fired.

She'd never been fired before. Piper Bradshaw didn't get fired. If anything, Piper Bradshaw did the firing. But she'd been called into her boss's office just after lunch. When she'd arrived, four people were present and Ian showed up only a couple seconds after her. She knew immediately what was happening, and even though she'd known it was a possibility, she never really expected it would happen. She'd been naïve. Naïve and stupid and arrogant. There had been talk, her boss said. Things had been overheard, he'd said. Bottom line: they knew both Ian and Piper had given their staffs heads-ups after they'd been warned not to.

"I'm afraid we have no choice but to let you both go, effective immediately."

Ian hadn't seemed surprised. Piper had stood there in disbelief.

God, her father would be so disappointed in her.

Ian had gently taken her arm and led her from the meeting.

Half an hour later, they were in the parking lot, having turned in their security badges and carrying their personal belongings. As they approached their cars, Ian said that he wanted to have a drink with her, but couldn't stay long. Piper had agreed. What the hell else was she going to do?

Now it was nearly four o'clock, and Ian finished up his second VT and stood.

"Piper, it's been an honor." He laid a hand on her shoulder and held out his other one.

She put her hand in his and they shook. "Same here," she said, surprised by the small lump that formed in her throat.

"You have my number. Keep in touch, okay?" He smiled then, warm and friendly and inviting, and Piper was reminded that he was a pretty great guy. "Take care of yourself. Let me know where you land."

Piper nodded, then watched him leave with mixed emotions that she didn't want to deal with. Instead, she ordered another drink.

She was angry. At a lot of different people. At Ian for being naïve (though he would disagree with her). At her father for not being here to talk to her about what she should have done. At Lindsay. God, she was angry at Lindsay. For being Lindsay. For her pie-in-the-sky simplicity of things. For her beautiful eyes and her ability to get under Piper's skin and for *changing her mind* about how she should handle the situation at work. But Piper was mostly angry at herself. For too many reasons to even articulate.

"I just want my father," she muttered aloud.

"Pardon?" the bartender said.

Piper shook her head. "Just another, please." She slid her glass his way. As he crafted her cocktail, she slipped the wine list out of its little holder and perused what they had. It was a much larger selection than she remembered in the past, and there were flights now. A couple of them looked familiar.

With a sigh, she put the menu back and sipped from the fresh drink the bartender gave her. The bar was dark, depressing, and she felt much the same way. Maybe some sunshine would help?

"Okay if I take this out onto the patio?" she asked the bartender.

He nodded his approval and she headed out into the light of day, knowing her train of emotions was headed to a bad place. Maybe she could cut it off at the pass.

❖

Lindsay would have liked it to be busier for a Friday night. It wasn't bad. They were a bit more than half full, but she hadn't scheduled a band for tonight, and now she wondered if she should have. Smooth hadn't been available, and that bummed her out. Unreasonably, but still. There were specials running, and those seemed to be doing fairly well, but she wanted more.

It was a gorgeous night, and while there were a few people milling out on the patio, it wasn't really ready for many, and that frustrated Lindsay no end. She really needed to talk to Piper about it. It was wasted space, a huge draw that wasn't being used. She had no idea why not, why the Bradshaws hadn't immediately furnished and decorated it. Seemed like a complete business failure. Sunset was scheduled for 8:40, according to the weather app on Lindsay's phone. If she could get the patio furnished, fancied up a bit, she could run some "sunset specials," that sort of thing. Might bring in more customers. She jotted a note in her little pad.

Moving from the window in the back that overlooked the patio, Lindsay headed into the office. Zack and Bridget were out front handling things just fine, which allowed her to get some paperwork and research done that she'd put off earlier. She had just opened her email when Bridget rapped on the door. Lindsay looked up into her worried face.

"What is it?" Lindsay asked, suddenly concerned.

Before Bridget could answer, Piper appeared behind her. "You have a visitor," Bridget said with a grimace. She waved Piper into the office, then made a show of closing the door.

Lindsay had an instant bad feeling.

She stood. "Piper. Hi."

Piper swayed on her feet a bit, and her eyes seemed slightly out of focus. "Don't hi me," she said.

Lindsay squinted at her. "Are you okay?"

Piper pointed at her. "I am a lot of things. *A lot* of things. But okay is not one of them."

"I see." It was clear by this point that Piper was drunk. Very drunk. And upset. "Please tell me you didn't drive here like this."

"What am I, stupid? No. I Uber'd."

Lindsay tried to stifle her relief at that. She wanted to know what was going on, but she'd have to tread carefully because Piper had the demeanor of somebody who was about ready to explode. Or maybe throw up. Lindsay had brought an unopened bottle of water into the office with her. Handing it to Piper, she said, "Here."

Piper snatched it from her hand, cracked the top open, and drank deeply from it. Lindsay took the time to scan over her. She was wearing a suit, so evidently she hadn't been home from work yet. But the skirt was wrinkled and the sleeves to the jacket were pushed up unevenly, giving her a slightly disheveled appearance. Which was very unlike the Piper Bradshaw Lindsay had gotten used to.

A moment of silence went by. "You want to tell me what's going on?" Lindsay finally asked, as gently as she could.

"Like you don't know." Piper flopped into a chair and glared at Lindsay.

Lindsay shook her head, sure her surprise was clear. "I really don't, Piper."

Piper sat forward, glared again. Lindsay hadn't really seen those unique hazel eyes when they were angry. They were still gorgeous, just…harder. Colder. "I just came from Lakeshore." Piper sat back clumsily, like her statement cleared everything up.

Lindsay lifted her hands, palms up, expectant. "Okay?"

"*Lakeshore.*" Piper enunciated the word, as if that would make her meaning clearer.

"Piper, you're going to have to help me here."

Piper inhaled loudly, then blew it out as if Lindsay was the thickest person on the planet. "Why isn't Smooth playing here tonight?"

Lindsay blinked at the seeming change of topic. "Um…they couldn't. I asked. They had another gig."

"Yes, they did. At Lakeshore. They're playing there right now."

Lindsay shrugged. "Okay."

Piper cocked her head and raised her eyebrows as if to say, "Really?"

Again, Lindsay turned her palms up. "Bands play in different places. Coincidence."

"Lakeshore has wine flights."

"Yeah, I know."

"Some of the same ones we do."

Lindsay did notice the plural there. When she'd looked, there had only been one. "How many?"

"Five."

"The same ones as ours?" This was a surprise.

Piper snorted. "Exactly the same. You know what else they have over there?"

Piper's face had gone hard. Lindsay could still tell she was drunk, but there was an unmistakable sharpness to her, in her eyes, like she'd sobered exponentially in the past minute or two. It made Lindsay uncomfortable. Slowly, Lindsay shook her head.

"An outdoor patio. A brand-new one."

That was news. "They do?"

"They do. And it's furnished with *exactly* the same furniture you wanted to use, the stuff we priced. And it's laid out the same."

"The same?" Lindsay pictured her own drawing, how thrilled she'd been to come up with the setup.

"Exactly the same."

It was then that Lindsay really heard Piper's tone. It was more than angry or surprised. It was...accusatory. Lindsay's brow furrowed as she looked at Piper who stared back at her with those cold, hard eyes. "What are you saying, Piper?"

"Seems pretty clear."

Lindsay expected to feel anger, but she didn't. Rather, she felt a stab in her chest. Pain. Betrayal. "Just say it," she said, her voice quiet.

"I think you're feeding our ideas to Lakeshore."

And there it was. Lindsay took it in, let her brain absorb it, was surprised by how much it hurt. "Why would I do that?" Again, her voice stayed quiet. Calm.

"Simple. Because I won't let you do what you want to here," Piper said, her voice seeming extra loud when compared to Lindsay's. "Because you don't control the money. I do. You're just the bartender. So you thought you'd go someplace else where they'd listen to you. Someplace that needs a boost."

Lindsay willed herself not to flinch at Piper's words, not to let her know how much they stung. Quietly, in measured tones, she told her, "I have put my heart and soul into this place. I have nothing but the utmost respect for your parents and their vision of this wine bar."

Piper scoffed, and the sound made Lindsay clench her teeth. "Right. That's why you're doing everything you can to erase my father completely." Piper's voice faltered for the first time, and Lindsay was shocked to see her eyes well.

"What?" Lindsay asked in disbelief. "Piper, I'm not...I would never..."

"You're trying to change *everything*." Piper stood up then, nearly knocking her chair backward to the floor. Lindsay stood as well while Piper ticked things off on her fingers. "You changed the wall color. You added decorations to replace his. You're adding wines he never would have." Her breath came in gasps now. "And where is his sign? The big Vineyard sign that's usually on the wall? He had that specially designed! *It's his.*"

Lindsay was stunned into silence. She didn't know what to say or how to say it or if Piper would even hear her in her current state. "Piper, I—"

Piper cut her off with a raised hand. "No. I don't want to hear it. I've had enough. I can take over running this place."

Lindsay's eyes went wide. "What?"

"Yeah. Seems only fair that *both* of us get fired today. Leave your keys with Bridget." And with that, Piper reached for the doorknob, missed, and tried again. Finally yanking the door open, she stumbled out into the back room as Lindsay watched in stupefied silence.

CHAPTER NINETEEN

The doorbell rang.

Was it the doorbell? Maybe not.

Piper reached blindly for a pillow and pulled it over her head. She was face down in her bed and, judging by the fact that the room was bright even with her eyes closed, she had to guess it was later than her usual wake up time. She felt Edgar tromp across the backs of her thighs, probably annoyed he hadn't gotten breakfast yet, but Piper didn't care. She couldn't move, and she knew if she tried to, the subtle throbbing in her head would turn into an unbearable pounding she didn't have the energy to deal with.

The doorbell rang again.

"Fuck," Piper whispered, still not moving an inch. Maybe they'd just go away.

She'd just about drifted off again when she heard a sound far more disturbing than the doorbell.

The stairs squeaked.

Specifically, the fourth stair from the living room. Piper knew it well.

Somebody was coming up her stairs.

She could jump up and grab the pepper spray from her nightstand. She could hide in the master bath, lock herself in. She could roll off the bed and then roll under it like a four-year-old.

She did none of those things. Instead, she slitted her eyes and waited for her murderer/rapist/Grim Reaper to appear in the doorway, resigned to her fate.

The figure that showed up was none of those.

It was Matthew.

"What the hell, Piper?" He stepped quickly to the bed and shook her.

"Stop," she ordered, but it came out more like an unintelligible groan that maybe started with an *S*.

"I've been texting and calling you all morning." He picked her phone up from the nightstand. "Why do you put this on silent all the damn time? What if there's an emergency? How will anybody get ahold of you?"

Piper focused on willing Matthew away, trying to telepathically get him to evaporate from her bedroom, but it was obvious to her that his voice was slightly panicked and she felt a little bad about that.

"Why are you here, Matty?" she finally asked.

"I'm here because people were worried about you." Piper felt him sit on the bed next to her. "Lindsay left me a weirdly cryptic text while I was in the shower. Said maybe I should check on you. I tried to call her, but she didn't answer or respond to my texts."

Piper turned her head so she faced the other way. Away from Matthew.

"So," he went on. "I see you're still wearing what used to be that very nice Ralph Lauren suit I helped you pick out. At least you managed to kick off your heels before you passed out."

Piper made no comment. Bits and pieces from last night were starting to filter in and none of them made her happy. She just wanted to sleep. Forever. She wanted Matthew to leave so she could fall back to sleep and not have to deal with her life, with the world, with anything. She wanted oblivion.

Silence reigned.

"What happened, Piper?" Matthew's voice made her flinch; she'd hoped he left.

"I don't want to talk about it," she said, her words muffled by the pillow.

A weight settled on her leg: Matthew's hand. "Come on. I get a weird text from somebody I hardly know telling me to check on you. I do that and find you passed out in bed at almost noon on a Saturday, still in your work clothes from the day before and smelling like a distillery. I know you pretty well, Piper, and this isn't you. At all. Now tell me what happened. Please."

There was genuine concern in his voice. Worry. Piper knew him well enough to know when something had him apprehensive. She also knew it wasn't fair of her to leave him twisting in the wind like that.

She inhaled deeply, let it out.

"I got fired."

Matthew was quiet for so long that she risked the discomfort of turning her head so she could actually see if he was still sitting there.

He was. "Are you okay? I mean, you're obviously not okay, since you got shitfaced last night. Are you okay now? What the hell happened?"

The questions came rapid-fire and Piper closed her eyes at the onslaught. But not before seeing the concern on Matthew's face that matched that in his voice. He was worried for her, about her. He was her best friend and she owed him an explanation.

"Tell you what," she said softly. "You go downstairs, feed Edgar, and get a pot of coffee brewing. I'll take a shower, get myself together, and come down. Then I'll tell you all about my day yesterday. Deal?"

"Yes, please." Matthew smiled and stood. "Come on, Eddie. Let's eat."

Edgar seemed to know exactly what had been said because he flew off the bed and out the door in a flash.

Getting herself out of bed and sitting upright was harder than Piper even expected it to be. Everything hurt and she was painfully slow, but she managed to shed her clothes (Matthew was right about the state of her suit) and get herself into the bathroom. Since it felt (and tasted) like something had crawled into her mouth and died as she slept, the first thing she did was brush her teeth. Three times. Once she felt better about not disintegrating a wall with her breath, she stepped carefully into the shower.

It took her nearly twenty minutes of simply standing under the water and making lame attempts at soaping things up before she felt somewhat human again. The idea of putting on makeup or blow-drying her hair was just too much to handle, so she slapped on some moisturizer, finger-combed her hair, donned a pair of yoga pants and a ratty old Ms. Pac-Man T-shirt, and headed carefully down the stairs, bottle of Motrin in hand.

The smell of fresh coffee was somehow divine, rather than turning her stomach, and Piper was surprised. The second she entered the kitchen, Matthew handed her a cup, doctored up just the way she liked it.

"Thank you," she said, and took the mug in both hands, holding it like a life preserver.

"Feeling better?"

"A bit, yes."

"Breakfast?"

The mention of food didn't send her stomach roiling as she expected, so Piper entertained the idea for moment. "Maybe just toast to start out."

With a nod, Matthew popped some bread into the toaster. He graciously allowed her several swallows of coffee before finally turning to her, eyebrows raised expectantly.

Piper sighed, crossed the kitchen, and took a seat at the small table in the breakfast nook. One more sip of coffee and she felt as ready as she'd probably get, so she launched into what had happened at work, from her initial discussion (and disagreement) with Ian to the same discussion with Lindsay to her own wavering to meeting with her staff to her and Ian both being let go.

"Wow," Matthew said, as he set a plate of buttered toast in front of her, then took the seat on the other side of the round table. "That's a lot."

"Sure seems like it, huh?" Piper took a hesitant nibble.

"Then what?"

"Then Ian and I decided to get a drink. We went to Lakeshore."

"Why? That's the opposite end of the lake."

"Ian lives over that way and had to be home at a certain time. I, with nobody waiting on me, didn't have that worry."

"And then you got drunk."

"No." Piper held up a finger. "Then I noticed some very odd things about Lakeshore. Then, I got drunk." A thought occurred to her. "Shit. My car is still over there. I Uber'd home."

"Thank God."

"Can you take me to get it?"

"After you finish telling me the rest of the story," Matthew said with a nod. "What 'odd things' did you notice?" He made air quotes and Piper squinted at him.

"You're mocking me."

"No. Not at all." Matthew made a rolling gesture with his hand.

Piper spilled it all. She told him about the wine flights, how they weren't just flights, they were the exact same flights they had at Vineyard. "Same brands. Same varietals. Same groupings."

Matthew nodded and sipped his coffee.

"Smooth was scheduled to play that night. They're a jazz band that's been at Vineyard a couple times now and brings in a good crowd."

More nodding from Matthew's side of the table. "Not unusual, really, but okay."

Piper arched one eyebrow, but continued with her story. "Then there's the patio." She explained the traditional-but-modern furniture style, the placement of it all, the outdoor heaters, the décor, all of it the same as the proposal Lindsay had given her. "It was *identical*, Matty."

"And what do you think that means?"

"Isn't it obvious?"

Matthew's face said, "not really," even though he didn't actually say the words.

"Okay, you know what?" Piper finished her coffee. "What time is it?"

"A little after one."

"Good. They're open. We have to go get my car anyway, so let's drop in for a visit and I'll show you what I mean."

❖

Piper's SUV was right where she'd left it, no worse for wear. Thank God. After giving it a quick once-over, she led Matthew into Lakeshore, which was about a third full with Saturday shoppers and families out for the day who'd stopped for lunch. They grabbed two barstools only a couple seats off where Piper and Ian had sat the night before. The bartender was a girl this time, maybe twenty-five, a tall blonde with bright blue eyes and an eyebrow piercing that made Piper wonder how uncomfortable it had been to have done.

Matthew ordered a beer and Piper water. She pulled the wine flight menu out and showed it to Matthew.

"See?" she said in hushed tones. "It's an exact duplicate."

"Their prices are a little lower," Matthew commented, then had the good sense to look sheepish when Piper shot him a look.

The bartender gave them their drinks. Piper took a sip, then pointed at a flyer on the wall that advertised Smooth playing again next weekend. "See?" Matthew was unimpressed. He may have thought she was crazy; she could see it on his face. At the very least, he thought she was overreacting and she hadn't even gotten into the meat of the situation yet. Her frustration mounting, she said, "Let's go out to the patio and I'll show you what I'm talking about."

"Wait." Matthew grabbed her arm, kept her from getting off her stool. "What's the conclusion you've jumped to here?" He knew exactly what the conclusion was, she could also see *that* on his face. Apparently, he wanted her to say it.

Fine.

"I think Lindsay got tired of my telling her no or cutting her budgets back from what she thinks she needs. I think she got fed up and decided to share her ideas with another business. This one. I think she's probably planning a move here."

Matthew studied her for so long that she wondered if he was going to say anything at all. Finally, he looked at his beer as he turned it in his fingers. He took a deep breath in, let it out very slowly, then focused on her. "So, let me see if I get this. You think that Lindsay—a woman who is very competent, somebody your mother adores and trusts enough to leave in charge while she's away, not to mention a woman you have developed some major feelings for—don't interrupt me." He held up a hand the second Piper opened her mouth, stopping any sound from coming out, and she was surprised to realize that he seemed angry with her. Frustrated somehow. "Somebody who has increased the wine bar's overall business with her ideas…you think she's been filtering those successful ideas over to here because…why again?"

Piper opened her mouth to speak, but no words would come.

"Yeah, that's what I thought. What's the matter with you, Piper? Seriously."

Piper closed her eyes and was horrified to feel the threat of tears. What was the matter with her? Really and truly, what was it? Because there was something.

Matthew's tone softened as he laid a hand on her forearm. "Talk to me."

"I miss my dad," Piper said, her voice almost inaudible, and the statement surprised her. It also squeezed her heart. She felt Matthew's gentle pressure on her arm and it reassured her. "So much has happened that I have no control over. I feel like my world is slipping out of my grasp, Matty. My mom left. The wine bar is looking more different every day. I slept with Lindsay. And I got fired because I took her advice, and now I guess I need to blame someone…" Her voice trailed off as a person caught her eye.

She was aware of Matthew staring at her, wide-eyed, most likely because it was the first he'd heard of her night with Lindsay, but Piper's focus was over his shoulder. On somebody else. A person who'd just come in through the patio door, papers in his hand, chatting with Mark Bloom, who Piper knew was the owner of Lakeshore.

Matthew turned in his stool as he followed her gaze. "Hey, doesn't that redheaded guy work at Vineyard?"

"Oh, no." Piper shook her head back and forth slowly as the realization of what she'd done grabbed her by the throat. Words wouldn't form. She had so many in her head, but they flitted around like moths and she couldn't grasp any of them.

"Oh, Piper." Matthew was looking at her, his disappointment in her so apparent, she wanted to hide from it. "What did you do?"

Piper swallowed hard. "I fired her." The pit of guilt and shame that formed deep in her gut was almost too much to bear, but she couldn't fight it back. All she could do was shake her head and watch as the redheaded kid and Mark walked in the other direction, the kid using his hands animatedly, causing Piper to wonder if he was sharing yet another of Lindsay's ideas for increasing business.

❖

There wasn't much more Matthew could do for her besides look at her with disenchantment—and Piper wasn't sure how much more of that she could take, deserved or not—so they said their goodbyes in the parking lot. He did hug her, and he told her he loved her, which he meant, Piper knew. But for now, she needed to get away from him. She couldn't stand being around somebody who knew what she'd done, how cruel she'd been. Even the rearview mirror taunted her as she sat in the driver's seat of her SUV. She couldn't bear to look at *herself*.

Her cell rang and her heart soared with hope, so she snatched it up and answered without checking the screen. "Hello?"

"Piper?"

"Yes. Who's this?"

"It's Bridget. From Vineyard."

"Oh." Piper tried not to sound as disappointed as she felt. "Hey, Bridget."

"I just drove past and realized there are no lights on." No preamble. No small talk. Bridget obviously didn't like her any more. Unsurprisingly.

"Okay," Piper said, drawing the word out, not sure what was wanted of her.

"We open at two on Saturdays. I left your keys under the big flowerpot on the patio."

All at once, a memory crashed through her skull and sat down heavily. *I can take over running this place*. That's what she'd told Lindsay last night. *Leave your keys with Bridget*. She was responsible for opening now. Shit. "Oh, right. Yes," she finally said to Bridget. "Okay. Thanks for letting me know."

Bridget hung up without saying goodbye.

Piper pressed the End button on her phone and slumped down in her seat. Like a powerful storm over the ocean, everything that had happened to her over the past week suddenly crashed over her, a tidal wave of feelings, of wrong decisions, of grief. And for the first time since her father's funeral, a sob tore its way up from her chest and burst out of her like a small explosion. She cried for her lost job. She cried because she missed her mother. She cried because Matthew was right: she had feelings for Lindsay, and instead of embracing them, she'd lashed out, been unspeakably cruel to her, and had most likely ruined anything good they might have had. She cried because she missed her father so badly, it made her chest ache. And she cried because she had no goddamn idea what she was supposed to do now. But everything had spiraled out of her control, and she felt utterly useless. Helpless. She wanted to fix things. Badly.

Instead, she cried some more because she had no idea how.

❖

Why did Saturday at the wine bar have to be so damn busy?

And when had that happened?

That question ping-ponged its way around Piper's head for nearly seven hours as she ran around like a chicken with its head cut off (a favorite euphemism of her father's that never failed to make her stomach clench in a little bit of horror at the thought of a headless chicken running around), trying to keep a handle on things. And failing.

Sharon was the only employee working aside from Piper herself, and though they could've used another staff member, Piper was glad she didn't have to get into detailed explanations about the situation. Sharon was an old friend of her mother's, so when she asked where Lindsay was, and Piper said that she'd be running things herself tonight (not the whole truth, but not a lie either), Sharon simply nodded and got to work.

Piper'd had to wing it when it came to opening Vineyard for the day, as she had no idea what the procedure was. She did her best, used common sense, which got her to turn on the lights and the music. Thank

God Lindsay had a list tacked to the office wall of the week's specials, so she copied Saturday's to the chalkboard behind the bar. Sharon had arrived at six, and Piper did her best *not* to ask a bunch of questions about how things were normally done. The last thing she wanted was her employees thinking she was utterly incompetent. Which she absolutely was.

The one good thing about having so much to do and so much to figure out was that it kept Piper from dwelling on the biggest issue of her life currently: Lindsay. And that had stopped her in her tracks, because how could the biggest current issue not be the fact that she was unemployed? Not just unemployed, but fired. How had Lindsay taken over first position that way?

Those questions would pop up here and there throughout the night. And then, inevitably, something regarding the wine bar would need tending and she was able to shove the Lindsay thing aside for a while. But over and over, she was faced with what she'd done, what she needed to fix, and how. She had lots of questions and very few answers.

"I'd like to sample the Chilean Malbec," the man at the bar stated, yanking Piper out of her reverie.

She turned her focus to him, recognized him as—what had Lindsay called him?—Mr. Can I Taste That. She gave him a nod, turned and then scanned the wine rack for a full minute before finding the right bottle. It took her another two minutes to pull the cork. She finally poured him what she decided was a sip and slid it across to him.

"That's it?" he asked, gray eyebrows raised.

With a quiet sigh, she splashed a bit more into his glass.

He sipped, made slight grimace. "Hmm. I don't know. It's a bit on the sweet side for me."

Piper reached for his glass, but he pulled it toward him. "So…not that sweet, though, huh?"

He squinted at her for a beat, then finished the wine. A quick glance down at the menu, then back up, and he said, "How about the Chianti?"

By the time he asked for his fourth sample—the Amarone, which Piper knew was expensive—she had been clenching her jaw so tightly, she was sure she'd cracked a molar. And just when she thought she'd reached the end of her rope with this man, Lindsay's voice echoed through her head.

"He's a pain, but I suspect he also has lots of money and possibly some influence. So I'm always careful to take good care of him, no

matter how ridiculous he gets. I don't ever want him to be able to trash Vineyard..."

Damn her and her business logic. Piper turned her back to him, located the Amarone, and forced herself to take in three deep, quiet breaths. Then she poured and smiled at him as she gave him the wine. It occurred to her how proud of her Lindsay would be, at the same time Piper realized she was really not fond of dealing with customers.

By 10:45, there were three patrons left in Vineyard and Piper was beyond exhausted. She was sure part of her fatigue came from the vestiges of her hangover and the fact that being passed out wasn't the same as sleeping. But the rest of it was from her day of working. She'd had no idea how hard it was to be running around, waiting on customers, and not only arranging cheese boards, but cleaning them up as well. She hadn't even touched on any of the paperwork to be dealt with. She couldn't begin to comprehend ordering and distributors and such. Oh, she could figure it all out in time; none of this was beyond her. The truth was, she didn't want to. Because it was Lindsay's job. And Lindsay was good at it.

Yeah...

Piper blew out a breath as the last three folks stood and gathered their things. They waved and thanked her and she waved back. "Come see us again," she said as she followed them to the door and locked it behind them. Then she hit the main lights, turned off the music, and went into the office in the back where she dropped into what used to be her mother's chair, but now what she thought of as Lindsay's. Interesting.

The office smelled like Lindsay as well. Some blend of scents. Coconut. Maybe a little citrus. A bit of musk. Piper wondered if it was a combination of things. Shampoo, lotion, perfume? She had no idea, but she inhaled deeply anyway, taking it in.

Lindsay...

Piper's head fell back against the chair and she felt her eyes well up. God, when had she become such a waterworks?

She needed to talk to Lindsay.

Without giving herself time to talk her way out of it, she picked up her phone.

Can we talk?

She clicked Send.

The clock on the wall ticked loudly, as if rubbing in how much time was passing with no response. Not that Piper was surprised. What

would surprise her? Was if Lindsay ever talked to her again. God, she'd
been horrible. Piper could be a lot of things—and she knew it—cold,
hard, precise, unemotional. But she'd never considered herself to be a
terrible human being.

Until today.

Gina had suggested more than once that she go see a therapist. A
grief counselor to help her deal with the loss of her father. And Piper
had waved it off. Dismissed it easily, saying she didn't need help. Yet
here she was, more than two years after her father's passing, and she
still had times when she felt simply buried by his loss. Literally buried.
She'd woken up in the middle of the night struggling for breath more
than once after dreaming about him, feeling like some enormous weight
sat on her chest, constricting her lungs, as if she'd been buried alive.

He would be so disappointed in her right now.

With a shake of her head, she glanced at her phone, which still
taunted her with no response from Lindsay. She typed out, *Please?* and
clicked Send.

By the time she'd shut everything down and locked the door behind
her, it was 11:30 and there was still no response from Lindsay. Yet
again, Piper's eyes filled with tears and she fought hard, but managed to
keep them from spilling over and running down her cheeks. She needed
sleep. She needed to put this day out of her mind and fall into oblivion.

At home, she gave Edgar some love—more than he wanted,
judging from his halfhearted struggle in her arms—and then located a
bottle of Tylenol PM in her medicine cabinet. Sleep was not going to
elude her tonight.

She tried not to think about how all of her concerns and issues
would still be here in the morning.

CHAPTER TWENTY

Piper had survived Sunday—barely—but getting out of bed on Monday proved to be difficult. She knew exactly why. It was the first official workday at her old company since she'd been fired, and she was having trouble accepting that she was no longer part of that team, that she no longer occupied that managerial role she'd worked so hard to achieve. The combination of that, the situation with Lindsay (who hadn't responded to any of her texts, including the four she'd sent yesterday), and not being able to talk to her father about any of it whirred inside her gut like some sadistic blender and kept her from moving. At all. She was reasonably sure a mild depression was setting in, and she lay there in her bed with no energy whatsoever to do anything, until well after nine.

It took Edgar's not-so-gentle kneading of her chest with his claws, along with his pathetic—and surprisingly loud—yowls to finally get her to groan in annoyance and actually shift a limb or two.

"Fine," she said to him. "*Fine*. I'm glad it's all about you, Eddie." She tossed off the covers, sat up, and rubbed at her eyes. She felt groggy. She'd used the Tylenol PM again last night, and this was the price she had to pay for a somewhat decent night's sleep.

In the kitchen, she popped a pod into the Keurig, then fed Edgar while her coffee brewed. Not even the scent of that first cup, which usually got her going in the morning, could lift her spirits. She felt flattened. It wasn't a feeling she was used to. She didn't like it.

Bridget had practically thrown her out of Vineyard last night.

Okay, maybe that was harsh.

Piper doctored up her coffee, then took it out onto her small back deck, deciding some fresh air might be good for her. She sat in the wooden Adirondack chair her father had given her as a housewarming gift when she'd moved in and watched two chickadees as they nibbled birdseed from the feeder she'd filled for the first time in months.

Sunday at Vineyard hadn't been that busy, and that was probably a good thing. It was the first time, though, that Piper realized just how organized and precise Bridget was at her job. The customers loved her. She knew her wine. She was bubbly and energetic, perfect for dealing with the public. Piper knew Vineyard was lucky to have her, but she was also worried about losing her because one thing had been made very clear yesterday: Bridget was *not* happy with Piper. And anything Piper screwed up annoyed her.

When Piper dropped and shattered a glass, it seemed Bridget had reached her limit.

"You know what?" Bridget had said to her, obviously working hard to keep her voice calm and normal. "Why don't you just go home? I've got this."

"No, it's okay," Piper had protested, even though she wanted nothing more than to simply abandon ship. She'd grabbed the broom and dustpan from the back and was doing her best to clean up the tiny shards of glass.

"Really." Bridget stopped Piper from sweeping with a hand on the broom. "It's not that busy tonight. I can handle it no problem. You look exhausted. Just go. I've got this."

Their gazes held, and there was so much in Bridget's dark brown eyes. Some genuine concern. A lot of irritation. And much to her own surprise, Piper had agreed to go. Honestly, she just needed to get away from that place that was making her feel so utterly incompetent. And she didn't like being there without Lindsay; it was like there was a huge hole nobody was talking about. A hole she'd caused. She'd nodded to Bridget, uttered a soft "Okay," and left the wine bar in Bridget's capable hands.

Then she'd sat in her car in the parking lot and cried for fifteen minutes.

She was a mess.

Piper sipped her coffee, watched the birds flit, and tried not to think about Lindsay. She failed, of course, because as soon as you tell yourself not to think about pink elephants, pink elephants are all you can think about.

Lindsay hadn't answered a single text. Nor any of Piper's three phone calls (which was probably good, as Piper had no idea what she'd say if Lindsay picked up). Piper understood. Completely. She was also frustrated as hell and knew she could not let go of the situation and take any steps forward unless she was able to clear the air with Lindsay. She needed to apologize. She needed to beg her to come back to Vineyard. Even if Lindsay laughed in her face, which she would be totally justified in doing, Piper needed to say it.

God, she needed to say so much to Lindsay.

And that was when she realized the true depth of her feelings. Right then, in that moment. She missed Lindsay physically, yes. In a big way. Despite the fact that they'd only been together that one time, it had left an impression. But even more than that, Piper missed talking to Lindsay. Just talking to her. Lindsay had snuck in, that was for sure. Piper hadn't expected that. She'd dismissed Lindsay right off the bat and Lindsay had surprised her. And now Piper sat on her back deck mentally listing all the things she wished she could talk to Lindsay about right then and there.

What would I say to her if she was right here?

Piper listed it all in her head, one thing at a time. Somehow, it made her feel better.

She watched the birds until she'd finished her coffee. Then she got herself a refill, returned to her seat, and did her best to simply take air in, let air out, hearing her father's voice once again telling her, *Just breathe. Just be.* It was so weird how reminding herself to do something her body did automatically actually helped.

At 1:00, Piper slid her key into the lock and let herself into Vineyard. It smelled clean, and the sun shone brightly through the windows. It felt like the first time she'd really looked at it in ages, which was strange. The first thing that caught her eye was the large, swirly Vineyard sign that was back in its spot on the wall...except it was clean and shiny and...

Piper walked up to it, reached out and ran her fingertips over it.

It had been repainted.

A lump formed in Piper's throat and her eyes welled. Lindsay had had it repainted. And sanded, by the looks of it, by the smoothness under Piper's hand.

She looked up at the ceiling, irritated at the Universe. "You know, I'm getting it. Okay? I know it takes me a while sometimes, but you don't have to *keep* hitting me with things. You can ease up for a day or two." Piper wondered when it had been brought here. Had Bridget called Lindsay to tell her Piper was gone last night?

They probably text all the time about what a disaster I am here.

Piper didn't like that idea, but knew it was likely.

God, she'd fucked up. Piper didn't use that word often at all, and she didn't use it lightly. It was most appropriate here, though. She made mistakes all the time, just like every other human being on the planet. But this wasn't a mistake. She had *royally fucked up*. And even though she intended to find a way to try and fix it, she had to accept that fixing it might not be possible, that she most likely damaged things beyond repair. That was a tough one to swallow.

She was just about to dive into the alarmingly full email inbox when her cell rang. A glance told her it was Gina, whom she'd blown off with a variety of "I'll call you later" texts over the weekend. Piper took a deep breath and answered.

"Hey there."

"For God's sake, Piper, when you tell somebody you're going to call, you have to call. Especially when they're worried about you and they've made it very clear they're worried about you." Gina's voice was a combination of frantic, hurt, and angry. Piper let her go on a bit longer.

"I know. I know. You're right. I'm sorry."

"Are you okay?"

"I am."

"Yeah, I'm going to need more than that." The warning edge in her sister's tone was all the clue Piper needed that Gina was going to blow soon.

"Okay." Piper took a deep breath and launched in. Gina had known about the firing because Matthew had shared that with her, but she didn't know details. Piper told her everything about it, why she'd done what she'd done, Lindsay's part in it, the resulting fallout. Without giving Gina any opportunity to interrupt with questions or comments, she launched into the details about Lindsay. The date at the fishing shack, the mind-melting sex. She finished up with Piper's ridiculously misguided blame and consequent firing of her.

"That's it." Piper felt a strange sense of relief having laid it all out like that.

There was silence on the other end of the call.

"Gina? You there?"

"Uh-huh."

"I'm done. You can talk now."

Another beat of silence went by before Gina finally said, "I have no idea what to say to all of that."

Piper grunted. "Yeah, well, if you're thinking of yelling at me and telling me what a complete asshole I am, please don't. I've told myself that enough times over the past couple of days. I don't need to hear it from others. I just…" She blew out a breath of frustration. "I need to fix it and I'm not sure how."

"I'm assuming you mean with Lindsay."

"Yes."

"I agree. You really do. You've texted?"

"About a dozen times," Piper said. "No response."

"You've called?"

"No answer." Piper pursed her lips. "I was thinking of going to her house…"

"No." Gina said it quickly. Firmly. "You can't do that."

"Why not?"

"Because that's her territory. One, you can't really invade *her* space to speak *your* piece. That's not cool. And two, it's not an even playing field. You're at a disadvantage. You have to catch her someplace neutral."

Piper was nodding as Gina spoke. "Yeah, that's a good point."

"You know what you want to say to her?" Gina's voice had softened a bit.

"Some, yeah. The rest will come to me. I hope."

"Well, you know some of her routine. Think about what she does each day and if there's a neutral place where she might be willing to talk to you."

"She won't answer my texts, so it's not like I can set up a date and time." Piper rolled her eyes.

"You're the one who messed up, so it's only fair that you're the one who has to do all the work here. You're a smart girl, P. You'll figure it out."

Gina was right, because even as she was speaking to her, Piper was already thinking of the perfect place. If she could just get Lindsay to stop and listen to her for five minutes, maybe she could fix this whole thing. Maybe she could get Lindsay to come back to Vineyard.

"I will. Thanks, Gina."

"Any time, little sister of mine." She paused before asking, "What about you? Are you okay? I mean, getting fired…"

"Sucks. Hugely." Piper sat back in the chair, somehow feeling a tiny bit lighter. "But I'll be okay. What about you? Enjoying your summer break?" The topic shift was obvious, but Piper needed it and Gina seemed to understand. As she talked about her upcoming vacation and how stressful the planning had become, how hard it was to wrangle the kids, Piper scanned the office. There were papers tacked to the wall, schedules and memos and ads. There were three piles on the desk, but they were neat. Lindsay was obviously organized and took pride in her work, things Piper knew but had conveniently forgotten in her drunken tirade. She listened to Gina with one ear, but much of her attention was elsewhere. She felt off balance, like she was standing on a precipice and the rocks beneath her feet were precariously unstable. She was either going to steady herself or she was going to plunge over the side of a cliff; she had no idea which. But it didn't matter because she was charging ahead anyway.

Piper was going to fix this, even if it killed her.

❖

Tuesday's forecast predicted hot and muggy weather, so Lindsay wanted to get Rocket outside, get him to burn off some energy, before it became too sticky for either of them to move.

It had been a rough weekend, so getting out into the fresh air, among the trees and near the water, felt good. Like a relief somehow. Lindsay had stayed holed up in her house for pretty much the entire past three days, aside from dropping the sign back off at Vineyard. She'd asked Bridget to let her know when Piper wasn't there so she could bring it by without having to run into her. The text had come Sunday night.

Had to send her home before I killed her. Safe to drop off sign if you want.

Bridget's words had been bittersweet. On the one hand, a part of Lindsay got a little tingle of satisfaction knowing Piper wasn't running things like the well-oiled machine she probably thought it would be. On the other hand, most of Lindsay did not find joy in Piper's failures. Despite how horrible Piper had made her feel.

Doing her best not to reflect back on that awful conversation didn't always work. Like now. Piper's words echoed in Lindsay's head as if she were standing right in front of her again.

You're just the bartender.

Of everything she'd said, of every hurtful sentence, that one was the worst. When Lindsay looked back, she saw the fight as a movie. Each terrible thing Piper said backed Lindsay up until she hit a window, fell through, and was dangling from the sill. And with *those* words—telling her she was just a bartender—Piper stepped on Lindsay's fingers, sending her plunging down into oblivion.

How could Piper think Lindsay was trying to erase Mr. B.? Lindsay had such a hard time with that...although when she really thought about it, she could sort of see how it might look that way from where Piper sat. But it wasn't at all Lindsay's intention, and she wished so badly Piper had given her the chance to say so, to apologize for making her feel that way.

For three days, Lindsay had done her best to cut Piper some slack. She'd obviously been fired on Friday—her comment couldn't really be read any other way—and Lindsay wondered if Piper had done what she'd been trying not to: warned her staff about upcoming layoffs. Lindsay secretly hoped she had. Even if it got her fired, it was the right thing to do, and Lindsay had to believe Piper knew that.

She whistled for Rocket, who'd gotten ahead of her. They were nearing the parking lot, and she liked to leash him so he didn't hop his overly-friendly, usually mud-covered butt into some stranger's car to say hello. When he didn't come right back, she picked up her pace and whistled again. She'd started to jog and was just about to the edge of the lot when she skidded to a stop.

Piper.

She was in a squat, giving tons of attention to Rocket who, of course, was ecstatic to see her. His thick tail wagged so hard it made his entire body sway from one side to the other as he made little whimpers of happiness. Piper looked tired. Spent. There were dark circles under her eyes and her color was drab. And yet she still looked beautiful. Lindsay didn't want her to. Lindsay wanted to see her, be completely turned off, and stand there stone-faced. Unaffected. What's that phrase? Best laid plans...? Yeah, because Piper was gorgeous, even in her state of obvious exhaustion. Even in her casual attire. Especially in her casual attire. She had workout pants on. Black. Tight-fitting. Knee-length so her bare legs were visible from the knees down and Lindsay had an unexpected flash of having her hands, her mouth all over those ridiculous legs. Her shirt was white, short-sleeved, with a small logo on the left chest that Lindsay couldn't quite make out. Flip-flops on her feet. Dark, wavy hair in a bouncy ponytail that Lindsay had decided the first time she'd seen it was her favorite look on Piper. It made her face more visible, those dimples easily seen. They only made a quick, peek-a-boo appearance as she looked up and saw Lindsay, though. Her smile was uncertain, hesitant, and came and went in a snap.

"Hi," she said as she stood up, one hand still on Rocket's head as he bumped against her thigh.

Lindsay tried to say hi, had to clear her throat first. "Hey."

"Do you have a minute?" Piper asked.

With a shrug, Lindsay replied, "I have a lot of minutes now. What with being unemployed and all."

Piper nodded, bit down on her bottom lip, which shouldn't have been sexy given the situation, but was anyway.

Lindsay silently cursed her.

"I know. I wanted to talk to you about that."

Lindsay closed the distance between them, but only long enough to clip on Rocket's leash. Then she stepped back again, putting a safe amount of space between them, having to drag Rocket with her.

Piper was nervous. Lindsay finally looked at her directly enough to see it. Her hands had a slight tremble in them, which Lindsay could see in the papers she held in one hand. The corners shook just a bit, as if some unseen force was sending a vibration through them. Her eye contact was there, but spotty. She'd look at Lindsay, then look away, then look back, as if holding it for too long was painful. Lindsay had the fleeting thought that she wanted to help her, wanted to ease her discomfort somehow.

You're just the bartender.

Yeah, that desire to help went right out the window. Lindsay stood silently, folded her arms across her chest, and waited.

Piper shifted her weight from foot to foot, then chuckled uneasily. "I had this all mapped out in my head, what I was going to say. Seems it's all left me."

Lindsay shrugged. "Well, I need to get Rocket home to—"

"No, wait." Piper held up a hand. "Please."

Lindsay ran her tongue around the inside of her mouth and waited.

"I'm sorry." Piper nodded once, as if coming to an understanding of some sort. "I guess that's the best place to start here. I'm sorry, and I should've said it sooner."

"You should have."

"I know. I'm sorry about that, too. So I'm doubly sorry."

Piper cleared her throat, and Lindsay wondered if she was buying time while she sorted out her words.

"I was in a really bad place on Friday." She held up a hand again as if Lindsay had been about to interrupt. "Which is not an excuse. I know that. But I wanted to let you know my state of mind, because it didn't help me with clarity." She cleared her throat a second time. "Thursday night, I had a secret meeting with my staff and I warned them that the upcoming merger would mean layoffs for them. My bosses found out, and Friday morning, I was fired."

Lindsay made eye contact then, wanted to say something, but thought better of it.

A very subtle smile tugged up one corner of Piper's mouth, though. "It was the right thing to do," she said quietly.

Lindsay gave a nod, feeling oddly proud of Piper, but again, deciding that it wasn't the right time to say so.

"I know that now, but on Friday, I was a wreck. I've never been fired before. I don't get fired. I didn't know what to do and I didn't handle it well. I got pretty drunk." At Lindsay's silent, "duh," Piper chuckled. "Yeah. Not my smartest decision. I would normally have talked to my dad about it, but..." Her smile faded. "You ended up taking the brunt of my frustration, my anger, my fear, my missing of my father. I piled it all onto you, and I'm so very sorry about that."

There was genuine emotion on Piper's face, something Lindsay hardly ever saw, and something about it seemed to mend her heart just a tiny bit. It was like her heart had developed a series of cracks, and Piper's words were the glue. They spread across one of the cracks, fusing the flesh back together. A small lump had developed in Lindsay's throat, preventing words. She nodded.

"I'd like for you to come back to Vineyard. I have many reasons for that."

Lindsay found her voice. "Like what?"

It was Piper's turn to nod, as if she'd expected this question. "One, we need you. The staff needs you. The customers are asking about you. It doesn't feel the same there without your energy. Two, I suck at your job."

Lindsay felt the smile, couldn't help it.

"Seriously. I almost killed Mr. Can I Taste That the other day. And I don't know how to place the orders. I know nothing about the cheese. The staff hates me." She tipped her head from side to side. "Rightfully so, really. And three, I thought you might like the opportunity to confront—and then fire—Zack."

Lindsay raised her eyebrows in surprise. "What?"

"Yeah, he's the one who's been taking your ideas over to Lakeshore. I saw him there on Friday, talking with the owner. He seemed pretty comfortable."

"Wow."

"Yeah. I mean, I'll do it if you want. I've fired people before." The shock on her face was immediate. "Like…other than you."

Lindsay stared at her for a beat before they both allowed themselves to laugh just a little.

"One more thing," Piper said. "I did a little research and noticed that you hadn't signed yourself up for the sommelier certification, so…" She handed the papers over to Lindsay. "I took the liberty of doing it for you. Whether or not you want to come back to Vineyard, you should do it. You're a natural and you love it. That's obvious." Piper kept her eyes on the papers as Lindsay slowly reached out and took them. "It's Tuesday and Thursday nights for six weeks. I can cover those nights at Vineyard. I mean, if you decide to come back. And if you don't decide to come back, you should go anyway. You're all registered. Your fee is paid either way. It's the least I can do."

And just like that, Piper seemed to run out of steam. She stopped talking. She toed the dirt on the ground. She nibbled on the inside of her cheek and kept her eyes on Rocket. Lindsay saw her swallow once and shift her weight again, like she wasn't sure what her next move should be.

"I'll need some time to think," Lindsay finally said, her voice quiet.

Piper nodded. "Oh, sure. Sure. Take all the time you need. That's fine. Totally."

"Okay. Is that all?" They stood there, gazes held. This was good. It was all good…but there was more. More Lindsay needed to hear. More she needed to feel. She waited until those hazel eyes darted away and Piper shifted her weight yet again. Lindsay swallowed, sighed quietly, shook her head slowly back and forth. "You just don't get it, do you?" She smiled sadly. She wasn't angry. She didn't raise her voice. Piper's eyes widened, her confusion obvious, and they stood there for another ten or fifteen seconds before Lindsay held up the papers and said, "All right. We've got to get home."

Piper stayed rooted to her spot, even as Lindsay watched her in the rearview mirror as she pulled away.

No. Piper didn't get it.

But would she ever?

"Wow," Angela said later that day as they sat on Lindsay's back deck sipping a velvety Merlot and munching on extra sharp cheddar with stone ground crackers. "I'm going to bet that took a huge amount out of her."

Lindsay squinted at her friend. "What do you mean?"

It was very warm out, but Lindsay had opened the umbrella that stood between their chairs, and the shade kept them comfortable. Rocket lounged on the wood by Lindsay's feet, exhausted from his day of running through the trees and chasing squirrels in the backyard. When Angela had called Sunday morning and Lindsay had filled her in on the latest happenings, they'd set up this date immediately, and she'd come right from her office, still in her dress slacks and high heels.

"I mean that from everything you've told me about this woman, apologizing isn't something she does often. Because she's usually right."

"Or thinks she is."

"That, too. My point being, she made some huge effort here. You've ignored her texts. You've ignored her messages. She could've just given up."

"And she didn't."

"And she didn't." Angela held up a finger while she took a sip of her wine. "*And* not only did she not give up, she found you."

"She stalked me."

"That, too. *And* not only did she find you, she registered you for the wine thingy." Angela raised her eyebrows and gave a nod, as if she'd just made a very important point.

Lindsay couldn't help the chuckle that bubbled up. "Always with the bright side," she said.

"Hey, the bright side is important." She joined Lindsay in her mirth, but then became serious again. "I just think you should take into consideration that it was obviously important to her to apologize to you. Yeah, she was late to the party with it, but some people need time to retreat and think about stuff, you know? And, call me crazy, but I think you really like this one. Like, really like her." They both knew what Angela meant, but left the words unspoken. "I think she moves you."

She moves me. That was an alarmingly accurate way to describe how Lindsay felt about the time she'd spent with Piper. She looked off in the distance and sipped her wine. After a beat, she said softly, "Yeah, that's exactly it. And I need to hear that I move her, too. You know?"

Angela nodded. "I do." Another moment of quiet passed before she reached over the space between them and grasped Lindsay's forearm. "Don't write her off completely until you think about it. Promise me."

Lindsay nodded her assent. "I promise."

She'd never broken a promise to Angela in all the time they'd been friends and she wouldn't start now. What amused her was that there was no way Lindsay *could* write her off, even if she wanted to. Because Piper Bradshaw had been pretty much all she'd thought about since Friday. And all the texts, all the messages had done nothing other than ensure she'd keep thinking about her. She didn't mean to sigh as loudly as she did, but Angela heard her and tightened her grip on Lindsay's arm.

"Did you talk to Maya and Bert about her?" Lindsay's responding snort was all Angela needed. "Let me guess. They told you to run away. Far and fast."

"Pretty much, yeah. Mostly Maya, but…"

"Bert will agree with anything her wife says."

"Pretty much, yeah."

A beat went by before Angela said quietly, "It'll be okay, Linds. You got this."

But did she? Lindsay wasn't sure. At all. She'd never been this undecided before. There were so many cons and just as many pros. Could Lindsay work with Piper? Would she want to? Could she survive it? Did Piper have the same feelings as she did? If so, could she admit it? If not, what then? Could Lindsay still handle seeing her every day? Could they concentrate on a friendship and nothing more?

So many questions. Endless questions. They ricocheted around Lindsay's head until she could barely remember where she was. Angela sat with her, still holding on to her arm, sipping her wine and watching the summer afternoon laze on by.

She was going to have to wait Piper out. It was the only solution. She couldn't nudge her. She didn't want to. Piper had to make the move.

The question was, how long could Lindsay wait?

CHAPTER TWENTY-ONE

It was late.

Piper glanced at her watch. 11:47 on Wednesday night. Vineyard had been closed for over an hour now, and Piper sat at Lindsay's desk, only a small lamp lighting up her work space, as she tried to get some things done. Things she'd been putting off because she not only hated them, but she was terrible at them. This had become the story of her life now.

Like ordering.

She was terrible at ordering.

Piper sighed. She couldn't *not* order wine. Hello? Wine bar? She also couldn't just continue to duplicate the weekly orders Lindsay had put in over the past month. Things needed to be changed up every so often to keep things fresh. A stale menu was a good way to keep customers bored and uninclined to return.

She scratched the back of her head and tried to focus on the email from Mike, one of the wine vendors Lindsay dealt with regularly. The email was addressed to Lindsay. Frankly, Piper hadn't gotten around to letting people know Lindsay was no longer here. Maybe that was because Piper didn't want to admit it to herself, even though it was her fault. She knew she should probably tell her mother as well, but if she was being honest with herself, Piper knew she was still waiting, still hoping that Lindsay would walk back through the door, ready to try again.

This entire train of thought had become circular for Piper since she watched Lindsay drive away from the lake...she checked her watch...almost thirty-nine hours ago. Around and around. Asking the same questions. Failing to answer any of them. She needed to stop or she'd drive herself nuts.

With a literal shake of her head, she squeezed her eyes shut to clear the sleep out of them, opened, and focused on the email. Mike was touting the wonderfulness of a new red blend and reported how blends were now selling more than both Pinot Noir and Merlot. Blends were big. Lindsay had been telling her that for weeks now. Mike had even included a link that detailed how it was made.

"Can't hurt to learn, I guess," Piper said to the empty office, sighed another sigh (she'd been doing a lot of that lately), and clicked.

The article detailed what went into the process of making Smoke and Mirrors Red, a new blend from a winery on the outskirts of Napa Valley. Piper was surprised to find herself drawn into the narrative. In the interview, the winemaker talked about how he started with a base, in this case, a Zinfandel. But he needed help, another opinion, so asked his wife to brainstorm with him. Together, they thought about food pairings, about occasions for the wine, and what kind of taste they were shooting for. They added a touch of Cabernet Franc to get a little bit of spice. They tasted again, added some Grenache to lighten things up. Tasted again. Put in a little Syrah for depth and richness.

The whole thing fascinated Piper, and she devoured the entire article right to the end. The last paragraph, which described the finished product, stopped her in her tracks. She read it. She read it again.

And then she got it.

Finally.

A weight lifted from her shoulders in that instant. That was what it felt like. As if a literal twenty pounds had been taken off her body, and she sat up straighter, breathed easier than she had in nearly a week.

You just don't get it, do you?

As Lindsay's voice echoed through her head, a huge smile broke across Piper's face.

"I do now, Lindsay. I do now."

She picked up her phone, typed out a text—deleting and rewording several times before hitting Send—and packed up her things.

She had plans to make.

Lindsay hesitated at the door.

She'd been sure. Then she hadn't. Then she had. Then she hadn't. This morning, she had and she seemed to stay there, at "sure," until she reached out and actually grasped the door handle of Vineyard. Then "not so sure" came squealing back like a zigzagging toddler, running through the room screaming at the top of its lungs.

So she stood there, gripping the door handle, and took in a couple big lungsful of air.

"Just breathe," she whispered to herself. "You're okay. Just breathe."

She lifted her chin, pulled the door open, and went inside.

Vineyard wasn't open yet, not for another hour, but the lights were on, soft jazz emanated from the speakers, and a table in the middle of the room was set. Well, sort of set. It was covered with a white linen tablecloth. There were two empty wine glasses and a bottle of wine sitting there, along with a small bud vase containing one red rose, and a set of small votive candles, both lit and flickering. Lindsay stared for a moment, brow furrowed, before looking up to see Piper standing next to the bar.

She looked radiant, and that was new. Lindsay had always thought Piper beautiful, from the very beginning, even when she was angry with her. But this…this was definitely new. There was something else there. She wore dark jeans with black sandals on her feet, her toes polished an apropos wine color. Her top was a black tank, form-fitting and alarmingly sexy. Her hair was in a ponytail, and as she stood with her hands clasped loosely in front of her, a soft smile on her face, Lindsay struggled to figure out this new…aura? She didn't know how else to classify it. But it was different and it was shimmery and Piper was *radiant*.

"Hi," she said, and took a step toward Lindsay with her arm held out to indicate the table. "Sit. Please."

Lindsay squinted at her slightly before doing as she was asked. Once she was seated, Piper picked up the bottle and used her wine key to open it. She only struggled a bit, and when Lindsay grinned, Piper grinned back.

"I got it," she said, cranking the corkscrew.

"You do. I see that."

The cork gave a pop as it was pulled free. Piper cleared her throat.

"This is Magical Vineyard's Smoke and Mirrors Red Blend." Piper poured the crimson wine into one glass, then the other. "I was reading about it the other night. It was nearly midnight and I was trying not to dwell on how bad I am at doing the ordering, on how much this wine bar misses you." She made eye contact then, those hazel eyes snagging and holding Lindsay's. "Needs you." She handed a glass to Lindsay, then picked up her own, held it to the light, swirled it. "So, I was reading about this *blend*." She stressed the word, which made Lindsay smile again. "And the more I read, the more interested I became. I learned all about how it was made, about the selection of different grapes and which made the most sense. But one thing really struck me."

Lindsay was captivated. She didn't understand it and she couldn't explain it. But she went with it.

Piper swirled the wine, as Lindsay had taught her to, and Lindsay did the same. They each held their glasses up to the light, observed the deep crimson of it, the tears that ran down the inside of the glass.

Lindsay continued to be mesmerized by Piper, couldn't seem to even begin to break eye contact. As Piper stuck her nose in the glass and inhaled—and Lindsay followed suit—their gazes held.

They sipped.

It was delicious. Complex. Lindsay could taste several different grapes, and the combination was velvety smooth and intricate. She gave a nod. "It's impressive."

"Isn't it? As I said, one thing about the process of making such a perfect blend stayed with me. I was struck by the final description of it. So struck that I memorized it." Piper cleared her throat, looked directly at Lindsay, and said, "With this blend, each component, though clearly present, is subordinate to the whole."

Lindsay swallowed, wondering at the intensity of Piper's gaze.

"It occurred to me that such a description also applies to us." Piper's voice had gone very soft, almost delicate. "All of our best attributes, yours and mine, come together to make a magnificent whole. None of them overshadows another. They simply…blend."

The lump in Lindsay's throat hadn't gone down with the last swallow, and she tried again as her vision blurred slightly.

"I want you to come back to Vineyard, Lindsay. It misses you. It needs you. But more than that…I miss you and I need you. I want you to come back to me." Piper's beautiful hazel eyes glistened with unshed tears as she stood there, gazing down at Lindsay. "Please, Lindsay. I love you. Come back to me."

Lindsay sat there for another beat as she felt her heart seem to expand in her chest. She searched Piper's face, saw nothing there but raw, pure emotion—something new for Piper. Maybe that was why she looked so different. It was as if she'd been cracked open and a warm, soft glow was now spilling out of her, lighting up the wine bar with its warmth. Lindsay couldn't get enough of it, wanted to simply bask in it for the remainder of the day, the week, her life. One tear spilled over and coursed slowly down Piper's cheek, and she didn't look scared. She didn't look sad. She looked hopeful. And loving. And Lindsay could barely believe what was happening, how it filled her heart, nourished her very soul.

She stood up, left her wine on the white tablecloth, and then took Piper's face tenderly in her hands. Using her thumb, she wiped the wetness from the tear away and smiled, then pressed a gentle kiss to those soft lips, lips she suddenly knew she was going to kiss for the rest of her days. In the quietest of whispers, she said, "Oh, Piper. You finally get it. I love you, too."

EPILOGUE

Three months later

When the door to Gina's house opened, Piper couldn't believe her eyes. It was her mother, yes, but some new and improved version. Before she had more time to analyze the view, she was wrapped up in her mother's arms. Tightly. Warmth and love enveloped her.

"Piper, my girl," her mom whispered in her ear. "I missed you so much."

Piper was no longer surprised to feel her eyes well up, as this seemed to be the new version of her—sappy and emotional—and she squeezed her mom tighter, using the extra time to pull herself together. When she felt it was safe, she pushed out of the hug, but kept a grip on her mother's upper arms, holding her at arm's length and making a show of looking her up and down.

"Mom. Seriously. You look amazing." It was true. She was tan—not overly so, but in a way that made her appear healthy and vibrant. Her hair was sun-streaked, the chestnut brown shot through with glimmers of golden blond. She'd put on a little weight around the middle, which was good, as Piper had worried about her being too skinny ever since her father died.

Her mom dismissed the compliment with a good-natured wave and reached both arms out past Piper. "Lindsay, sweetheart, come here."

Piper watched as her mother pulled Lindsay into a big hug, Lindsay's gaze locking on Piper's over her shoulder, a smile on her face. "I missed you, Mrs. B. I'm glad you're back."

"Get in here, you guys," Gina called from the dining room. "It's chilly out."

Piper and Lindsay took off their jackets and draped them over a chair, then followed Ellen into the dining room where Gina had laid out enough munchies to feed twenty people.

"Um, Gina? Who else is coming?" Lindsay asked as she handed over two bottles of wine she'd brought. "Did you invite your entire class and not tell us?"

"Ha ha. You're hilarious." Gina took the bottles.

"Girls," Ellen said, and her tone had softened considerably as she moved to stand next to a handsome man who stood quietly off to the side. He was tall with salt-and-pepper hair, a neatly trimmed mustache and goatee, and kind blue eyes. "This is Jeffrey."

Piper stood still, not exactly staring at Jeffrey, but unable to stop looking at him, at the way his arm rested on her mother's shoulders. A gentle nudge in her back told her Lindsay was prodding her. "Um. Sorry. Hi." She held out a hand. "I'm Piper."

Jeffrey's hand was large, warm, and he didn't try to out-firm Piper with his grip. "Piper, it's so nice to finally meet you. Your mother talks about you girls nonstop."

Piper could feel Lindsay's hand on the small of her back, and somehow, that made things right. "It's nice to meet you as well." Jeffrey's existence—and his new role in her mother's life—weren't a surprise. She'd brought him up in phone conversation about two months ago, so Piper and Gina had had time to get used to the idea of their mother with a boyfriend, but it was still just as weird to see it as Piper expected it would be.

"Hi. I'm Lindsay." Lindsay's voice yanked Piper back to the situation at hand.

"Piper's girlfriend," Mrs. B. said quietly, but not so quietly that both she and Piper didn't hear it.

"Lindsay." Jeffrey's face lit up as he shook her hand. "I've heard all about you as well." To Mrs. B., he said, "You're right. They're gorgeous together."

Piper felt her face heat up as Lindsay glanced at her, eyebrows raised in a clear statement of *what was that?* Piper gave her a subtle shrug as Gina ushered them into seats. Gina's husband was out of town on business and the kids were both off with friends, having seen their grandmother the night before, so it was just the five of them.

For the next hour, they relaxed, laughed, drank and ate as Ellen regaled them with tales of her travels, how she'd only been in Florida alone, then had met up with Jeffrey and spent the rest of her time crisscrossing the country with him.

"I can't believe you met him online and never told us," Piper said, trying hard to keep any irritation out of her voice. She felt Lindsay's hand on her thigh, squeezing gently.

Ellen nodded. "I know. But I'd never met him in person, and if it hadn't worked out, if we hadn't clicked while face-to-face the way we did in messages, what would have been the point?"

"Yeah." Piper could admit to understanding that.

"Plus, I wanted to spend time with him without other eyes on us." She gave him a glance so filled with happiness that it brought tears to Piper's eyes. Not for the first time, she cursed Lindsay for having cracked her open to emotion—it seemed like everything made Piper tear up lately. "And you two," Ellen said, pointing a finger at Piper and Lindsay and moving it back and forth between them. "This. I knew you'd make a great couple. I knew it." She laughed again, obviously thrilled, then turned to Gina. "Didn't I tell you?"

Gina had the good sense to look at least slightly sheepish. "You called it, Mom."

"Wait, what?" Piper looked from her sister to her mother and back.

"Though it was close." Gina went on as if Piper hadn't spoken. "Your daughter is a hardhead and almost screwed it all up. Thank God she worked hard to fix it. And that Lindsay gave her the chance to." She popped a cracker topped with bruschetta into her mouth and grinned at her little sister.

There was a beat of silence before Piper asked, "What is happening right now?"

"I think," Lindsay said, reaching for a knife. "I *think* your mother and sister are saying that leaving you and me to work together wasn't totally innocent on their parts. That it was a plan of sorts." She looked at them. "Yes?"

Ellen picked up her wine glass and hid her smile behind it as she nodded.

"Mom!" Piper burst out. "You...I can't believe it." She snapped her head to the left to glare at Gina. "And *you*. You're my big sister. You're supposed to look out for me."

"Oh, I did," Gina said, then sipped her own wine, completely unaffected by her little sister's bluster. "You needed somebody. You needed *Lindsay*. I agreed with Mom. It was time. That *was* me looking out for you."

Piper blinked in disbelief. She tried to speak but could only stammer, words seeming to refuse to form in her mouth as she tried to absorb what she'd just heard. Her mother and sister both looked infuriatingly satisfied with themselves. Jeffrey sat, quietly eating some cheese, his face a canvas of entertained amusement as he chewed. Piper shifted her focus to Lindsay, who was spreading tapenade on a piece of baguette. When their eyes met, Piper raised her eyebrows in expectation.

Lindsay shook her head. "Don't look at me. I kind of like how things turned out. I'm not going to argue. The ends clearly justify the means here." Her smile was radiant as she reached up and stroked Piper's cheek with the backs of her fingers. "I made out like a bandit, so..." She shrugged.

And just like that, all the tension drained out of Piper like water near an open drain. She had no idea how Lindsay did it, but she created calm for Piper. Safety. She held the world at bay if that's what Piper needed. She was steadiness, certainty. Piper had never felt as relaxed as she had over the past two months. She grasped Lindsay's hand, kissed the knuckles, and entwined their fingers.

"It took a while, though," Lindsay added playfully as she looked at the others around the table. "I made her work for it."

Laughter erupted around the table as Piper grinned at her. "I wore you down, though."

"You did. I couldn't take your sad puppy dog eyes anymore." Lindsay groaned. "And the sad sighing. Oh, my God, the *sighing*!"

Piper laughed and playfully slapped at her shoulder. "Hey, it worked."

"It did," Lindsay said. Gina, Ellen, and Jeffrey began talking about something, but their voices faded. Lindsay stopped laughing, but that gorgeous smile stayed in place, and for just a moment, the world fell away until it was only the two of them, only their hearts beating, only two pairs of eyes looking deeply into the other.

I love you, Lindsay mouthed, her eyes sparkling like sunlight off the water.

"Love you back," Piper whispered.

Then they turned back to the others and the volume on the world increased again. They were part of this family. They were part of something bigger than themselves.

They were together.

About the Author

Georgia Beers is an award-winning author of nearly twenty lesbian romances. She resides in upstate New York, where she was born and raised. When not writing, she enjoys too much TV, too little wine, not enough time in the gym, and long walks with her dog. She is currently hard at work on her next book. You can visit her and find out more at www.georgiabeers.com.

Books Available From Bold Strokes Books

A Call Away by KC Richardson. Can a businesswoman from a big city find the answers she's looking for, and possibly love, on a small-town farm? (978-1-63555-025-2)

Berlin Hungers by Justine Saracen. Can the love between an RAF woman and the wife of a Luftwaffe pilot, former enemies, survive in besieged Berlin during the aftermath of World War II? (978-1-63555-116-7)

Blend by Georgia Beers. Lindsay and Piper are like night and day. Working together won't be easy, but not falling in love might prove the hardest job of all. (978-1-63555-189-1)

Hunger for You by Jenny Frame. Principe of an ancient vampire clan Byron Debrek must save her one true love from falling into the hands of her enemies and into the middle of a vampire war. (978-1-63555-168-6)

Mercy by Michelle Larkin. FBI Special Agent Mercy Parker and psychic ex-profiler Piper Vasey learn to love again as they race to stop a man with supernatural gifts who's bent on annihilating humankind. (978-1-63555-202-7)

Pride and Porters by Charlotte Greene. Will pride and prejudice prevent these modern-day lovers from living happily ever after? (978-1-63555-158-7)

Rocks and Stars by Sam Ledel. Kyle's struggle to own who she is and what she really wants may end up landing her on the bench and without the woman of her dreams. (978-1-63555-156-3)

The Boss of Her: Office Romance Novellas by Julie Cannon, Aurora Rey, and M. Ullrich. Going to work never felt so good. Three office romance novellas from talented writers Julie Cannon, Aurora Rey, and M. Ullrich. (978-1-63555-145-7)

The Deep End by Ellie Hart. When family ties become entangled in murder and deception, it's time to find a way out... (978-1-63555-288-1)

A Country Girl's Heart by Dena Blake. When Kat Jackson gets a second chance at love, following her heart will prove the hardest decision of all. (978-1-63555-134-1)

Dangerous Waters by Radclyffe. Life, death, and war on the home front. Two women join forces against a powerful opponent, nature itself. (978-1-63555-233-1)

Fury's Death by Brey Willows. When all we hold sacred fails, who will be there to save us? (978-1-63555-063-4)

It's Not a Date by Heather Blackmore. Kade's desire to keep things with Jen on a professional level is in Jen's best interest. Yet what's in Kade's best interest…is Jen. (978-1-63555-149-5)

Killer Winter by Kay Bigelow. Just when she thought things could get no worse, homicide Lieutenant Leah Samuels learns the woman she loves has betrayed her in devastating ways. (978-1-63555-177-8)

Score by MJ Williamz. Will an addiction to pain pills destroy Ronda's chance with the woman she loves, or will she come out on top and score a happily ever after? (978-1-62639-807-8)

Spring's Wake by Aurora Rey. When wanderer Willa Lange falls for Provincetown B&B owner Nora Calhoun, will past hurts and a fifteen-year age gap keep them from finding love? (978-1-63555-035-1)

The Northwoods by Jane Hoppen. When Evelyn Bauer, disguised as her dead husband, George, travels to a Northwoods logging camp to work, she and the camp cook Sarah Bell forge a friendship fraught with both tenderness and turmoil. (978-1-63555-143-3)

Truth or Dare by C. Spencer. For a group of six lesbian friends, life changes course after one long snow-filled weekend. (978-1-63555-148-8)

Children of the Healer by Barbara Ann Wright. Life becomes desperate for ex-soldier Cordelia Ross when the indigenous aliens of her planet are drawn into a civil war and old enemies linger in the shadows. Book Three of the Godfall Series. (978-1-63555-031-3)

A Heart to Call Home by Jeannie Levig. When Jessie Weldon returns to her hometown after thirty years, can she and her childhood crush Dakota Scott heal the tragic past that links them? (978-1-63555-059-7)

Hearts Like Hers by Melissa Brayden. Coffee shop owner Autumn Primm is ready to cut loose and live a little, but is the baggage that comes with out-of-towner Kate Carpenter too heavy for anything long term? (978-1-63555-014-6)

Love at Cooper's Creek by Missouri Vaun. Shaw Daily flees corporate life to find solace in the rural Blue Ridge Mountains, but escapism eludes her when her attentions are captured by small town beauty Kate Elkins. (978-1-62639-960-0)

Twice in a Lifetime by PJ Trebelhorn. Detective Callie Burke can't deny the growing attraction to her late friend's widow, Taylor Fletcher, who also happens to own the bar where Callie's sister works. (978-1-63555-033-7)

Undiscovered Affinity by Jane Hardee. Will a no-strings-attached affair be enough to break Olivia's control and convince Cardic that love does exist? (978-1-63555-061-0)

Between Sand and Stardust by Tina Michele. Are the lifelong bonds of love strong enough to conquer time, distance, and heartache when Haven Thorne and Willa Bennette are given another chance at forever? (978-1-62639-940-2)

Charming the Vicar by Jenny Frame. When magician and atheist Finn Kane seeks refuge in an English village after a spiritual crisis, can local vicar Bridget Claremont restore her faith in life and love? (978-1-63555-029-0)

Data Capture by Jesse J. Thoma. Lola Walker is undercover on the hunt for cybercriminals while trying not to notice the woman who might be perfectly wrong for her for all the right reasons. (978-1-62639-985-3)